D0949731

ALSO BY KIMBERLA LAWSON ROBY

Changing Faces

The Best-Kept Secret

Too Much of a Good Thing

A Taste of Reality

It's a Thin Line

Casting the First Stone

Here and Now

Behind Closed Doors

Love and Lies

KIMBERLA
LAWSON ROBY

wm

WILLIAM MORROW
An Imprint of HarperCollinsPublishers

LOVE AND LIES. Copyright © 2007 by Kimberla Lawson Roby. All rights reserved. Printed in the United States of America. No part of this book may be used or reproduced in any manner whatsoever without written permission except in the case of brief quotations embodied in critical articles and reviews. For information address HarperCollins Publishers, 10 East 53rd Street, New York, NY 10022.

HarperCollins books may be purchased for educational, business, or sales promotional use. For information please write: Special Markets Department, HarperCollins Publishers, 10 East 53rd Street, New York, NY 10022.

FIRST EDITION

Designed by Janet M. Evans

Library of Congress Cataloging-in-Publication Data has been applied for.

ISBN: 978-0-06-089249-4
ISBN-10: 0-06-089249-8

07 08 09 10 11 ❖/RRD 10 9 8 7 6 5 4 3 2 1

For my husband, Will. Know that
I love you with all my heart. Know that
I appreciate the unconditional love you
have shown me since the
very beginning.

For my brothers, Willie Jr. and Michael
Stapleton. Know that I love both of you,
that I am proud to have you as my
siblings, and that the bond we share
can never be broken.

Acknowledgments

First and foremost, I am thankful to God for continuing to bless my life over and over again and for continually guiding me down the path You want me to follow.

An abundance of thanks goes to my husband, Will, who, after sixteen years and all that we have endured, still remains the love of my life. My brothers, Willie Jr. and Michael Stapleton; my stepson and daughter-in-law, Trenod and LaTasha Vines-Roby, for loving me and supporting everything I do. To my step-grandchildren, Lamont and Trenod Jr.; my nieces and nephews, Michael Jamaal, Malik, Ja'Mya, Ja'Mel, and Alanna, for loving me as much as I love you. To my cousin Patricia Haley (Jeffrey) Glass for always remembering Jr., Mike, and me on Mother's Day—it means more than you'll ever know—and Patricia, know that my prayers are with you as you continue your journey in ministry.

To my aunts and uncles, Cliff and Vernell Tennin, Ben Tennin, Ada Tennin, Fannie (Haley) and Earl Rome, Mary and Charlie Beasley, Luther Tennin, and Robert Thomas; and my cousins,

MacArthur and Leona Tennin, Katie Jordan, Lynn Beasley, Dr. L. C. and Julia (San) Tennin, Fred Haley, Willie Beasley, Alphonso Beasley, Darlene Patterson and Greg, Celei Patterson, Jenia Tennin, Michelle Tennin, Ryan Alexander, Dora Lee Tennin and Marlene, Donald Tennin, and Treva Tennin for, after nine books, still attending my local booksigning events and/or calling to check on me to make sure things are going well both personally and professionally. My schedule is sometimes a bit overloaded, and I don't call or visit as much as I would like, but I hope you know that I am always here for each of you if you need me.

To my second family for taking the time to attend all of my booksigning events and for letting me know regularly that you are proud of what I do for a living. My mother-in-law, Lillie Roby; my brothers-in-law and sisters-in-law, Ronald Roby, Robert and Tammy Roby, Terry Roby, Gloria Roby; and my little niece Bianca who I can't believe is already in high school!

Then I must give special mention and acknowledgment to my wonderful friend Kelli Tunson Bullard as we celebrate thirty-five years of friendship (in 2006). I also want to acknowledge you for being such an amazing mother to your daughters Kiara, Kaprisha, and KaSondra. I am so, so proud of you for the way you are raising all three of them and it is the reason you saw me shed so many tears of happiness during KaSondra's high school graduation weekend. You remind me of my mother when she was raising my brothers and me (you're always there for them) and you certainly deserve to be commended. Not to mention, since we have been friends for such a long period of time, your girls are nothing less than real nieces to me. I am so thankful that God placed you in my life and that you have always made me feel comfortable enough to confide in you just about everything I can think of. Is there anything at all that you don't know about me?

To my wonderful friend Lori Whitaker Thurman, as we celebrate twenty years of friendship (in 2006) and for being the most loyal and dependable person anyone could ever pray for. I've tried to recall a time when you weren't there for me over the last twenty years and can you believe I simply can't think of one? Needless to say, I thank God for you and for making you the kind of friend you are. And of course, I have to congratulate you on your new business, Book Connections, which actually isn't so new anymore! It is so very needed in the publishing industry, and I'm glad you finally made the decision to go for it. I am so proud of you for taking that entrepreneurial leap, and I look forward to seeing your business grow leaps and bounds now and in the future. But most of all, thank you for being the wonderfully compassionate person you are.

To my wonderful friend and cousin Janell Francine Green. I LOVE your new body products, and I'm happy to know that Drippinnectar.com will be up and running real soon so that the rest of the world can see just what they have been missing! Words cannot express how proud I am of you and how much I appreciate the way you never change. Your bubbly and caring personality is always a true breath of fresh air and it has proven to be a great blessing to me.

To four of my other childhood friends who I don't see or talk to as much as I'd like to but who always let me know that our friendship is still very special, Venita Sockwell Owens, Tanya Marks Hand, Aileen Blacknell, and Veronda Johnson Harris. To my friend and e-mail buddy Pamela Charles, who resides in Dallas, Texas, for making me laugh just about every single day. To Sonya Pearson Francis, my friend whom I grew up with in church here at home and who, like Pamela, always comes out to see me whenever I'm signing in Dallas.

To my wonderful friend and fellow author Victoria Christopher Murray, for all of our e-mail exchanges and phone conversations that always end up lasting longer than we plan for and for always being so optimistic about everything I'm involved in. I am so proud of you and your awesome writing talent.

To Janet (Jai Lynn) Salter, my hairstylist and friend who has no problem doing my hair, sometimes as early as 6:00 A.M., just to accommodate my travel or event schedule. Of course, I must admit I'll be sad to see you leave once you have that huge gospel music recording contract (which is coming), but happy that you'll finally, on a new level, be able to use the amazing voice God has so generously given you.

To my agent, Elaine Koster; my editor, Carolyn Marino; my publisher, Lisa Gallagher; my publicist, Pam Jaffee; and all the other wonderful people at HarperCollins/William Morrow who work hard at elevating my career. Thank you for everything.

My website designer, Pamela Walker-Williams at Pageturner.net, and my national book-club packager, Lori Thurman of Book Connections (BkConnections@aol.com), for all that both of you do to promote my work.

Dr. Betty Price at Crenshaw Christian Center for consistently encouraging and supporting what I do as a writer. Visiting with you and speaking to your Women Who Care program attendees is always the highlight of my year.

Donna Fontana, Kristi Widmar, Jennifer Mitchell, Lisa Craig, Holly Garman, and everyone else at Weight Watchers for supporting *Changing Faces* and for allowing me the opportunity to share my amazing Weight Watchers experience with women all over the country.

To all of the bookstores who sell my books, every person in the media who publicizes them, and all of the FABULOUS book clubs and individual readers who read my stories. Know that I will never, ever forget you.

Much love and God bless you always,

Kimberla Lawson Roby

Love and Lies

Chapter 1

CHARLOTTE

It was all I could do not to curse my husband out—my husband, a man who was never home more than a few days at a time, a man who didn't seem to care about his wife in the least, a man who was probably sleeping with only God knew whom. Which is why after five years of pleading with him to change and begging him to spend more time with me, I had finally had enough. I was finally in a place where I would no longer tolerate the world-renowned Reverend Curtis Black or the adultery I was sure he was committing.

"So when exactly are you going to be here, Curtis?" I asked now, gripping the phone tightly.

"I just told you. In a couple of days."

"I realize that, but I need to know a specific day. What I need to know is the time your flight will be arriving at O'Hare."

"Well, Charlotte, as much as I hate to disappoint you, I don't know what time."

"*You don't know?* How could you not know?"

"Because I just don't."

"Curtis, please. Do you think I'm that stupid? Do you really think you can get me to believe that you're coming home this week but your travel reservations still haven't been arranged? Do you really think I'm that crazy?"

"Like I said . . . I'll be there in a couple of days."

See, it was comments such as this that made me want to do unspeakable things to Curtis. Made me want to snatch him down from that nice little pedestal that thousands of people nationwide had placed him on. What I wanted to do was show him firsthand that being a *New York Times* bestselling author didn't mean that he could do whatever he wanted whenever he wanted to.

But I decided instead that I would calmly try to reason with him one last time.

"Curtis, have you even thought about the amount of time you spend on the road? I mean, are you even aware of the fact that you've now been gone for two weeks straight, and that once you return, you'll only be here for five short days?"

"Charlotte, why are we doing this? Huh? Because you know just as well as I do that my speaking engagements are very necessary. You've known for the last five years that this is what I have to do if you want to keep living the wealthy lifestyle you so desperately wanted when we were first married."

"But baby, there has to be some sort of balance," I said, remembering just how miserable I'd been before his publisher had offered him a contract with an initial advance worth seven hundred fifty thousand dollars for one book.

"Look, either you want luxury or you want average," he said, sounding impatient.

"What I want is for you to be here with your family. Matthew and Marissa need you, Curtis, and I'm tired of feeling as though I'm a single parent. Twelve-year-old boys need their fathers."

"All three of my children, including Alicia, know that I love them and that I have a job to do. I've explained to them that it won't always be this way, but for now, this is what I have to do."

"Curtis, all I'm asking is that you please cancel some of your commitments. I need you to spend more time at home."

"It's not going to happen. Not right now, and to be honest, I'm tired of repeating the same words to you over and over again."

"Oh, so now you've got the nerve to be irritated?" I said, my last bit of tolerance evaporating second by second.

"No, I just don't see a reason to continue discussing a situation that isn't going to change."

"Well, maybe the problem isn't your speaking engagements, Curtis. Maybe it has more to do with the fact that you're out there sleeping around. Because, knowing you, you've probably got a different woman lined up in every city."

"You mean like the way you slept with Aaron behind my back? How you slept with that deceitful lunatic even though he claimed to be my best friend? Or do you mean like how you lied about Matthew being my son when you knew full well that he might not be? Or maybe you mean like how because you slept with Aaron, we had to get a paternity test just to make sure Marissa was actually mine? So tell me, Charlotte, which sin of yours are you talking about exactly?"

At that moment, I wondered when Curtis would ever stop wallowing in the past and would eventually forgive me for the way I had betrayed him. Because whether he wanted to admit it or not, it wasn't like any of this had happened one month ago.

As a matter of fact, it had been five whole years since Marissa had been born, and to me it was high time for us to move on. Not to mention it wasn't like he'd been this perfect little Boy Scout himself.

"You know what, Curtis, as far as I'm concerned, you need to get over it. What you need to do is stop making all these lame excuses and get your priorities in order."

"No, what I need to do is the same thing I've been doing all along. Making a ton of money so that you can continue living like the queen you *think* you are, and so that I can maintain the type of freedom I've definitely become accustomed to. End of story."

His tone was razor sharp and more than anything I wanted to hurt him back. What I wanted was for him to feel more pain than he was now causing me, but for some reason I couldn't find the words. I was speechless and the only thing I could think to do was slam the phone down on its base.

Which is exactly what I did, and then I covered my face with both hands.

It was so hard to believe that after all the lying and scheming I'd done over the years, making sure I obtained everything I wanted, I was still living in complete turmoil. To put it plainly, I was living a life of pure hell and I didn't know how much more I'd be able to stand before exploding.

I walked out of the sitting room inside our master bedroom suite and over toward the balcony. Once there, I folded my arms and gazed out, trying to settle my nerves. This just didn't make any sense, being so unhappy. Not when we had this massive three-level mini-mansion, a Lexus 470 SUV, a Mercedes S500, and a BMW two-seater. Not when I'd hired a five-day-per-week housekeeper who also cooked our meals. Not when we had an enormous bank account and a whole slew of investments.

Although maybe this overly aggressive attempt at gaining the whole world really was grounds for losing one's own soul, because that's exactly how I had been feeling for more than a year now. I'd tried my best to make things right with Curtis, but no matter what I said or did, he no longer paid much attention to me. And even on the rare occasion when he was home, he spent all of his time with the children and even visited Alicia on her college campus, which was only a couple of hours away. He did everything with everyone except me, his wife of seven years, and now I knew, just at this very moment, that this wasn't going to change. After all, he'd slept with me when he was married to his first wife, Tanya, and his second wife, Mariah, so how in the world could I have ever thought I would be an exception? How could I have ever thought Curtis was going to be the loving, faithful husband until death do us part?

Of course, in the beginning, when we'd first gotten married, I had to admit that Curtis was in fact the loving husband and father. I also had to admit that I was the one who'd blundered into this ridiculous world of insanity the day I'd made the decision to sleep with Aaron Malone—or Donovan Wainright, which we'd learned was his real name. Oh, how this had proven to be an absolute nightmare, and to think I'd almost lost my life because of it. The man had taken the fatal attraction theory to a whole new level, and he'd gone to major extremes to ruin everything. He'd blabbed to Curtis practically every comment that I'd been naïve enough to confide to him, and in the end he'd tried to burn our house down with me still inside it.

Just the mere thought that I'd risked each of our lives for the likes of Aaron, a schizophrenic who'd masked himself as a stable and intelligent born-again Christian, was enough to make me cringe. It was enough to make me wonder if that mental institution he'd been dragged back to was now keeping closer watch on him. Because for the life of me I still couldn't understand how in the beginning he'd been able to convince his psychiatrist that he'd somehow made this miraculous recovery, how he'd been able to leave the state of Michigan, set up shop in Illinois with a whole new identity, and then find a good-paying job. Although Curtis had learned from one of the detectives that this had all been possible because Aaron had been good about taking his medication.

I stared through the window a while longer almost in a daze and then finally walked back toward our California king-size bed. And then it hit me. No matter what I'd done with Aaron five years ago, Curtis still didn't have the right to treat me as if I didn't matter. He had no right because his own history was full of dirt, and as far as I was concerned we were even. He'd gotten me pregnant before I'd turned eighteen, which by law was statutory rape, and I'd committed adultery with Aaron. We'd both committed sins that we would surely have to answer for, but from this day forward, I was going to handle things a lot differently. I wouldn't give up my affluent way of living, not under any circumstances, but I was going to live my life the same as Curtis, any way I chose. At the same time, I would find out who my husband was sleeping with, because no matter what he refused to admit, I knew him better than he knew himself. I knew my husband, the Reverend Curtis Black, couldn't go more than a day without having sex, even if it wasn't with me.

So, starting today, my primary focus would be my own happiness and raising my two adorable children. I would live even better than I had been and Curtis would come to realize that soon enough. He'd learn the hard way, once again, that I truly was his match. He would learn that just because he was the sole provider of our household didn't mean that I wasn't in a position to

collect half of everything. Which is exactly what I would do if
he forced me.

Over the next hour, I phoned my friend Janine at work, called
to speak to my parents, and now I was heading down the wrought
iron and wood winding staircase that led to the foyer. I strolled
across the black-and-white marble flooring, down the long hallway, and into the kitchen.

I gasped when I saw Marissa playing with fire.

She was standing her little five-year-old behind in front of
the stove, switching one of the front burners from low to high,
high to low, and then waving her hand through the flame, back
and forth and back and forth again.

"Marissa!" I yelled out to her. "Have you lost your mind?!"

But she never even flinched. She seemed almost mesmerized
by what she was doing and, strangely enough, fascinated by the
whole scenario.

"Marissa!" I screamed louder than before, and this time she
snapped out of her trance. "What are you doing?"

Instead of responding, however, my little girl stared at me,
turned back toward the stove, politely turned off the burner,
and walked right past me. She walked right out of the kitchen
and headed up to her bedroom like I hadn't said a word to her.
She acted as if nothing out of the ordinary had just happened,
and this worried me more than anything else. Especially since
as of late, Marissa had begun acting so bizarrely, and I also wondered why at times she was so cruel toward Matthew and me but
was always the perfect little angel when Curtis was around. I'd
tried to ignore these signs, but I feared that something was very
wrong with her. I feared that maybe Marissa wasn't Curtis's daughter after all and that instead she was Aaron's and had inherited
his schizophrenia. Because it wasn't like I'd ever actually seen

the results of the paternity test. It wasn't like I'd even wanted to see them, because I'd immediately decided it was better if no one, not even I, knew the truth. It had been better that way because as long as Curtis had believed wholeheartedly that he was Marissa's father, there hadn't been a thing for me to worry about.

And the more I thought about it, there still wasn't.

I decided that Marissa *was* Curtis's daughter and that she was merely going through some weird childhood phase—one she would grow out of any day now.

Truthfully, I refused to accept anything different.

Chapter 2

JANINE

I opened the door to my condo, walked inside, and saw Antonio laid back on my red leather sofa, consumed with some PlayStation video game. Which wouldn't have been so bad except for the fact that Antonio was thirty-seven, had no job, wasn't seriously looking for one, and spent most of his time doing only what he preferred—which was, for the most part, nothing. This of course had become very old, and I was now only days from telling him to pack the few rags he owned and to get out.

As I slipped off my shoes and dropped my keys into my handbag, I realized how engrossed Antonio was in his game. It angered me to see that he was so caught up he hadn't even noticed my presence. Either that or he simply didn't want to break his concentration. This was also the reason I intentionally strolled very slowly in front of the flat-screen television set, blocking his view.

"Hey, baby," he said, smiling. "I didn't even hear you come in."

"Obviously."

"So how was your day?" he asked, still pressing various buttons.

But I purposely ignored his question and left the family room abruptly. As soon as I did, though, I heard him drop the video controller onto the table. Next he followed me into the bedroom.

"Baby, what's wrong?" he said, sounding deeply concerned and trying to embrace me. But I pushed him away.

"*What's wrong?*" I repeated. I was so livid I could barely breathe.

"Yeah. What's wrong? I mean you act as if you're upset about something."

"What's wrong is the fact that you have the nerve to even ask me how my day was."

"But why wouldn't I ask you?" he said, frowning. "I ask you all the time."

I shook my head in disgust. "Well, if you must know, my day was the same as it was for every other responsible, hardworking American in this country. But I guess you wouldn't know anything about that, now would you?"

"Whoa, whoa, whoa. Where is all this coming from?"

"It's coming from the fact that I'm sick of you sitting around here all day, taking advantage of me. You've been doing it ever since you moved in here and I'm sick of it, Antonio."

"But how many times have I told you? There aren't any real jobs out there for me to pursue."

"Really?" I said, folding my arms. "And what exactly does *real* actually mean?"

"Real means finding a job at a company that can appreciate my associate's degree in general studies. And on top of that, there just aren't any companies out there that are willing to utilize my natural wisdom. At least not the way I would expect them to."

I laughed out loud. I did this because there was no way he could have been serious about what he'd just said. He just couldn't have. Not if he had a brain in his head.

"Oh, so now I guess I'm funny?"

"Actually, you are. But that's neither here nor there because the bottom line is that you don't have a steady income."

"But I just explained to you why I don't."

"Well, maybe you need to accept the fact that a general studies degree is exactly that: general. And since you haven't really specialized in any particular field, you might need to use your *natural wisdom* and take whatever entry-level position you can find and then work your way up to something better."

"Your sarcasm is becoming very old," he spoke coldly. "And it still doesn't change what I just told you. There aren't any jobs out there for me."

"Oh, I think there are. And to prove it, I checked our employment directory at the university and they have a number of openings. They had listings for a janitor, a library assistant, and a groundskeeper. And as a professor on staff, I know I could get you hired pretty quickly."

Antonio gazed at me with a staggered look on his face. "You can't be serious."

"As long as you're bringing a paycheck in here, it doesn't matter what the position is."

"You know what, Janine, let's end this conversation before it goes too far."

"It's already gone too far, and it's like I said before, you need to find a job."

"And I will. Just as soon as the right position comes along. One that pays well and one that fits my qualifications. But until then, you'll just have to be patient."

"No, that's not going to happen. I've been patient for almost two years, and as of right now, you have thirty days to find a full-time job and start paying some of these expenses."

His laugh was cynical. "You know . . . this is so typical. A black woman not wanting to stand by her man simply because he isn't sitting behind some wooden desk, pulling in six figures."

"That's not it and you know it. This is about bills and how they need to be paid."

"But you would have to pay these same bills even if I wasn't living here, so I don't see what the problem is."

What nerve. I couldn't believe he'd already analyzed the entire situation and then decided that I could afford to pay for everything. He'd stood right there in my face and basically told me that my complaint wasn't valid.

"Look," he said in a more relaxed tone. "You know that I love you, right? Because if you do, then why isn't that enough? I mean, remember how lonely you were when we first met and how you've told me on more than one occasion that you never want to feel that way again?"

"That's all beside the point."

"Is that right?" he said, raising his voice again. "Well, maybe this new attitude of yours is nothing more than some excuse you've come up with just so you can start dating other men . . . that is, if you haven't started already."

"Just stop it, Antonio. You know I'm not seeing anyone else, and no matter how hard you try avoiding the truth, this is only about you not taking responsibility. I mean, here you are, two years older than me, yet you don't have a penny to your name or even a car to drive around in."

"But I keep telling you that when the right opportunity comes along, I'll gladly take it. And if you love me the way you've been claiming you do, then my being unemployed shouldn't matter one way or the other. Especially since I'm faithful to you, and without question I'm the best you've ever had when it comes to sex. I mean, now let's just be real about this whole thing. Most women would kill to be in your shoes, so it seems to me that you should stop all this whining and just thank God that I'm even here."

I couldn't believe how stupid he was sounding, and the sad part was that he really was that full of himself. Which was interesting because no matter how many idiot remarks he made, he was still broke.

"Your thirty days begin now," I said matter-of-factly, and Antonio stormed out of the bedroom. Minutes later, I heard him slam the front door and speed off in my second vehicle. It was at that moment that I wondered how I'd been foolish enough to connect with such a loser. I wondered how I could have ever believed that a grown man, an unemployed one at that, who'd still been living with his parents, would somehow miraculously evolve into this perfect companion. I must have been crazy to think he'd ever be my ideal husband. I was crazy to let him move in with me, knowing he had nothing to offer.

But I knew there was no sense pondering any of the above because as much as I hated to admit it, I'd fallen for Antonio the very first day I'd met him. Partly because he had treated me so well in the beginning and we always had so much fun together, and partly because he was Denzel Washington gorgeous. Not to mention Antonio had been right about how lonely I'd been before meeting him, and while I would never tell him, he really was the best when it came to sex.

Nonetheless, his love for me, the fun we had, and our overall relationship just weren't enough. I deserved so much more than that, and settling for anything less was no longer an option I wanted to explore. What I wanted was a decent, hardworking man in my life, the same as my best friend, Charlotte, had.

What I wouldn't give to trade places with her, to be married to a man who was as intelligent and successful as Curtis, a man who was such a good father to his children. I didn't envy Charlotte, at least not in the same way so many other women did, but I did want the same type of life she was living, or at least something similar. I already had a wonderful career as a professor of business, but for whatever reason, I just couldn't seem to get things right in my personal life. It had been that way most of my adult years, and as confident as I was, I was starting to question what was wrong with me.

I wondered why I consistently attracted the wrong men and why I always seemed to give so much more than I received. A few years back, I'd cosigned a personal loan for a man I'd been seeing for more than a year because he'd claimed he was in a financial bind. But after about a month, he'd skipped town and I never heard from him again. Then, about a year before meeting Antonio, I'd been dating this guy named Raymond, but it hadn't been long before I'd made the mistake of showing up at his house unannounced and had caught him with his other woman—a woman who he wasn't married to but had five small children with. Information he'd somehow forgotten to tell me.

I removed my clothing, slipped on a knit lounging set, pulled back the black velvet comforter, and stretched across my bed. What a day this had been. Worse, I knew this was only the beginning, because I had a feeling Antonio wasn't going to leave quietly and might have to be forced out of my condo. I had a feeling this whole process would become uglier as time went on and that there was simply no other way to handle it.

I knew that from this day forward, Antonio and I would practically be at war with each other and that I had better start preparing myself. I needed to prepare for the worst because I just couldn't see Antonio—penniless, homeless, arrogant Antonio, leaving without a fight.

I knew this because only a few months ago, I'd learned from a cousin of his that he had beaten the last woman who'd kicked him out of her house so badly that she'd had to stay in the hospital for an entire week. It was the reason I'd mustered the courage to confront him only minutes ago in a bold fashion, even though, deep down, I'd been scared to death. I'd decided that if this was going to become a violent and very difficult situation, it was better for me to go ahead and get it over with.

It was better for me to face whatever was to come.

Better to do it now rather than later.

Chapter 3

CHARLOTTE

What a beautiful autumn day this was. It was barely the end of September, but the leaves on most trees were already changing into breathtaking colors and the warm weather felt like Indian summer. The sun shone brightly, the sky was clear, and the slight breeze was exhilarating.

"I am so glad you decided to take the day off from work," I said to Janine, turning into the parking lot of the day spa I frequented at least four times per month.

"I'm glad, too," she said. "Because I really do need this. More than I thought I did."

"For me, going to the spa isn't a luxury, it's a necessity. Especially the massages, because by the time I run Matthew and Marissa to and from school events and church activities, I'm so stressed."

"I can imagine," Janine said, but I could tell she was preoccupied with something else.

"Are you okay?" I asked, turning off the ignition.

"Not really."

"What's wrong?"

"I don't even know where to begin, and to be honest, all I want to do right now is go inside and enjoy my services."

"That's fine, but before the day is over, I want to know what's bothering you. Because now you've got me worried."

"Please don't be. I'm good. And I promise we'll talk when we leave here."

We stepped outside the car, and all I could think was that this probably had something to do with that no-good Antonio. He'd been using Janine for the longest time, and it was the reason I never had much to say to him whenever I went to Janine's condo for a visit. I'd met Janine right when she'd moved here two years ago from Cincinnati, and she'd met Antonio around the same time. Of course, I'd known immediately that he would never amount to anything, but Janine had been taken with him from the beginning. The man had made promises to her that he clearly hadn't planned on keeping, and Janine had believed him. Either that or she'd been hoping that he really was going to get his act together.

Still, I didn't understand how a woman who was so intelligent and who had such a warm heart could be attracted to the likes of Antonio. Yes, he was good-looking, but from where I was sitting, looks couldn't buy a doggoned thing. Money, on the other hand, could get you almost anything you wanted. It was also the reason I'd never dated a man who wasn't earning a very respectable income and why I had no intentions of divorcing Curtis. Our marriage definitely left much to be desired, but no matter how bad things got, I knew we would always be okay financially. I loved money and lots of it, and I wasn't ashamed to admit it.

We walked inside the building and told the receptionist our names. She keyed in our information on her computer and located our appointment times.

"You're scheduled for a shea butter wrap, a hot stone therapy massage, and a facial, correct?" she asked me.

"Yes, that's correct."

"And actually, you're getting the same," she said to Janine.

"Yes. I am."

"Great," she said, and then she told us the names of each therapist who would be providing our treatments. "I'll take you back to our locker room area so that you can change into a robe and slippers, and after that you can have a seat in our waiting area. We have fruit, whole wheat snacks, and water with lemon, so please feel free to help yourselves to whatever you want. Mina and Teresa will be with you shortly."

"Sounds good," I said as we followed behind her.

When she left us, we removed our clothing and locked everything away. Then we headed out to the lounge area and took a seat. The lights were dim, candles were lit, and as always, the atmosphere was soothing. I loved being here and I often wondered why there were so many women who'd never even been to a spa, because they couldn't have possibly known what they were missing.

"I feel relaxed already," Janine said. "What a tranquil setting this is."

"I know. I was just thinking the same thing, and you really do need to come here with me more often."

"Well, I would except I can't afford to spend this type of money every single week like some people," she said, teasing.

"Yeah, but how many times have I offered to take care of it for you?"

"True, but you know I don't feel comfortable with that."

"And we've been best friends for how long?"

"Two years."

"Exactly. So I would never feel as though you were trying to use me. You're a good person, I love you like a sister, and by now you should know that I would do anything for you."

"I do know, and I love you, too."

"And I'll always be here for you. The only other best friend I'd ever had was my cousin Anise, and of course you know how I ruined that. I still miss her, but it's my own fault because I never should have betrayed her the way I did."

I'd told Janine about my sleeping with Anise's ex-husband, David, while they were still married, but I just hadn't been able to admit to Janine that Matthew was David's son. Not many people knew this although Aaron had told Anise, and I'd always been worried that one day Anise would end up telling David that he had a son living barely ninety miles away from him and that David would decide he wanted to see him. I worried about that a great deal because while Curtis wasn't Matthew's biological father, he loved him unconditionally. He loved Matthew the same as he loved Alicia and Marissa, and Matthew loved Curtis more than anything. Even now, Matthew was still a daddy's child and his face still lit up whenever he spoke to Curtis by phone or saw him walk through our front door. The bond they shared was one of the reasons I wished Curtis and I could be happy with each other again.

After about four hours of soothing and relaxing treatments, Janine and I returned to the locker room area, slipped our clothing back on, reapplied our makeup, and groomed our hair.

"So you just about ready?" I said, doing a final once-over in the mirror.

"Yep. Pretty much."

"I made our lunch reservation for one o'clock, so we still have about a half hour, but I'm sure they'll be able to seat us a few minutes early."

"Where are we going?"

"Basil Café."

"Really? You know I love that place."

"That's why I chose it."

"You're too much and you're such a good friend," she said, her eyes tearing up.

"Look, Janine. What's wrong? I can't stand seeing you this way."

But before she could answer, two other women entered the room. So instead we spoke to them and headed out to the reception area to pay our fees and gratuity and so that I could schedule my appointments for next week. After that, we left and drove over to the restaurant.

When we arrived, we were seated right away, and as soon as the hostess left our table, I asked Janine, once again, to tell me what was up.

"It's Antonio."

I knew it. I'd known it all along and I could only imagine what Janine was about to say.

"What's he done?"

"It's more what he hasn't done. He just won't get a job. He won't do anything except sit around the house all day or hang out with his loser friends."

"Well, J," I said, "as much as I hate to say it, you know I've never thought Antonio was right for you."

"I know, but I wanted to give him the benefit of the doubt and there was a time when he really made me happy. He really made me feel special, and I honestly thought he had a lot more ambition. Especially since I know he's capable of doing so much more."

"But it doesn't matter how capable he is if he's decided that he doesn't have to. I mean—and please don't take this the wrong way—but as soon as you allowed him to move into your condo with no sign of employment and you pretty much gave him your other car to drive around in, he was set. He decided right then and there that you were okay with who he was, regardless of whether he worked or not."

Janine sighed deeply, and I knew I'd hurt her feelings. I hadn't meant to, but it was time I told her how I felt.

"I'm sorry, J, but Antonio clearly doesn't mean you any good. He never has, and what you need to do is kick his butt out on the street where it belongs."

"But that's just it. I told him last night that he has a month to find a job or he has to leave."

"And?"

"He wasn't happy about it, so I don't know what he's going to do."

"Well, my guess is that he's going to continue doing what he's always done, which is nothing."

When the waiter with smooth dark skin approached us, Janine leaned back in her chair and I couldn't help admiring his thick salt-and-pepper mane.

"How are you ladies?"

"We're good," I said. "And you?"

"Wonderful. Can I start you with one of our wine specials or an appetizer?"

"Sure, I'll have the Chablis," I said, thinking about how after seven years of being married to Curtis, he still despised the fact that I, on occasion, had a glass of wine. He couldn't stand it, but as of late, I couldn't have cared less what he thought.

"I'll have the same," Janine added. "And I'll also have a side salad with no croutons."

"I'll have the shrimp cocktail," I stated.

"Very well. I'll bring your drinks and appetizers, and then I'll take your lunch orders."

"Thanks," I said, and he left the table. Then I looked at Janine. "Do you know which entrée you're going to have?"

"Maybe grilled salmon."

"I was thinking the same thing. Either that or the stuffed flounder. I haven't tried it here before, but I've heard it's really good."

"You must think I'm the craziest and most naïve woman you've ever met," Janine said, getting back to the subject we'd been discussing.

"No. Absolutely not. I mean, I wish you had been able to see Antonio the same way I saw him, but hey, we all make mistakes, and somewhere along the way we all end up believing in someone we shouldn't."

"Still. I feel so stupid. Especially at thirty-five years old."

"What you have to do now is throw that jerk out and move on with your life."

"I'm just hoping it'll be that easy," she said, and then told me how she'd heard that Antonio had beaten up the last woman who'd tried to get rid of him.

"Are you serious?"

"Yes."

"Then you definitely have to be careful. Because even though that fool has a degree, I've always thought he had thuglike tendencies. And the more I think about it, maybe you should just call the police and have them come wait for him to pack his things and leave."

"I don't know. I told him thirty days, and if I change it, I'm betting it will only make things worse."

"Gosh, J, I hate to see you going through this."

"Makes you appreciate how good a man Curtis really is, doesn't it?"

At first I just stared at Janine, and then I decided that it was time I confided my suspicions to at least someone. I didn't want to worry my parents, and outside of the two of them, Janine was the only other person I trusted completely.

"Curtis is a good provider, but I don't think I would go as far as saying he's a good man."

"And why is that?" she asked, and I could tell she was stunned by my comment.

"Because Curtis isn't the person you think he is. You don't know the whole story on the good reverend, and now I think he's messing around with someone else."

"Why?"

Because he's cheated on every woman he's ever been married to. That's what I wanted to tell her, but for some reason I couldn't. I guess there was a part of me that still wanted everyone to believe I had it all. Love, money, and a perfect marriage. Maybe at some point I would tell her how ruthless Curtis had been since the day I'd met him, but not today. I also didn't want to have to tell her how he had in fact changed for the good when we'd first gotten married, but then I'd nearly destroyed our relationship forever.

So instead I took a different approach. "Haven't you ever noticed how much Curtis is on the road?"

"Yeah, but you've always said it was because he's out doing speaking engagements at churches as well as promoting his books."

"I know, but with three titles in print and all of them being national best sellers, Curtis doesn't have to be gone as much as he is. He tries to claim that all of this traveling is still necessary, but I know it's not. Curtis is gone simply because he doesn't want to be here with me."

"Wow. I'm speechless."

"Only because Curtis and I both know how to put up this

huge front when other people are around. Although lately he hasn't really been doing that as much as I have. His attitude toward me has gotten a lot worse over the last six months, and that's why I think someone else has his attention."

"Have you asked him?"

"I've mentioned it during a number of arguments, but to be honest, he hasn't confirmed or denied anything."

"Well, I think you should sit down and talk to him when he gets home."

"That's the plan, but I will say this: I'm not going to fret over whatever Curtis is doing and I've already decided that life goes on and that I'm going to live mine even better than I have been."

"Meaning?"

"Meaning, I'm not giving up my home or anything else, and that I'm going to do whatever I please, the same as him."

"I don't know what to say."

"I'm sure this all comes as a surprise to you, but like I said, you really don't know Curtis. Most people don't."

"Maybe you guys just need to get away for a while."

"Maybe. But I doubt it'll happen because Curtis's calendar is booked on and off throughout the rest of this year and well into next spring."

"Charlotte, I am so sorry."

"Don't be. Because I'll be fine no matter what."

"I believe that, but still."

"Really, I'm okay. And you just worry about kickin' that bum Antonio to the curb as soon as possible."

"Don't remind me."

"I'm here if you need me. Day or night."

"I know that. And thanks. Your friendship means more to me right now than ever because I really don't have anyone else. It's at times like this that I wish my mom was still here with me.

I miss her so, so much," she said, referring to her mother passing just before she'd moved here to Mitchell.

"I can only imagine."

When we finished our meals, we left the restaurant and I dropped Janine at her condo. I prayed that Antonio wasn't going to be trouble and that he wouldn't do anything to harm her physically. I could tell he was already upsetting her emotionally and that was enough in itself.

As I drove away and onto the main highway, heading home, my cell phone rang and I saw that it was an unknown number.

"Hello?" I answered. But no one said anything. "Hello?" I said again, and heard someone breathing, but still there was no response.

So I flipped my phone shut and dropped it onto the seat.

As soon as I did, it rang again.

"Hello?" I said, but this time the other party hung up first.

I despised hang-ups and prank calls, and if this kept up, I was going to have my number changed. Something I wasn't going to be happy about because I'd had this same number ever since we'd moved to Mitchell and everyone who meant anything to me had it.

I drove a few more miles before my phone rang yet a third time.

I snatched it up, opened it, and yelled, "Hello?"

"Hi baby, how are you?" the voice said.

"What? Who is this?" I said, and a wave of nervousness penetrated my soul.

"Come on now, baby, you know who this is."

"Oh my God, no," was all I could manage, and even that was in a whisper.

"Oh my God, yes," Aaron mocked me. "So how are you? Or better yet, how's our little girl?"

"Aaron, why are you calling me?" I said, pulling to the side of the road and placing my gear in park.

"Because I needed to hear your voice and I needed to check on my daughter."

"You don't have a daughter."

"Of course I do. I saw my boy Curtis on television doing an interview and he said he had a five-year-old daughter. Which of course we both know that the daughter he's talking about is actually mine. Plus I did the math. And back then, you and I were definitely sexing each other up every chance we got."

"Just stop it. You're not her father. Curtis and I had a paternity test done before she was even born, and it proved beyond a doubt that he was the father."

"Like I said, Charlotte . . . how's our little girl?"

"Aaron, I'm calling the police as soon as I hang up."

"And you think that's going to stop me from coming to get my child?"

"Donovan," I heard someone call to him in the background. "Who are you talking to?"

"No one," he lied.

"Hello?" a male voice said to me.

"Yes."

"Who am I speaking with?"

"Who's this?" I asked.

"Dr. Goldstein."

"Are you Aaron's doctor?"

"I'm *Donovan's* doctor."

"Well, I don't know if you're aware of this or not, but your patient went by the name of Aaron when he moved here to Mitchell, Illinois, and he tried to burn my home down with me in it. My name is Charlotte Black."

"Oh dear God, Mrs. Black. Yes, I know the whole story and

I'm so sorry that Donovan has bothered you. I left him alone in my office for only a few minutes, and I guess he took advantage of the situation. He knows that he's only allowed supervised phone calls, and I can assure you that this won't happen again."

"Is he still in Michigan?"

"Yes, and you don't have a thing to worry about. I would, however, get my phone number changed. Just to make sure he's not able to contact you again."

"I will."

"Again, I apologize for the inconvenience."

"Take care, Doctor."

When I dropped the phone back down on the seat, I hung my head back against the headrest, held my chest, and tried to breathe again.

I tried to breathe and at the same time believe that Aaron truly wasn't going to be a problem. All I could hope was that I'd never hear from him ever again.

I hoped and prayed like my life depended on it.

Chapter 4

JANINE

Why couldn't Antonio just leave on his own? was all I could think as I climbed out of bed and dragged myself into the bathroom. I was terribly exhausted and it was all because I'd tossed and turned the entire night and hadn't gotten more than a couple hours of sleep. Antonio had never come to bed and we still hadn't said more than two words to each other since two days ago when I'd given him that ultimatum. Although his demeanor and facial expressions had spoken a thousand words, and I was now sure that he was waiting for me to say or do the wrong thing. It was as if he was hoping for some sort of confrontation, and I couldn't deny that I was doing everything I could to avoid him. It was the reason I'd spent most of my time in my bedroom yesterday afternoon, right after Charlotte had dropped me off from lunch.

I turned on the faucet, wet my face, and then cleansed it with this product I'd purchased over the phone. I'd seen it on an infomercial, and interestingly enough, it was actually working. My adult acne was finally gone for the first time in almost five years, and I couldn't have been happier.

After drying my face and moisturizing it, I went back into my bedroom, over to my closet, and slipped on a pair of black workout pants and a sweatshirt. I chose a sweatshirt over a T-shirt because the warmer I was initially, the more sweating I would do, meaning I would eliminate any excess water I had retained from the day before. I loved working out because it kept my body in such great shape and it gave me so much energy, but today I was more interested in the release of endorphins. I needed a pick-me-up, so to speak, and whenever my endorphins were released, I felt amazingly better. It was almost as if I rose to this natural high and couldn't get enough of it.

Next, I pulled on my socks and gym shoes and went down to the lower level where I'd transformed most of the space into an exercise area. I'd been adding piece by piece over a short period of time, and now I owned a high-end treadmill, not much different from the one I used at the health club whenever I went there, a Bowflex machine, a set of free weights, and a bicycle. Exercise equipment was the one thing I didn't mind investing in since staying fit had definitely become one of my top priorities.

Once there, I picked up the remote to the television, flipped it on, and searched for the *Today* show, and then I straddled the center of the treadmill and chose a manual program. But as soon as I stepped onto the belt, Antonio came down the stairs.

"So how long are we going to keep doing this?" he said, dressed in the same sweater and jeans I'd seen him in yester-day.

"Doing what?"

"This. Not speaking to each other. Acting like we don't care one way or the other."

"You seemed upset when you left out of here the other day, so I thought it was better not to say anything," I said, choosing my words very carefully.

"I left because you were basically saying that you want me out of your life."

And I do. "It's not that, Antonio, but at the same time, I can't keep paying for everything. I can't keep taking care of you and me with one income."

"Oh, so is that how you see it? That you're taking care of me?"

Now I wished I'd kept my mouth shut altogether, because just that quickly his tone was beginning to shift and it wasn't for the better.

"What I mean is that I need your help," I said, trying to fix my comment. "There are so many other things I want to do, and if I had help, I could save a lot more money. We could save so much more together."

"And we will. But at the same time, you can't expect me to take just any job. You can't expect me to stoop to such menial levels."

I wanted to tell him that *menial* paid a lot more than what he was earning, and that as far as I was concerned, there was no such thing when it came to employment. More than anything, I wanted to tell him to get over himself, to grow up, and to start acting like a real man.

But I wasn't crazy. So instead I said, "You're right, and I'm sorry I even suggested those university positions to you the other day."

"You know, I was thinking. Maybe it's time we got married. Because it's not like it's right for us to be living in sin the way we are anyhow."

He was ridiculously unbelievable. I'd been foolish enough to think he had potential and even more naïve for letting him freeload off of me, but the temperature in Maui would drop well below zero before I took his hand in holy matrimony. This, I promised, would never happen.

Still, I went along for the sake of peace, but answered him very cautiously. "Maybe, but I still think it would be better if we took some time to plan our lives out and work toward getting you a job. I know you don't want to keep hearing that, but there has to be something out there for you."

"Yeah, but in the meantime, why do we have to wait? Why don't we just go down to the courthouse and do it there."

"Because that's not the kind of memory I want for us," I said, glancing at the readout on the treadmill. The incline was moving higher and I was already feeling the effects of it.

"What do you mean, 'that kind of memory'?"

"I've always wanted a huge church wedding, and that takes money."

"Exactly. It'll take the kind of money we don't have, so I say we go before a judge and maybe take a honeymoon somewhere you've always wanted to go."

I bumped the speed up another mile per hour, breathed in and out, and wondered how I was going to discreetly change the subject.

Then I finally said, "I don't know."

"Well, you think about it," he said, winking at me.

I, of course, didn't like the route this whole fiasco was taking, because once Antonio learned that I had no intention of becoming his wife, there was no telling what he might do. Although I was sure he'd claim it was that I didn't think he was good enough to marry and that I wanted a man who could offer me a lot more than he could. If he did, he'd be right on both accounts.

When he left, I pumped the incline up a bit higher than what the program currently called for, watched Al standing outside Studio 1A chatting with a few people in the crowd after reporting the national weather forecast, and then I listened to Ann report the news. I tuned in for at least another twenty minutes, and now sweat was pouring from my face and I could feel how drenched my chest, back, and stomach were as well. I worked another five minutes and then switched the machine into cool-down mode, and as expected, I felt better already. My adrenaline was cranking and it was definitely what I had needed.

Next, I spent twenty minutes on the Bowflex machine, then went up to the kitchen, grabbed a bottle of water from the refrigerator, and drank all 16.9 ounces at once. Then I looked at the clock and headed toward my bedroom. This was my late day and I still had about two hours before my first class would begin, but I decided to go ahead and take my shower and get dressed. I hated rushing, and if I left in time, I'd be able to stop at Starbucks for a caffè mocha.

But when I walked into the bedroom, Antonio was lying across the bed without one stitch of clothing on. He lay there smiling and motioning with his hand for me to join him.

"I can't," I said, and quickly looked away from him, because while I hated to admit it, I wanted him. I wanted him to make love to me the same as he always had, and at this very moment, I didn't care about how irresponsible and lazy he was. What I cared about was the exceptional pleasure he was capable of giving me and how satisfied I would still feel a number of hours from now if I gave into him.

"Baby, come here," he said, and my body weakened. I knew this wasn't going to help matters in the least, but I simply didn't have the strength to fight him off. Sadly, I didn't want to. I knew having sex with him was wrong, sinful even, but the man had incredible skills. He had an ability I was sure most men would envy if they ever saw him in action, wishing they could learn his expertise.

Still, I tried to walk away, but the next thing I knew, I was standing in front of the bed and Antonio was undressing me. I guess he didn't care about the fact that I was perspiring all over the place because he pulled me across the bed and was now having his way with me. So much so that all I could do was close my eyes, moan, and enjoy all that he was doing. I moaned and decided that for now, I wouldn't concern myself with the negative aspects of our relationship. I wouldn't worry about the ultimatum I'd given him or that our time together was limited. Instead, I would selfishly take from him what I could get while I could get it and I wouldn't feel bad about it. Especially since he had taken a whole lot more from me than I cared to think about. More than he would ever be able to repay me for, so this was the least he could do for me.

The very least indeed.

I'd just finished teaching my last class of the day and my students were walking out of the room, one by one. At the same time, I found myself reminiscing about Antonio and how wonderfully he'd made me feel just hours ago. Sex had always been excellent with him, but today had been the absolute best. It was as if he'd worked harder than usual at satisfying me, making sure I knew just what I'd be missing once he was gone. And I did know. I felt the pain of being alone and the fear that I would never find my soul mate.

I sighed deeply, picked up a stack of quizzes that my students had just taken, and prepared to head up to my office. But when

I looked up, Antonio was heading toward me. He was holding an enormous bundle of long-stemmed hot pink roses and was smiling from ear to ear. He was also holding a tiny box wrapped in silver paper and adorned with a shiny white ribbon.

"What's all of this?"

"It's my way of saying I want to spend the rest of my life with you," he said, passing me the beautiful flowers—which were nice, but the little silver box was what worried me.

"Open it," he said.

I didn't want to, not here at the university, but I could see that I didn't have much choice. So I did what he asked. I untied the ribbon, removed the wrapping, and pulled the lid off of the box. Then I pulled out a black felt case and eased it open. At first I couldn't believe what I was seeing, but when I pulled out a white gold princess-cut diamond solitaire that was at least a carat and a half, I knew I wasn't dreaming. It didn't have the best clarity I'd ever seen, but it was pretty obvious that he'd paid good money for it. The question was...

"How were you able to afford this?" I asked.

"Oh, here we go. Is that all you care about?"

"Well, no, but Antonio, you have to admit that my curiosity is definitely warranted."

"Well, for now let's just enjoy the moment. Let's enjoy the fact that I love you and that I want you to be my wife."

"I don't know what to say," I said for lack of a better response.

"Say yes."

"It's not that simple," I said, stalling. Now, all sorts of terrible thoughts were crossing my mind. I mean, had he stolen this from some jewelry store or purchased it from some pawnshop? Was he doing something illegal that I didn't know about? Because there was no way he could afford this.

"So are you saying no?" he said, and this time his tone wasn't as cordial.

"No, I'm not saying anything, but I really need you to tell me how you bought this."

"Fine. You'll have to find out sooner or later, anyway, so I might as well tell you now. I used one of your credit cards."

"You what? How?"

"I used one of your credit cards."

"But I haven't given you any of them, Antonio."

"I know, but for a long time I'd been trying to figure out a way to buy you an engagement ring, and then about three months ago this preapproved letter came for you, I opened it, filled it out, and then requested a second card in my name as an authorized user."

I stood there, batting away tears, and I couldn't say a word.

"I know it wasn't right for me to forge your name, but since we're going to be married anyway, I figured you wouldn't mind."

"But I do mind, Antonio."

"Oh, give me a break, Janine. Money, money, money. I'm so sick of you whining about money all the time," he shouted.

"Will you please keep your voice down? This is a university."

"Do I look like I care about any of that? Do I?" he said, invading my space. I stepped backward.

"Let's just discuss this at home," I hurried to say before one of my colleagues suddenly walked by and witnessed our disagreement.

"No, we'll discuss it right here, and since we're on the subject, you might as well know that I've already maxed out the ten-thousand-dollar credit line they gave you. That ring I went out of my way to get you was almost four thousand, I spent another couple thousand on some new clothes and shoes that I needed, and I spent the rest here and there through cash advances."

"And you just started using it this month?"

"No, I've been using it ever since it came."

"Then why haven't I seen any statements?"

"Because I've been filing them away and trying to figure out how to pay the bill."

"Antonio, no. Please don't tell me that my account is past due."

"Well, it is. And maybe if you hadn't been harassing me all the time about money, I would have felt more comfortable telling you about this, and then at least you could have made the minimum payments. So if you want to blame someone, blame your damn self, because this is basically all your fault."

Was he kidding?

"You know what, Antonio? I want you out of my house by this weekend. Today is Thursday and I want you gone by Sunday."

"What? You want me gone? Huh!"

"Yes, because I can't live like this anymore," I said, gathering together the quizzes and placing them in my leather briefcase. I also picked up a textbook and a few other documents and attempted to walk around Antonio.

But he snatched me tightly by my arm and I dropped the book and a few papers onto the floor. "I'll leave when I'm good and ready to leave, and if you even think about trying to force me out any sooner, you'll regret it for the rest of your life. Do you understand me? Because I'm not playing with you."

I wanted to tell him that he was hurting me, but somehow I knew it would be safer if I didn't say anything.

"I'm not one of those little students you teach, and I suggest you recognize that before you end up like the last two women who tried to *put me out*," he said, turning me loose and shoving me at the same time against the desk. Then he picked up the roses and slammed them against the floor and placed the ring box inside his jacket. "I guess I'll see you at home," he said, and walked out.

I breathed freely again but my nerves were shot. My worst nightmare was finally happening and I knew Antonio wasn't joking. His threats were more like promises and I couldn't help wondering what it would take to get rid of him. I wondered how I would rid myself of this monster I'd helped create, but deep down I was terribly afraid.

I was sure I must have looked pretty stupid to Charlotte and anyone else who knew that I'd allowed a man to take such blatant advantage of me, but what they didn't know was that I had a very good reason: my sister and only sibling had once found herself in the same situation three years ago and she'd lost her life because of it. She'd been living with a man who, like Antonio, didn't see a reason to work and who had ultimately begun abusing her physically and mentally. She'd even gotten to the place where she didn't call Mom, Dad, or me because her boyfriend forbade it. But finally, after everyone had kept demanding that she call the police and put him out, she did, and the next evening he'd waited outside her apartment and then stabbed her to death. She'd just arrived home from work and was preparing to step outside her car, but he'd killed her before she was able to.

Still, I never talked to anyone about the way my sister died because I'd been one of the family members who'd been upset with her for not getting rid of him sooner, and talking about what happened only intensified my guilt. I remember thinking how kicking him out once and for all should have been the easiest thing for her to do. Yes, I'd allowed men to use me financially, but I just couldn't see allowing a man to move in with you, take over everything, and then slap you around whenever he felt like it. I hadn't been able to fathom it. Yet now, here I was in the same predicament, and it was the reason I knew I had to be very cautious in the way I handled Antonio.

Chapter 5

CHARLOTTE

hank God it was Friday. It was the end of another school week and this meant the children and I would be able to sleep in a few hours longer tomorrow morning. Tracy, our full-time housekeeper, always helped out with the children, but I still got up every morning at six like clockwork. I'd never been a morning person and was never going to be, but I felt an obligation toward seeing the children off to school and I also drove them when it was my week to carpool. Although there were times when Marissa refused to ride with one of the other parents or those "silly children," but Matthew loved traveling to school with any of his friends and schoolmates. He'd been that way for as long as I could remember and he got along with everyone. For a twelve-year-old boy, he had a real heart and he cared about others. He had not a selfish bone in his body, and I was extremely proud of that.

But that little Marissa was a completely different story. All she cared about was herself and she didn't mind stepping on whomever she had to in order to get what she wanted. She was mean-spirited and manipulative and she didn't have many friends. But the thing was, it didn't seem to bother her. She didn't care that none of the girls at her school invited her to their birthday parties or sleepovers or that no one ever asked her to go on any outings with them. It was almost as if she had no real emotions to express about anything. Sure, she loved her father, but that was pretty much where it ended. Of course, I wanted to believe that she loved me, too, a mother who would give her life for her, but Marissa honestly didn't act like it. And her feelings and actions toward her brother were worse. She did terrible things to him whenever she felt like it, and the only time she pretended to love him was when she wanted something he had or she wanted him to take her to the movies.

Needless to say, Matthew, being the child he was, would always do what she asked, I guess hoping she would eventually love him unconditionally, but I had to admit that there were days when I wished he would treat her the same as she treated him. Because maybe then she'd see how it felt to be misused by another human being. It was hard to believe that I had all this to say about a five-year-old.

"Mommy, I need five dollars," Marissa announced, and drank some of her orange juice.

"Five dollars, for what?"

"Because I don't have any money in my purse."

"Little girls don't need that kind of money. Especially to take to school."

"I'm telling Daddy you wouldn't give it to me. He's coming home this afternoon."

"I don't care who you tell, and just for your little information, your father won't be here until tomorrow."

"No he won't. Because this morning when I got up, I called him and he told me he'll be here when I get home from school," she said with a smirk, and I wanted to slap her. She'd reported this major news flash and was practically taunting me with the fact that she knew more about my own husband than I did.

Matthew looked at her and then me, but didn't say anything.

"Honey, do you need me to drive you to your dance at school tonight?" I asked, ignoring Ms. Thing altogether.

"Yes, and we need to pick up Jonathan and Elijah on the way," he said after swallowing more of his oatmeal.

"No problem. Just let me know what time you want to leave."

"Dances are stupid," Marissa complained, and I could tell she envied her brother and the time he spent with his two best friends.

"No they're not," he disagreed. "Dances are the bomb."

"You make me sick, Matthew," she said, shoving her bowl of cereal away from her and pouting. "I hate that I even have a brother."

Again Matthew looked at her, then at me, and didn't say anything.

And it was at that very moment that I realized Matthew thought his sister was crazy. I hadn't paid attention to it before, but now I could see it in his eyes.

"Marissa, that's enough," I told her. "And I don't ever want to hear you say anything like that again. Your brother loves you, and I want you to stop being so mean to him."

"He's mean to me, too."

"When?" Matthew said. "When am I ever mean to you?"

Marissa just rolled her eyes at him and then played with her food. I suppose because she knew her accusation was false. She knew her brother was kind to her and had been since she was born. Even then he would go into her nursery, admiring her and talking to her when he was only seven years old.

"Matthew," the housekeeper, Tracy, sang, and patted him on

the back. "It's almost time for you to get going. Your ride's going to be out there in a few minutes."

"Yes, ma'am," he said, smiling and finishing the rest of his food.

"You, too, Miss Marissa."

"Yes, ma'am."

Interestingly enough, Tracy was the only other person besides Curtis and my parents that Marissa seemed to love and respect. Although since we all loved Tracy, that wasn't so surprising. The woman was a sweetheart and she was the best cook in the world. She was only forty-five but she cooked as well as my grandmother and she made almost everything from scratch. She kept the house spick-and-span, too. And while she and Curtis were the same age, I was glad she was a little country, sheltered, and homely, because that way I never had to worry about Curtis coming on to her. Unattractive women weren't his thing. This I knew for sure.

"Miss Tracy, can you drive me to school today? Pleeease."

"I thought you were riding with Mrs. Rhinehart."

"I don't want to anymore. So, *pleeease*, can you?"

"Well, I am heading to the store, so if it's okay with your mom, I will."

"Mommy, can she?"

It was amazing how friendly and smiley Marissa was right now. All because she wanted me to say yes to what she was asking. What a scheming little thing she could be.

"Don't you think it would be better if you rode to school with the rest of the children?"

"No, Mommy. I don't want to."

"Fine, Marissa." I gave up because arguing with a kindergartner just wasn't worth the headache.

"See you later, Mom," Matthew said, kissing me on the cheek and then rushing out of the house.

But Marissa grabbed her book bag and the miniature purse Curtis had bought her during one of his trips to Miami, and sashayed out to Tracy's car like she was an adult. She was too grown for her own good, and I didn't know what we were going to do with her. I'd tried my best to teach her good manners, so all I could hope was that at some point she would somehow change for the better.

As soon as the children and Tracy had left, I grabbed the phone book and thumbed through the yellow pages. I'd been debating whether or not this was the route I should take, but this morning I'd finally decided that it was time I hired a private detective. I hadn't wanted to go to such extremes, but I didn't see where there was any other choice. Not with Curtis traveling all over the country the way he was. If he spent most of his time right here in the city, it would be a lot easier for me to follow him, but since he didn't, I had to do what I had to do. I desperately wanted to know who the tramp was, the one he was sleeping with, and whether she was only one of many.

After searching through the "P" section, I saw a few agencies listed, but when I came to an ad that said, "If your husband is cheating, we'll catch him—guaranteed or your money back," I reached for the phone and dialed the number.

"KP Investigations," a female voice answered.

"Hi, I'd like to make an appointment to speak with an investigator."

"Sure. When would you like to come in? Mr. Perry is going to be out of town on a job all day Sunday and won't be back until late Monday night, but he's pretty open for the rest of today."

"Let's see," I said, realizing it was only after 7 a.m. and that the receptionist was in the office rather early. "What about, say, around ten?"

"Ten is fine, and just so you're prepared, if you decide to hire Mr. Perry to handle your case, you'll need to pay an up-front retainer before he begins working."

"Not a problem, and thanks so much for getting me in so quickly."

"Okay, then. We'll see you in couple of hours or so."

Well, this was it. I'd scheduled my initial consultation and now it would only be a matter of time before I found out everything. I had to admit, though, this whole idea made me a little nervous. It even made me a bit sad, because what I really wanted was to find out that Curtis wasn't messing around on me after all. I knew it was wishful thinking, but what I wanted was for Curtis to love me the way he once had. I wanted us to recapture the love we'd genuinely shared together—love we'd had before I began sleeping with Aaron. I wanted life to be good between us again but I didn't know if it would ever be possible.

Before I went upstairs to get dressed, I realized I hadn't spoken to Janine, so I called her cell number. I knew she had an eight o'clock class that she taught on Fridays, so chances were she was sitting at her desk, reviewing her lesson, or she was still in the car driving.

"Hey," she said, obviously seeing my number on her Caller ID.

"Hey, yourself. How's it going?"

She sighed deeply and I knew something was wrong.

"Girl, I didn't even want to bother you last night, but you won't believe what happened yesterday!" she exclaimed.

"What? And where are you?"

"I'm about two minutes from the university. But yesterday Antonio came to my last class of the day, right when it was over, and he brought me a bunch of roses and an engagement ring."

"I know you're kidding?"

"No, but the killing part is that he used a credit card of mine to pay for it. That jerk actually forged my name on some preap-proved letter and he's had the card in his possession for three months. He even had one authorized in his own name."

"J, this is crazy. You have got to put that deadbeat out. Not next week, not next month, but now."

"I tried, but he threatened to do bad things to me if I brought it up again. And Charlotte, I believe him. I'm so afraid I don't know what to do."

"You have to call the police."

"I thought about that, but that will only make him angrier than he already is."

"Then what are you going to do?"

"For now, I'm going to go along with what he wants, but eventually I have to take care of this. I don't know how, but I will. I just can't move too quickly, though, because I've seen too many women lose their lives because they thought the police were going to protect them."

"I guess you're right, but gosh, J. I can't believe this is hap-pening to you."

"I can't believe it either, and while I know Antonio hasn't been the best man for me, his nature is so violent now. It's almost as if he's a totally different person."

"No, I'll bet he's the same. The only difference now is that you told him you wanted him to leave and he realized he was going to be on the street. So now he'll do anything he has to just to keep a roof over his head."

"This is terrible. And not only did he charge the ring, but he charged up the entire limit, which is ten thousand dollars."

"He didn't!" I said, trying to figure how and why Janine had fallen in love with this man. I'd asked myself both ques-tions on a few different occasions, but today I really wanted to know.

"Hey, I'm turning into the parking lot now, so I'll have to hang up, but I'll give you a call this afternoon."

"That's fine. I have to run out for a while this morning, but I should be back here by noon."

"I'll call you after that."

"Janine?"

"Yes."

"Are you going to be okay?"

"I'll be fine."

"I'll talk to you this afternoon, then."

"See ya."

This was horrifying and something was definitely going to have to be done about Antonio. There was no way I could simply sit back and allow him to bully Janine the way he was and then get away with it. I wasn't sure how I would proceed, but if Janine didn't get rid of him fairly soon, I would have to do it for her. I would take care of this one way or the other, even if it meant paying the right person to take care of it for me. I would do whatever was necessary to free my best friend from that maniac.

Chapter 6

CHARLOTTE

Thank you for seeing me," I said, taking a seat inside Mr. Perry's office, which was located right here in Mitchell.

"It's my pleasure. So what can I do for you?"

"Well, as embarrassing as this is for me, I need you to get some information on my husband."

"Okay," he said, leaning back in his leather chair. "What type of information do you want exactly?"

"I need to know if he's having an affair. He travels extensively, and for the most part, our marriage is not what it used to be."

"Is he a salesman?"

"No, he's a minister."

Mr. Perry raised his eyebrows and said, "Oh . . . okay."

"He and I are cofounders of Deliverance Outreach. Have you heard of it?"

"Of course. So your husband is *the* Reverend Curtis Black?"

"Yes, but he's no longer the residing pastor. We hired someone else to take that position once Curtis's first book was published and he started traveling around the country promoting it. He also has a lot of speaking engagements."

"I see. And you think he's having an affair with someone out on the road or right here in town?"

"Out on the road, because usually when he's home, it's only for a short period of time and he spends it with our children."

"Well, if I take your case, you do know that I'd have to charge you traveling and incidental expenses over and above my normal fee, right?"

"Whatever it takes, because I really need to know what's going on."

"Is he in town right now?"

"No, but he'll be home sometime this afternoon."

"I'm sure my assistant told you that I'm heading out of town on Sunday, but if it's okay with you, I'd like to get started tomorrow. Which would mean monitoring your house and tailing him wherever he goes. I just want to get an in-person look at him and see what his patterns are when he's home."

"Fine."

"Before you leave, I'll ask Melanie to give you a form that I'll need you to fill out. This way I'll have all of your contact information and the addresses of places your husband usually frequents. It would also be good if you could list the names and addresses of everyone he's close to or interacts with on a regular basis, and I'll also need his future travel schedule."

"No problem."

"And then, for starters, I'll need a retainer of five thousand dollars."

I'd said I was willing to pay whatever it took, but I hadn't planned on paying this much.

"That's pretty steep."

"Maybe, but I'm the best there is around these parts, and I guarantee my work. Plus I also have to consider the fact that I'll be traveling to other cities."

"Will this include those expenses as well?"

"For now. And what I'll do right from the beginning is get you receipts for everything I incur."

"But you're pretty sure you can get me what I need to know?"

"Mrs. Black, I'm positive. Your husband is nationally known, and thanks to you, I'll know where he is at all the time. Because he does give you the names of his hotels, am I right?"

"Yes. He never hides where he's staying."

"Good. Then this should be fairly easy and it won't take more than a week. Although, as I said, I'll get started tomorrow, and then on Wednesday morning I'll be flying to wherever your husband is headed to."

"I don't think he's going back out until then anyway, so that'll be perfect."

"Well, unless you have any questions, I'll be in touch."

"No, I think that's all, and thank you," I said, standing and shaking his hand.

"I'll call out to Melanie's desk right now so that she can get you the form I spoke about."

"I appreciate it."

"And Mrs. Black?"

"Yes."

"For whatever it's worth, your husband would be crazy to have an affair on someone as beautiful as you."

"Well, thank you."

"I'm serious. I'm not trying to disrespect you or come on to you in any way. I'm simply stating the truth."

"Thank you again," I said, smiling, and left his office.

Interestingly enough, I'd noticed how attractive Mr. Perry was from the moment I'd laid eyes on him, too, with his baby-smooth skin and coal-black hair. But ever since that whole debacle with Aaron, I tried my best not to look at any man except Curtis in that way. Although with the way Curtis was treating me, it was becoming a lot harder for me not to.

When I arrived home, I was shocked to see Curtis's luggage sitting on the floor, right in the center of our foyer. It was only a few minutes past noon, and I was surprised he'd decided to fly home so early. Especially since he usually never arrived home until it was time for the children to come home from school.

I scanned his luggage, briefcase, and a couple of large shopping bags from Saks and wondered how he'd been able to carry them on the plane. Because the last I'd known, the airlines were only allowing two carry-on pieces. Needless to say, I couldn't help wondering who had carried on one of them for him. There was no telling, and this small suspicion helped justify the five-thousand-dollar check I'd just written for KP Investigations.

When I walked up the stairs and into the bedroom, Curtis and I immediately made eye contact. The man still looked as fine as ever. After all these years, after all the trials we'd had to overcome, Curtis still took my breath away. It was also the reason it was so hard for me to simply let go, walk away, and move on without him.

"Hey," I said.

"Hey, yourself," he responded, and while I wasn't completely sure, he seemed to be in a much better mood than he was when we'd argued on the phone a few days ago.

"So did you have a good flight in?"

"I did. No turbulence and the weather was clear all the way."

I removed my Chanel blazer and dropped it onto one of the chaises and kicked off my Via Spiga pumps.

"You must've had a meeting at the church or something," he said, and I wanted to laugh because that statement alone told me that regardless of what Curtis was doing outside of our household, he still cared about my whereabouts. Still, I told the first lie I could come up with.

"No, actually, I had a few errands to run."

"Must have been some pretty important errands if you needed to get all dressed up like this," he said, smiling.

"Are you saying I look good?"

"Well, I wouldn't want this to go to your head, but yes. You look wonderful."

I smiled, but after a few seconds tears rolled down my face.

"What's the matter?" Curtis said, and I could tell he was confused.

"Us. We're what's wrong, and it's tearing me apart."

Curtis looked at me and it was obvious that he didn't know what to say.

"Don't you agree?" I continued.

"I do, but I don't know how we can fix it," he admitted.

"Well, can we at least talk about it?" I said, sliding over my blazer and sitting down on the chaise.

"But that's just it, Charlotte, we've grown so far apart that I honestly don't know if we can ever get back to where we were. So much has happened between us, and while I know it's been five years since you slept with Aaron, I still feel so much resentment toward you. But I will admit that there are times like today when I wish we could be happy with each other again. As a matter of fact, that's why I flew home earlier than I'd planned."

"And we can," I said, reaching for his hand and pulling him down beside me. I moved my body flush with the back of the chaise and he positioned himself on the edge of where I was sitting.

"But there are times, Charlotte . . ."

"Times?"

"Times when I literally hate you and wish I had never married you."

I finally knew what it felt like to have a dagger pounded straight through my heart. His comments hurt terribly, and worse, I could tell he meant every word he was saying.

"*Hate* is such a strong word," was all I could muster.

"I know. But I can't help the way I feel."

"Even though I've apologized to you for everything I did, over and over again?"

"Yes, even though you've done that. Because the thing is, no matter how hard I try, I can't seem to forget everything that happened. You sleeping with Aaron behind my back. You lying about Matthew being my son. It's all enough to make me sick."

"But I didn't lie about Matthew."

"But you knew you'd slept with your cousin's husband around the same time Matthew was conceived. Right?"

"Yes, but . . . okay, I made a mistake. A huge, huge mistake, but Matthew loves you no differently than if he was your biological son. He worships the ground you walk on."

"And I feel the same way about him. Still, though, that's beside the point."

"Well, baby, the only way we're going to get through this is if you can somehow find a way to forgive me."

"I know that, and I struggle every day with the idea of not forgiving you. But nonetheless, I still can't seem to get past what our history is with each other."

"And it doesn't matter to you that I love you with all my heart?"

"No. As much as I hate to say it, that doesn't change anything."

"Then maybe the real question is do you love me?"

When he didn't saying anything, I got nervous.

"Just be honest," I said.

"I guess a part of me does still love you, but it's not in the same way as when we were first married."

"Are you in love with someone else?" I asked without planning to.

"No. I'm not."

"Are you sure?"

"Positive."

I so wanted to believe him, but I knew it was better to just wait and see what Mr. Perry came up with.

"Then why do you seem so irritated with me when you're out on the road? I mean, whenever we talk, all we do is argue. It's almost as if my phone calls are a distraction to you."

"But it's only because when I'm traveling, I have a lot going on and I'm usually exhausted."

"But still, Curtis, you don't have to talk to me so rudely."

"I'm sorry."

"We used to have such a good time with each other," I said, leaning toward him and caressing the side of his face. "Remember?"

"I do."

"Baby, make love to me?" I said, shocked at my own request.

"What about Tracy? And by the way, where is she?"

"She's taking the afternoon off."

"Oh really? Why?"

"Because I told her we would probably order pizzas for dinner. She went to the grocery store this morning after dropping Marissa at school, but since you and the kids usually like to have pizza when you're home on Friday nights, I didn't see a reason for her to cook anything."

"That's fine."

"So, baby, come on," I said, pulling him toward me.

I could tell Curtis was hesitant, but today I wasn't taking no for an answer.

"I really need you," I said, and kissed him.

And before long, whatever hatred and resentment Curtis had for me was a distant memory. So distant that he was now kissing me in a ravenous fashion and moaning the way he used to. I moaned with him, and more than anything, I wanted my husband inside of me. I wanted him to give me the kind of love that would linger long after today was over. I wanted him to realize that it was possible for him to fall in love with me again and that no one else was worth his time.

Curtis kissed me up and down my neck and then unbuttoned my silk blouse. Then he removed it, slipped my bra straps down my arms, and burrowed his head into my chest, giving each breast equal attention.

I tried my best to control the quivering sensation I knew would overtake my body in a matter of seconds. I tried hard to prevent this from happening so quickly, but I just couldn't help myself. I just couldn't deny myself something I'd been thinking about and dreaming about for two whole weeks. Because, sadly enough, Curtis had been gone all that time. Of course, about a week ago, he'd come home for a couple of days, but we'd barely even spoken to each other so to me it was as if I hadn't seen him at all. It was as if I hadn't even had a husband and now I was making up for lost time.

Curtis stood and pulled me toward our bed and we both removed the rest of our clothing. Then we held each other, kissed for longer than usual, and slowly relaxed across the bed.

"I love you so much," I professed.

But Curtis didn't speak. Just kept turning me on in a way that forced me to breathe heavily and whimper like a child.

I whimpered and pretended that our life together was good.

I pretended it was perfect.

Chapter 7

No matter how many times I'd come to this particular nursing home to visit Antonio's mother or anyone else, it always reminded me of the one my grandmother had resided in until the day she'd died. She'd been stricken with Alzheimer's disease, and while my mother had moved her into her home and taken care of her for five years, it had finally come to a point where Grandmother had needed professional twenty-four-hour care and my mother had had no choice but to admit her. It had been the hardest decision she'd ever had to make, and it had been obvious that she'd never gotten over it. She'd always felt guilty even though she'd known deep down that the nursing facility had been the best place for Grandmother. The worst part of all, however, had been the fact that Grandmother had eventually lost most of her memory and was no longer able to recognize my mother, her sister, me, or anyone else she'd known most of her life. But nonetheless, we visited her daily, making sure she received the best care possible, and that was the one thing that gave my mother at least some comfort.

As I walked off of the elevator and down the carpeted corridor, I saw Mrs. Johnson, a sweet old lady, sitting in a wingback chair with her legs crossed—Mrs. Johnson, a lady who had no business living in anyone's nursing anything. The woman was completely in her right mind, extremely outgoing, and she dressed as well as all her thousands in the bank would allow her. She wasn't a millionaire, something she made clear every time we spoke, but she didn't have to worry about how her nursing home bill would be paid every month either. She was set for life, but the sad part was the fact that she had two sixty-something daughters who didn't see a reason to visit her more than a couple of times per month, let alone invite her to come live with one of them. Which was ridiculously shameful because Mrs. Johnson was still able to take showers without any assistance, walk around with the use of a cane, one that she didn't always need, and she knew everything that was happening throughout the world.

But sadly enough, Mrs. Johnson was only one of many residents in their late eighties who were healthy enough to still live a normal life, but too old to continue living alone. This of course—adult children not taking in their parents—was something I would never understand, and it was the reason I gave her a few minutes of my time whenever I came here.

"So, Mrs. Johnson, how are you today?"

"Still going the same as always," she said, smiling.

"Well, I'm glad to hear it," I said, sitting down next to her and admiring how sharp she looked. She was sporting a chic-looking lavender lamb's wool sweater and navy blue dress pants with lavender pinstripes.

"So how was work?" she asked.

"It was good but I'm glad it's the end of the week."

"I know the feeling. It's been over twenty years since I taught at the college, and while I loved it, there were still those days when I was glad to see the weekend come. I guess at some point we all need a break of some kind."

"I think so."

"And how's that boyfriend of yours?" she asked, and my spirit dropped to a new low. Still, I would never share with her the problems Antonio was causing for me because I didn't want to upset her.

So I lied as best I could. "He's doing well."

"Good. I like to see young people getting along and working hard at building a good life for themselves."

I wanted to comment, but instead all I did was smile.

"Are you okay?" she asked.

"Yes, I'm fine."

"And how's his mother doing? I haven't gone down to the rehab wing much this week at all because I've been participating in a different outing almost everyday. Bingo, shopping, Old Country Buffet, you name it."

"You've definitely been busy. And actually, I've been sort of busy, too, so I haven't seen her myself in over a week."

"Well, make sure you tell her I said hello and maybe I'll get to come see her sometime tomorrow."

"I will, and actually I'd better go on down to her room now myself."

"You do that, sweetie, and take care of yourself."

"You, too, Mrs. Johnson," I said, standing and hugging her.

"Your mother must have been so proud of you," she said.

"I hope so."

"I'll bet she was, and I know she would be proud to know that for over a year now you've been coming by the nursing home to sit and visit with some little old lady that you met by chance. I'll always be thankful for the day you came here with some of the ladies from your church, and for whatever reason you sat down and started talking to me. I was so sad and lonely that day, but when you left I felt better than I had in a long time."

"You're a wonderful person, Mrs. Johnson, and I always enjoy our time together."

"Me, too. But now you go on and see about Sadie, and I'll see you next time, okay?"

"You know you can count on it. And have a good weekend."

"You, too, dear."

It was so interesting how I always hated to leave this woman I saw only once a week and twice at the most. She'd been right about our chance meeting, but for some reason I'd been drawn to her immediately, something that had happened during my very first visit to the nursing facility. I'd come with a women's group I had joined at Deliverance Outreach, but even when some of the women had begun slacking off on making trips to see some of our members, I had continued coming on my own and always made sure I stopped to see Mrs. Johnson. Still, though, I wished her daughters would find it in their hearts or simply just find the time to come and visit her as well because I knew this would make her even happier.

I went through the hallway, past the nurses' station and down toward Sadie's end of the building. When I arrived in front of her room, I knocked and eased open the door, which was semi-closed, and peeked my head around it.

"Hi, sweetie," she said, sitting upright in her bed and holding the remote control for the television set.

"How are you, Sadie?" I said, hugging her and still feeling uncomfortable with calling her by her first name. My mother hadn't raised me that way, but I did it because Sadie had told me she wouldn't answer me otherwise. She just couldn't see having me call her anything else because she saw me as her friend and had decided a while ago that I was going to someday be her daughter-in-law. This was also the reason I regretted what I was going to have to tell her about Antonio.

"So how's my favorite young lady?"

"Well . . ." I said, sitting down in the chair next to her bed and placing my purse on her nightstand.

"Well, what?"

I could tell she was already trying to figure out what was wrong, and this made it even harder for me to tell her I definitely wasn't going to become a member of her family. It was also hard because Sadie was nothing like her son and didn't have a bitter bone in her body toward anyone.

"Antonio and I have broken up."

"What? Why? Sweetie, what happened?"

"It's a long story, but to begin, I just can't take his sitting around all day while I'm at work trying to make a decent living. I want so much more in life, but no matter what I say to Antonio, he just won't get a job."

"Hmmph."

"I'm sorry," I said, because she sounded as if she was sort of angry with me.

"*Sorry?* Baby, there's nothing for you to be sorry about, and to be honest, I always wondered how in the world you ever got mixed up with my son in the first place. Then, when you let him move in with you, I was even more taken aback. But after a while I figured you must have really loved him and that maybe some of your good character would rub off on him. After a while I was just glad he had someone so wonderful in his life. Especially since I knew he didn't deserve you. Not to mention I would never interfere in other grown folks' business."

I was stunned, to say the least, because I'd had no idea that she felt this way. She'd never said one negative word about Antonio the whole time I'd known her, but now I knew it was only because she probably felt a sense of loyalty to her own child.

"I guess I don't know what to say."

"You don't have to say anything because I know who my son is. I've known him his entire life and I certainly know what he's capable of. That boy has been trouble from the start because even as early as ten years old, he was already stealing candy from grocery stores. Then, by the time he was a teenager, he was running with the wrong crowd and stealing big-ticket items like TVs and stereos."

"And he never got caught?"

"He was sent to juvenile a couple of times, and that's why he didn't finish high school."

"But he told me he had a two-year degree."

"Yeah, the one he got while he was in that low-security prison for two years. He got his high school equivalency and his associate's."

"Not once has he ever mentioned being incarcerated."

"I'm sure he didn't. Antonio is very intelligent and that's why he's so good at fooling people. He knows exactly what to say and do in order to get what he wants, and when he doesn't get it, he goes crazy."

"Tell me about it. Two days ago I told him that if he didn't have a job by the end of the month, he has to move out. But then yesterday he brought me roses and an engagement ring, and when I told him he still had to go, he lost it."

"Where did he get the money to buy all that?"

"He used one of my credit cards."

"And you're still giving him thirty days to get out?"

"No, I told him I wanted him gone by this weekend, but he said he wasn't going anywhere."

Sadie sat up straighter in the bed. "He didn't put his hands on you, did he?"

"No, not really . . . well, yes. He grabbed my arm and threatened me."

"Lord have mercy on my child, but even more so on you."

"I just didn't know things would end up like this. Until now, Antonio has always been loving toward me."

"Only because you've been providing a roof over his head, clothes on his back, and food in his stomach," she said matter-of-factly, and I couldn't help thinking about how Charlotte had stated almost the same words.

"I've got to get him out but I'm so afraid of what he might do to me."

"Look, sweetheart," she said, reaching her hand under my chin and turning my face in her direction. "That's my child and I love him. But you get that lazy, freeloadin' poor-excuse-of-a-man out of your house and don't look back. You hear me? Get my son out of your house before you end up more sorry than you are now."

Tears streamed down my face and I wiped them away with both hands. I was upset because if his own mother didn't think he was worth the ground he walked on, how could I have thought any different? I'd asked myself this question at minimum a thousand times, and what was so disheartening was that I still didn't have an answer. I still couldn't come up with anything except that all this time, I'd been an extremely naïve college professor who should have known better. Or maybe love really was this blind.

"Go ahead and cry," Sadie told me. "Go ahead and cry your eyes out so that after today, you won't feel the need to shed any more tears over the mistake you made."

It was if she'd been reading my mind.

"Honey," she continued, "we've all been there and done that at one point in our lives, because even if we haven't allowed a boyfriend or husband to take advantage of us, we've allowed some other dreadful human being to do so. It's simply the way life is, but what you have to do is get over it and move on."

"But that's just it. I do want to get past this and go on with my life, but Antonio has made it clear that he's not having it."

"If he won't leave voluntarily, then you'll have to force him out. Call the police or do whatever else you have to, because him threatening you is just plain ridiculous. As a matter of fact, why don't you pass me that phone so I can have a nice little talk with him."

"No. I appreciate you offering to help, but if Antonio finds out that I told you anything, he's really going to go off. He'll say that I was here trying to upset you while you're trying to get well."

Sadie was only sixty, and the only reason she was in a nursing home was because this facility had one of the best rehabilitation departments in the city. Two weeks ago she'd had her hip replaced, but once she completed all the necessary physical therapy, she'd be going home.

"Are you sure? Because I certainly don't mind calling him. Plus it would give me a chance to let him know that when he does leave your house, he'd better find someone else to lay up on. Before he moved in with you, he was living with his daddy and me, but never again. We decided that a long time ago, and we mean what we say."

"I think it would better if I kept you out of it and just handled it the best way I can."

"Well, just don't take too long, because the longer you take, the more he'll think he owns the place, and you'll end up being a prisoner in your own home. He did that very thing to the last woman who let him live with her."

I wanted to ask her was this the same woman he'd sent to the hospital, but for some reason I already knew the answer. It was also the reason I was terrified of what he was going to do to me. I just wished he would wake up tomorrow morning, decide he could no longer stand the sight of me, and move out for good. I wished it could be that easy so I wouldn't have to deal with any more drama.

But so much for wishing, because I knew that when it came to Antonio, wishing wasn't going to help me. I knew prayer was an option and that it truly did work, but the thing was, I was already praying practically every waking moment yet nothing was actually happening. I also knew that God worked in His own timing, but with this, the horrible predicament I'd carelessly gotten myself into, I prayed that He would move faster than usual. I prayed that He would give me the courage and strength I needed to rid myself of Antonio. I prayed because I knew there was no other way out.

As soon as I turned the key and opened my front door, marijuana fumes welcomed me with open arms. The reason I say "welcomed" is because it was quite obvious that this illegal drug, along with Antonio and his three low-life friends, seemed to be the real owners while I seemed to be nothing more than a visitor.

"Antonio, can I speak to you for a minute?" I said, ignoring the Three Stooges relaxing on my furniture.

"See me for what?"

His tone was already curt and I knew this wasn't going to be pretty.

"Antonio, can I please speak with you in another room?"

"Whatever you have to say, you can say right here. These are my boys and I don't keep secrets from them anyway. And don't act like you don't know them because you met Killer a few weeks ago at Red Lobster and you've known Chad and Nate since the beginning."

To think I'd actually been in love with a man who had a friend named Killer. And while I hadn't thought much about it before, I was glad my mother wasn't around to witness any of what I was experiencing. The woman would be mortified.

"What's up, Antonio's Girl?" Nate said, the same as always.

"Yeah, what's up?" Chad echoed.

"Hey, what's happenin'?" Killer said, greeting me with bloodshot eyes and two solid-gold teeth. Although as I scanned each of their faces, I realized that they'd all been getting as high as the price of gas.

"Antonio. Just let me talk to you and then you can come right back in here."

"Look, girl. Say whatever the hell it is you have to say or leave me the hell alone. Damn."

My first reaction was to go ahead and tell him that I didn't appreciate his getting high in my home and that his friends had to leave this instant. But instead I cowardly left the room and returned to the place where I seemed to be spending an awful lot of my time. I went into my bedroom, closed the door, and began shedding my suit. I was so angry I could scream, although I must say that while I was still fearful of Antonio, this new slap in the face, him and his friends smoking drugs in my home, was just a bit too much. He was now breaking the law on my property, and the last thing I wanted was to find myself locked up for possession of something I didn't use and had never even tried as a teenager.

"So what was so important that you couldn't say it in front of my friends?" Antonio yelled, bursting into the room.

"Nothing."

"You made all that noise about nothing, huh?"

"It's not even important anymore."

"You know, you get sillier by the minute. And to think you're a college professor. All that book sense and no common sense."

"Why are you treating me this way?" I couldn't help asking.

"Because you deserve whatever you get. Thinking you could just use me for sex and companionship and then throw me out when you got ready. I told you before, I'm not someone to be played with, and now you know I was serious."

"Regardless of what has happened between us, Antonio, you could still respect my home better than you have been."

"Meaning what?"

"Meaning, you have no right bringing drugs into my house."

"So is that what you wanted to talk to me about? Because if it was, let me make something clear to you. As long as I'm living here, I'll do whatever I damn well please, and I don't want to hear another word about it."

I stared at him in a defeated manner, but all he did was sigh and shake his head. He sighed in a way that said I was pathetic, and that whether I liked it or not, he was now running the show.

Next he slammed the door and left the room.

And it was at that very moment that I wanted to call the police. I wanted to call them but I knew Antonio wouldn't think twice about telling them the drugs belonged to me. In the end, I knew it would be my word against his and that I had to figure out another way to handle this.

And soon.

Chapter 8

CHARLOTTE

Daddy, I'm so glad you're home," Marissa said, squeezing her arms around Curtis's neck so tightly that he had to be near strangulation. We were all sitting in the family room and Marissa obviously couldn't be happier.

"It's good to be home, baby girl. It's good to be here with you, Mommy, and Matthew."

"Then why do you have to be gone all the time?"

Normally I never agreed with anything Marissa had to say, but I was glad she was asking this particular question because I wanted to see if Curtis had a new excuse or if he would stick with the same reason he'd been giving both of us for months now.

"Well . . . Daddy has to be gone because he has to work. If he didn't, you wouldn't be able to have all the nice clothes you wear, you wouldn't have this nice house we live in, and we wouldn't be able to take trips to Disney World and some of the other fun places we've been."

"But I don't like it when you go away. I miss you."

"And I miss you, too. I miss all of you, but I have a job that I have to do."

I looked at Curtis and he looked at me because he knew Marissa, probably Matthew, too, and I were tired of hearing that same played-out story. We were tired because the truth was we had more than enough money to live on. Not that he should never write another book or spend time on the road promoting it, but it was time he took a break. It was time he took off at least six months so we could spend time together as a family. I loved money and I never denied it, but I still wanted so much more than that. I wanted to have consecutive days and weeks with no gaps in between where Curtis and I could make unexplainable love the way we had this afternoon.

"Matthew, don't you wish Daddy didn't have to travel to all those cities?" Marissa said.

"Yep," Matthew responded, and then smiled at Curtis.

"Don't you, too, Mommy?"

"Yep," I said, and realized the other benefit to having Curtis at home was that for the most part, Marissa acted like a normal child.

"See, Daddy, we all want you to be here with us."

"And I will. I have to travel a quite a bit over the next month, but after that, I'll see if I can be home all of November and December. That way I'll be home for the holidays."

"*Yeaaahhh!*" Marissa squealed, and hugged her father again. "I love you so much, Daddy."

Then she did something that left me speechless. She slid down from Curtis's lap, walked over to me, and embraced me tightly. "I love you, too, Mommy." Then she did something even more out of the ordinary. She turned and looked at Matthew and said, "I love you, too, Matthew."

"We love you, too, Marissa," we all said at the same time.

"Can we order the pizza now?" she said, leaving me and going back over to Curtis.

"Sounds good to me. What kind do you want?"

"Just cheese, please."

"Matthew, why don't you call it in?"

"Okay, Dad. So you want me to order a small cheese for Marissa, a large double cheese and double sausage with green peppers for you and me, and then, Mom, you want a small cheese, mushroom, and onion, right?" he said, turning his attention to me.

"That should do it," Curtis said.

"Yes, that'll be good," I added.

I watched Matthew head toward the kitchen to call Giordano's and then I leaned back in my chair, noticing Curtis flipping through the channels on our plasma television and Marissa sitting Indian-style on the floor right next to him. Had anyone dropped in on us at this very moment, they would swear our lives couldn't be better. They would swear life inside the Black household was the ideal way of living and that it just wasn't possible for any family to be happier. Of course, I had to admit that today had been one of the best days in a long while and Curtis did seem different. He'd been much more attentive to me ever since we'd made love, and now he seemed content with simply relaxing right here at home. Which was a blessing because only three days before, we'd argued like two enemies, and it was the reason I'd finally decided to contact that investigator. Although maybe this was still a good thing because if it turned out that Curtis wasn't seeing another woman, it would be good to know for sure that our marital problems stemmed only from Curtis being stressed and that it was a result of his being on the road so much. But time would tell soon enough.

After the pizza had been delivered, we ate until we were uncomfortably full and were now watching the last half of a kiddie movie Curtis had allowed Marissa to purchase at Wal-Mart a few weeks ago. She'd seen it multiple times, but now she wanted us to see it with her and we all went along with her wishes. Actually, it wasn't all that bad because even though it was animated, it had a plot to it and I had to admit I was sort of enjoying it.

We sat quietly, the way Marissa preferred, until the movie credits began rolling, and Marissa clapped like she'd never seen it before. But now it was time we checked out one of the DVDs Matthew had been dying to see.

However, our plans were halted when the doorbell rang.

"Are you expecting anyone?" Curtis asked me.

"No."

"You, Matthew?"

"Nope."

"Me either, Daddy," Marissa chimed in.

"Oh well, let's see who it is," he said, going through the hall and into the foyer.

I stood and walked behind him, but when I stepped toward the front door, I heard Curtis say coldly, "What are you doing here?"

"I was in the area, so I thought I'd look you up," a man said, one I'd never seen before.

"Well, you should have called."

"Call my own brother?"

"Like I said, you should have called."

"Well, I would have but I didn't have your number."

"Really? You didn't have my phone number but you were somehow miraculously able to get my address."

"Well, it wasn't all that hard. Not with you living like the

Rockefellers on the outskirts of a city that barely has over a hundred fifty thousand people. Which means all I had to do was ask a couple of them in terms of how to get here."

"Whatever."

"So, man, are you going to invite me in or what?"

"Well, to be honest, this isn't a good time."

"Curtis," I said, moving closer to the entrance, "who's this?"

"I'm his long-lost brother. But I'll bet you didn't even know about me," the man said, smiling.

"Curtis," I said, confused.

"It's a long story and I'll have to tell you about it later."

"Well, can't I even come in for a few minutes just to meet my niece and nephew?"

"How do you even know I have any children?"

"Curtis," he said, "this is Larry, remember? Your little Alicia used to play with my Jalen every time you and Tanya came to visit your in-laws in Atlanta. No disrespect to you," he said, looking at me. "And by the way, it's nice to meet you."

"Same here, and I'm Charlotte."

"Larry, why don't you leave me your number and I'll give you a call." Curtis was starting to get impatient and I knew it was just a matter of time before he said something indignant. I knew this because while I didn't have the story on Larry, Curtis's body language and facial expressions screamed a noticeable dislike toward him.

"I can't believe you're being this cold, man. To your own brother."

"Well, maybe it's because I don't feel all that safe inviting in some drug dealer who stole from his own family, lost his wife and child, and ended up on the streets. I mean, would you want someone like you being around your children?"

Larry stood there in silence but I could tell he was ashamed of what must have been the truth. Which now explained why Curtis had never mentioned him to me before now. Still, though, I wanted to know why Larry hadn't even bothered to show up at his mother's funeral, because no matter how down on his luck he was, I couldn't imagine anyone forgoing one last chance to see their mother.

"Curtis, man, that's all in the past. I've been clean for over two years and I'm trying to make amends to everyone. Everyone I hurt in any way, including you."

"Daddy, who's that at the door?" Marissa wanted to know.

"I'm your Uncle Larry," he said, smiling, and Marissa leaned against her father and smiled back at him. She only did this when she immediately liked someone, and of course this wasn't very often.

I turned around when I heard Matthew walking toward us.

"Curtis, it's chilly out there, so why don't we let Larry come inside?"

"Can we, Daddy?" Marissa asked.

"I guess. But just for a few minutes or so," Curtis said, and left us all standing where we were.

"Come on in, Larry, and make yourself at home," I told him.

"Thanks," he said, following us into the family room.

"Have a seat. Can I get you something to drink or eat?"

"I'll take some juice or soda if you have it."

"All we had tonight was pizza, but you're welcome to it if you want it."

"Well, if it's not too much of a bother," he agreed, and I saw Curtis giving him a dirty look.

"It's no bother at all."

"Curtis, you've got a beautiful family, man. You're really blessed, you know that?"

"And so were you once upon a time."

I continued into the kitchen and wondered why Larry had suddenly shown up out of nowhere. Especially since he had to know that Curtis wasn't going to be happy to see him. But maybe he'd been hoping that bygones would be bygones and that things would be fine in the long run. Although if he thought that, he couldn't possibly have known Curtis as well as I did, because Curtis was not the most forgiving man on earth whenever someone crossed him. I knew that reality better than anyone, and before the evening was over Larry would understand it, too.

When I came back into the family room and put down a plate of pizza and glass of soda in front of Larry, he was making himself more acquainted with the children.

"So, little Marissa, how old are you?"

"I'm five, but I'll be six in December and Daddy says that's only three months away."

"That it is."

"And what about you, Matthew?"

"I'm twelve."

"Man, you'll be a teenager pretty soon, then."

"Uh-huh," Matthew agreed proudly.

Larry and the children continued their small talk for another twenty minutes or so, but in the meantime Curtis said nothing.

"So how'd you know Curtis was living in Mitchell?" I asked.

"Well, to be honest, I was watching a broadcast on television for one of the megachurches in Atlanta, and it just so happens that Curtis was the guest speaker. And, of course, you know Curtis, he was bragging on his wonderful wife, son, and daughters and he mentioned that he lived in Mitchell. So I decided it was time I paid my brother a visit."

This time Curtis looked at him directly and I wondered when he was going to finally blow. I was hoping he wouldn't lose it in front of the children, but if Larry didn't leave fairly soon . . .

"Larry, man, I don't mean to be rude, but I just got home this afternoon and the plan was for my family and me to spend some quality time with each other. You understand, don't you?"

I almost laughed because Curtis was the only person I knew who could tell you to get your behind up and get out of his house in such a cordial tone.

"Oh, I'm sorry. Because I definitely didn't mean to intrude."

"Maybe you can come back another time," I said, trying to sweeten the atmosphere.

"Can he, Daddy?" Marissa asked. "Because I like Uncle Larry."

"We'll see."

Yeah, right. Because no matter what Curtis was saying to Marissa, I knew he would never approve of Larry being in our home ever again.

"Well, I guess I should go," Larry said, downing the last of his soda.

"Let me walk you to the door," Curtis quickly offered, but we all escorted him. Me because I wanted to make sure Curtis didn't end up punching Larry, and the children because they clearly did like him.

"Uncle Larry, maybe sometime you could come play football in the backyard with my friends and me," Matthew said.

"Absolutely."

"Will you play one of my games with me, too?" Marissa said.

"Of course. I look forward to it." He paused. "Okay, well, I guess I'll be going."

"Bye," Matthew and Marissa said in unison.

"See you, Larry," I said, but I was shocked to see him walk down the sidewalk into the driveway and then out to the street. I'd just assumed he'd driven here, but from the looks of it, he'd walked.

"Curtis, it's cold outside," I said when the children went back to the family room.

"I'm sure he'll be just fine," he said, and closed the door.

"Why are you so angry with him, and why haven't you ever talked about him to me?"

"Charlotte, baby, not tonight, okay?"

"But all I want to know is—"

"Baby, please. I said I don't want to do this right now, so can't you just respect that?"

"Whatever," I said, walking in front of him and into the kitchen.

I hated when he took out his frustrations on me, specifically when I had no clue as to what the situation was between him and his brother. It certainly wasn't my fault that the man had shown up here unannounced. And it definitely wasn't my fault that he was charming and just as gorgeous as Curtis and that I liked him as much as the children did. Larry was just one of those people. You know the kind, extremely intelligent but seemed a little rough around the edges? Almost sort of like Antonio, except it was obvious that Larry had once been very successful professionally and had lived a very good life. I wasn't sure why I believed that, but for some reason the man screamed class. Yes, he had no transportation and was apparently down on his luck, but he clearly hadn't lost his charming ways. He was just as charismatic as Curtis and he was someone you couldn't help wanting get to know better, even if you knew he hadn't always been the upstanding citizen he should've been.

I put the dishes in the dishwasher and wondered when Larry would be calling on us again. Because no matter how badly Curtis had treated him a few minutes ago, I knew Larry wasn't giving up that easily. I could tell that giving up just wasn't part of his personality.

Chapter 9

CHARLOTTE

It had been a while since Curtis had preached at Deliverance Outreach, but when he'd learned that he was going to be home for a few days, he'd decided to preach this morning's sermon. The congregation, of course, would be excited because most of the members had known Curtis and me since when we'd founded the church, and now with Curtis being well known throughout the country, they felt even more honored to be in his presence.

Right now we were getting dressed but I was still waiting to find out why Curtis had such animosity toward his brother. I'd wanted to ask him again yesterday, but with us traveling down to Champaign to see Alicia at her college campus, I hadn't wanted to upset Curtis or cause any friction between us overall. I'd wanted all of us to enjoy the time we had together, but the more I thought about Larry, the more I needed answers to my questions.

"So when are you going to tell me the story on Larry?" I said while sitting on the chaise and pulling on my panty hose.

Curtis stood facing the dresser mirror and sighed deeply. "You're just not going to let this go, are you?"

"No, because when a man shows up announcing that he's your brother and I've never heard one mention of him before, well, that's a problem. I mean, it's not like you and I just met, Curtis. We've been married for seven years."

"First of all, I think I need to clarify that Larry is not my brother."

"Then why did he say he was two nights ago, and why haven't you said otherwise?"

"He's not my biological brother."

I pulled my panty hose up to my waist. "Now I'm confused."

"There was a time when everyone thought we were blood brothers, but we aren't."

"It still doesn't make any sense."

"Okay, look. This is the deal. When I left home and went down to Atlanta to attend Morehouse College, Larry and I became best friends. I had already disassociated myself from my mother and sister, and the closer Larry and I became, the more time I spent with him and his parents on weekends, holidays, and summer breaks. And I guess because his parents treated me like their own son, I started calling them Mom and Dad and I began telling everyone that Larry was my brother. And before long, everyone around us started to believe it. Which was fine with me because you already know what a terrible father I had, so Larry's parents were a dream come true for me. It was so much easier to pretend that I was a member of their family because, unlike mine, they were always happy."

"Well, if that's the case, then why do you hate him so much now and why did you lose touch with him?"

Curtis raised up the collar of his pure white, medium-starched, French-cuffed dress shirt and slipped on a black-and-white diagonally striped tie.

"We lost touch because right after Tanya and I divorced, Larry turned to drugs and lost everything. Including his wife, his daughter . . . everything."

"Had he ever done drugs before?"

"No. At least not that I was aware of, but since I knew everything about him back then, I really doubt it. And even worse, he found some shady mortgage company and they refinanced his house without Tammy's signature. So, of course, after he lost his job as a CPA and withdrew a ton of money from their savings accounts to support his crack habit, Tammy and their daughter, Jalen, ended up losing everything."

"That's too bad."

"So now you see why I cut him off and why I don't want anything to do with him. I even had to send money down to Tammy so that she and Jalen could put down a deposit on an apartment and pay their first month's rent. Plus Larry's parents had to help her quite a bit until she got back on her feet. She ended up having to file for bankruptcy . . . and just having to think about all this again makes me sick. It really pisses me off and that's why I don't want Larry calling here or stepping foot inside this house ever again."

Curtis was hot, and while I was preparing to ask him why he thought Larry had shown up on Friday evening after all these years, Curtis blurted out the answer before I could say anything.

"The only reason that Negro showed up here after all this time is because he found out what I do for a living and because he thought he could scheme his way into a lot of money. But what he doesn't know is that it'll be over my dead body."

"But what if that's not the reason?" I carefully suggested. "What if he's been clean for a while and he really is sorry for what he did? I mean, what if he really wants to turn his life around?"

"Once a schemer, always a schemer. Right?"

"And what is that supposed to mean?"

"Nothing, Charlotte. Just forget it and let's just change the subject."

We could change the subject all he wanted but I knew when he'd said "Right?" he was trying to say that I was a perfect example. He was saying loudly and clearly that if I'd schemed behind his back the way I had in the past, I was certainly capable of doing it again. Although I wondered if he'd forgotten about all the low-down things he'd done over the years. I wondered if he was willing to point the gun in his own direction, because Lord knows his history of moral values was seriously lacking.

"You're wrong," I said, heading into our walk-in closet to get the black suit I'd purchased a couple of weekends go.

"Wrong for what?"

"You're wrong for having such a nasty attitude toward me just because your brother dropped over here."

"I told you he's not my brother."

"Well, your play brother, acquaintance, or whatever he is. But regardless, I didn't ask him to ring our doorbell and I never knew one thing about him until then."

"You're right. And I'm sorry. But Larry hurt so many people that it angers me to no end. He even stole a television, a microwave, and his mother's diamond earrings from their home just so he could buy drugs."

It seemed that the story only got worse as Curtis continued talking, but the sad part of it all was that Larry didn't seem like the type. Maybe I was naïve and only saw what I wanted to see, but while I'd already said this before, he was very likable.

I also was a believer that everyone deserved a second chance. I knew Curtis wasn't too keen on that philosophy and neither was my cousin Anise, but I believed that forgiveness was a necessary sacrifice. I had believed this most of my life, and all I could hope was that Curtis would eventually come to his senses. I doubted it, but I knew anything was possible.

Curtis drove the SUV out of our subdivision and headed toward the church. The temperature had dropped considerably over the last few days, but rightfully so since we were only days from entering October. Matthew was dressed in a navy blue cable-knit sweater and a pair of navy dress pants, and Marissa had on a hot pink corduroy jean-style jacket and skirt, all of which I'd purchased a few days ago from the Ralph Lauren outlet store. Curtis looked as sharp as always, and no matter how many years seemed to pass, he still looked as handsome as ever. He still caught the eye of most women, and no one would guess that he was forty-five. Thirty-eight or thirty-nine maybe, but definitely not a year more than that. And to top that off, he smelled good at all times. Today I wasn't sure what he was wearing, probably something brand new, but the scent reminded me of musk and some sweet aroma I couldn't think of at the moment. Then there was his perfect skin and perfectly cut hair—all reasons why I knew there had to be loads of women in every city throwing themselves at him.

"Daddy, when can we see Uncle Larry again?" Marissa asked, and I looked over at Curtis.

"I know you won't understand what I'm about to say because he seemed so nice the other night, but your Uncle Larry is not a good person. A long time ago, when he and I were both a lot younger, he was, but not anymore."

"But why isn't he a good person?"

"I wish I could explain it, baby girl, but I can't. Although I will say that sometimes grown-ups lose their way."

"Well, I like him. And Matthew likes him, too, don't you, Matthew?"

"Yep," Matthew said, not taking his eyes off the electronic game he was playing.

"See, Daddy?"

Curtis ignored Marissa's last comment, and surprisingly, she didn't say another word. This of course meant she wasn't happy about what her father had just told her but unlike when I told her something she didn't like, she kept quiet.

When we arrived at the church lot, Curtis parked in his designated parking space, which was also next to mine, and then we all walked inside the back way. Just as we did, Aunt Emma and Anise were walking up the stairs. I wanted to speak to my aunt but dreaded seeing my cousin. However, I knew Curtis was happy to see them both.

"Now, I know neither one of you is going to pretend like you don't see me," he said, teasing.

"Curtis," Aunt Emma said, "honey, it's so good to see you," she said, hugging him.

"It's good to see you, too. It's been a long time."

"Yes, it has."

"And how're you, Anise?"

"I'm good, Curtis," she said, the two of them embracing. "It's wonderful to see you."

"Hey, Aunt Emma," I said, interrupting.

"Hey, sweetie. How are you? And why haven't you called or been over to see me?"

"I'm fine and I guess I've just been busy with these two here," I said, referring to the children.

"I can imagine. They're growing up so fast."

She reached her arms out to both of them and they went over to greet her. Marissa only did so because Curtis was standing there watching. I knew this because Aunt Emma and Anise were two more individuals Marissa had never cared for. Her reason for not liking them was anyone's guess, and to be honest, I no longer tried to figure it out. Not just why she didn't like them, but why she didn't like most people.

Matthew, on the other hand, loved his aunt and cousin, and the smile and excitement on his face proved it.

"Well, I guess we'd better get in here and get a seat because with you preaching today, you know it's going to be a packed house," Aunt Emma said to Curtis.

"You think so, huh?"

"Come on now, you know the entire congregation looks forward to hearing you preach."

"That they do," Anise said, and I couldn't resist making her speak to me. Especially since she was speaking so freely to my husband.

"Hi, Anise."

"Charlotte," she said, and turned her head away from me.

That witch. She hadn't even said "Hi, Charlotte." I knew she had every reason to be upset with me, but after five years, this was starting to get ridiculous. I'd been walking around on eggshells, praying that she would start speaking to me again, but I was now becoming tired of it. I was losing my patience with her slowly but surely, and before long I was going to dismiss her for good. I was sorry and had told her so on a good number of occasions, but I wasn't going to do it anymore. Either she would finally accept my apology or she wouldn't, but either way I was moving on.

Once we'd had devotion, altar prayer, and the choir had sung a couple of songs, the Reverend Tolson, the residing pastor, stood at the pulpit.

"Today is a very special day," he began. "Today is special because we have in our presence the founder of Deliverance Outreach."

"Amen," said most everyone in attendance.

"We have in our presence a true man of God who along with his wife had the vision to start this great church and who went on to write and sell millions of copies of his books, the kind that are helping millions worldwide. The man we have in our presence today has gone on to become one of the most sought-after speakers in this country, delivering a message to sometimes thousands at a time. The man we have in our presence is none other than our own Reverend Curtis Black."

Everyone stood with applause and Curtis shook hands with the Reverend Tolson and stepped to the podium. He stood there for a few seconds, but the applause only continued. Which was always the case every time he was able to be here. It was almost as if most of the members worshiped him and wouldn't have missed hearing him speak, not under any circumstances.

"Thank you," Curtis said, and motioned for everyone to take their seats.

"It's good to be here with all of you. It's good because no matter how many places I travel to, the saying still stands . . . There really is no place like home."

Amens resonated again, but what I wanted to do was stand up and ask Curtis why, if he felt this way, did he seem to do everything he could to stay out on the road? I wanted to ask him why over the last thirty days, he'd only been home for maybe a total of seven.

"And I have to admit, the hardest thing of all is being away from my beautiful wife and three wonderful children," he continued. "It's hard being away from the people you love most and then trying to decide whether it's really worth it. Because over the last couple of days, Charlotte," he said, looking directly at me, "whether you realize it or not, I've been thinking a lot about how important you and the children really are to me. I know it hasn't been easy for you, being left alone all the time, but I promise you things are going to be different."

The church was mesmerized and in total agreement with what he was saying, but I couldn't tell whether he was telling the truth or putting on a show the same as always. Curtis was so hard to read, because less than a week ago he'd been rude and cruel to me on the phone and had pretty much told me to get used to all his traveling because he had to do what he had to do, but now he was acting as if he couldn't live without me. Although I had to admit that we had had a blissful weekend thus far. It hadn't been perfect, mainly because of Larry's surprise visit, but overall we'd been happier with each other than we'd been in five years. Maybe Curtis had finally come to realize that he did love me, that we both had our faults and that our marriage was truly worth fighting for. But with Curtis, who knew for sure? The most I could do was wait and see.

"Before I have you turn your Bibles to the Book of Luke, I just want to say to the Reverend Tolson, keep doing what you're doing. I knew when I first met you that you were the best man to lead the church in my absence, and I'm proud to know that you have done over and above what I ever expected. So thank you and may God continue blessing you with this ministry."

Curtis read Ephesians 5:25, which talks about husbands loving their wives even as Christ also loved the church, and then spoke on the subject "All in the Family." He talked about the importance of family and how so many people, including him, were guilty of taking their families for granted.

He preached what seemed straight from the heart and the congregation agreed with every word he said. The spirit was moving in a way that couldn't be explained, and even I found myself shedding tears of joy. Maybe because it seemed that my life with Curtis was about to take a turn for the better, and maybe it was because I couldn't deny how proud I was to be married to someone in Curtis's position. I was proud to be married to someone who was loved by most everyone.

"The doors of the church are open," Curtis said, nearing the end of his sermon and stepping down from the pulpit. At the same time, five people made their way to the front of the church and sat on the front pew. The music played, the choir sang softly, and Curtis asked if there was anyone else who was tired of being out in the street, tired of fighting a losing battle without God in their lives.

"Is there another?" he said, wiping the perspiration from his forehead with a handkerchief.

And I thought I would pass out when Larry stood and walked down the aisle. I didn't have a problem with him coming forward and turning his life over to God, but I was desperately concerned about the way Curtis might react to him.

As Larry walked over to Curtis and hugged him, the congregation applauded and a couple of people spoke in tongues. Shortly after, the music stopped and Curtis asked the names of each person who had come. Most of them hadn't wanted to make any particular remarks, but Larry took the cordless microphone from Curtis and turned to face everyone.

"First, I just want to say that I really don't know God, but the reason I came up here is because I want to get to know Him."

The church roared with amens, hallelujahs, and "Thank you, Jesus."

"Because I'm finally at the end of my rope and I'm tired of struggling the way I have been. I'm ashamed to tell you that I was once a drug user who ruined the lives of his wife and child and stole from his own parents. I'm ashamed to tell you that crack became more important to me than any human being I could think of and I was willing to do whatever I had to to get my hands on it."

"My Lord!" one of the older women in the church exclaimed.

"Please have mercy on us today!" another added.

"But now, I've been clean for two years and I want to be a better person. I also want to apologize to my brother Curtis," he said, and I heard gasps throughout the sanctuary. "Curtis and I are not blood brothers, but he's as much of a brother as I could have ever prayed for. We were close until I turned to drugs and allowed them to take over my life. And Curtis, man . . . I'm sorry."

Tears flowed down his face and he hugged Curtis so firmly that I wondered if Curtis could still breathe.

Curtis went along with what Larry was saying, but while Curtis's pleasant demeanor may have been working for everyone else, I could see as clear as day that he still wasn't happy about Larry. He still didn't trust him, didn't believe a word he was saying, and still didn't want him around.

But for me, I wasn't sure what to think. I couldn't tell whether Larry was feigning his sincerity the way Curtis obviously thought he was or if he was maybe being on the up and up.

I couldn't tell one way or the other, but what I did know was that learning Larry's true mission was inevitable.

Chapter 10

CHARLOTTE

Right after service, we'd stopped at Smokehouse, a barbecue and soul food restaurant. Curtis and Matthew had ordered rib dinners, I'd ordered roasted chicken with macaroni and cheese and green beans, and Marissa had gotten her usual: French fries, a side of coleslaw, and peach cobbler. I wasn't sure why, but she'd never liked eating meat. She'd eaten chicken a few times when she was three years old, but over the last two years she'd gone straight vegetarian. Well, not straight exactly, because she did eat eggs and lots of dairy products, which I was happy about because at least she still got the protein she needed.

We'd laughed and talked and had a great time together, and now Curtis and I were in our bedroom changing out of our dress clothes and the children were in their respective quarters doing the same.

"Can you believe that fool had the audacity to show up at church this morning?" Curtis said, loosening his tie.

I'd been wondering when he was finally going to bring up

the subject of Larry, although now I knew he was simply waiting to do it when the children weren't around. Still I didn't say anything because I didn't want a discussion to turn into an argument.

"He had a lot of nerve walking his behind down that aisle, trying to fool the entire congregation into believing he's a changed man," Curtis continued. "Because I'm here to tell you right now, he's not. He's still the same conniving manipulator he was when he was still out there using, and to be honest, who's to say he's not still out there doing it now?"

"All I'll say is that he doesn't look like he's strung out on anything," I finally said.

"Maybe not strung out, but there's no way for you to tell if someone is drug free until you've been around them for a while. Plus Larry had one of those slick, charming personalities even when he was clean and living a normal life."

Well, wasn't that the hair weave calling the curly wig fake. But maybe Curtis just didn't see himself in the same light. Maybe he didn't know that he was exactly the same way, and had been since the day I'd first met him.

"People do change," I tried to explain. "I know you don't believe that, but what if he's really trying to get his life together and just wants a shoulder or two to lean on in the process?"

"Please. Just mark my word. Larry Reynolds means nothing but trouble."

"But what if we're turning away someone who really needs our help? Someone who isn't simply trying to get over on us?"

"You just don't get it, do you? And that's fine, but I'm telling you, I don't want him coming around here. I've said this more than once over the last couple of days, but I'm saying it again so that there won't be any misunderstandings. I don't want him having any contact with you, Matthew, or Marissa. Period."

"Whatever you want," I said, pulling the black three-quarter-sleeved, V-neck sweater over my head and down over my body. Then I slipped on a pair of black riding pants and reached for my ankle boots with three-inch heels. "Are you sure you don't want to go over to Janine's with me?"

"No, I think it's best for me to stay here with the kids, because if that fool Antonio steps out of line with me, I'll end up hurting him."

I laughed because I knew Curtis was partly being humorous and partly serious. Serious because he cared about Janine the same as I did and he certainly wasn't happy about the way Antonio was treating her. Yesterday I'd told him what was going on with them, just before we'd driven down to see Alicia, and Curtis had had more than a few words to say.

"I'm really worried about her because I know he's threatening her exactly the way she's saying," I said.

"Well, you know I've never understood why she ever started dating him in the first place."

"Me neither. But the thing is she really loved him, and while I keep telling her to kick him out, there's no telling what he'll do to retaliate."

"I feel bad for her, and when you see her tell her that I'll be praying for all this to come to an end."

"I will," I said, and kissed him on the lips. But when I prepared to step away, Curtis pulled me into his arms and kissed me again.

"You do know that I meant what I said during service this morning, right?"

"No. I don't."

"Well, you should because I was serious. I know I've been distant and, as you say, 'rude' to you, but I'm going to do everything I can to make things better between us. I was also serious when I told Marissa that I'm going to finish out my engagements over the next month so I can be home through the end of the year. And then, next year, I'm going to cut my normal traveling in half and do some more writing, and maybe you can go with me some of the time and the kids can do the same during the summer months."

"That's all I've been asking for," I said, smiling, but deep down I couldn't help wondering why Curtis's attitude toward me had changed so drastically and if it was going to last for any real length of time. But maybe it would.

"And just for the record, I do love you. I know I said it wasn't the same as in the beginning, and that's still partly true, but I do love you the way a man should love his wife."

"I love you, too, and I've never stopped. I've disliked you on a number of occasions, but I never stopped loving you."

He kissed me again and said, "You'd better get going so you can check on Janine."

"I know. See you when I get back," I said, and realized I hadn't felt this happy in months.

But when I walked down the stairway I heard Marissa telling Matthew that she hated him. I was carrying my boots in my hand because I wasn't in the habit of walking across the carpet or any other flooring with them on, and this allowed me to ease closer to the family room without Marissa or Matthew realizing it. The television was on but Marissa spoke softly yet loud enough for me to hear everything she was saying.

"Nobody likes you, not even Daddy, so why don't you go live somewhere else?" she told him. "Because I don't want a brother or a mother. I just want it to be Daddy and me living here," she said, pausing. "And that's why I wish someone would run you over with their car or shoot a bullet in your head," she said.

That's when I'd finally had enough.

But as I walked into the family room, preparing to yell at Marissa, Curtis came in behind me and Marissa ran over to him, smiling.

"Daddy, I'm so glad we went to church today, and I love you so much. I love Mommy and I love Matthew, too. I'm the luckiest girl in the world."

"There's no such thing as luck, young lady, but yes, you are very blessed," he said, picking her up—he picked up this demonic five-year-old who had just admitted that she wanted her brother or me terminated.

And the same as every other time Marissa had shown how unstable she was, Matthew looked at her, then at me, and didn't say a word.

Today, though, I wanted to scream. I wanted desperately to tell Curtis about the stove incident, about the inexcusable way Marissa frequently treated Matthew and me, and about every other malicious act she had committed. But I couldn't. I couldn't tell him anything because I couldn't take the chance that he might start thinking that Marissa wasn't his. I couldn't take the chance of him believing that Aaron might be her natural father regardless of the paternity test results he'd been given. And although I knew keeping Marissa's obvious issues a secret wasn't the right thing to do, I didn't see where I had a choice. Not when things were looking up for Curtis and me. Not when it seemed that our marriage finally had a chance at making it.

So instead I kissed Matthew on his forehead, told him I loved him, and then did the same to Marissa.

"I love you, too, Mommy," she said, and then climbed into Curtis's lap. "See you when you get back."

And it was only then that I realized who Marissa reminded me of.

Rhoda Penmark, the little girl in *The Bad Seed*.

I strode up the walkway to Janine's condo but in the back of my mind I couldn't help thinking about the horrible things Marissa had said to Matthew. I thought about the fact that this couldn't have been the first time and how Matthew had kept quiet about all of it. Marissa had always spoken to him in a more than nasty tone, but until today I had never caught her wishing such tragedy and violence on him and it scared me. It also angered me, and I knew, for Matthew's sake, I was going to have to do something about it. I wasn't sure what, but there was no way I could continue allowing my son to be subjected to such abuse.

When I rang the doorbell, it only took a few seconds for Antonio to answer it.

"Is Janine here?" I said, even though I already knew she was because I'd called her from my cell phone.

"She's back there somewhere," he said, leaving me at the door and heading back into the living room, totally dismissing me.

I'd never liked him, but now I flat out couldn't stand the sight of him. And I just *knew* that wasn't marijuana I was smelling. Couldn't be. Although from the looks of his scary-looking three-man posse, I wouldn't be surprised.

"Tonio, man, who's that fine-ass mofo right there?" one of them said, and I cringed.

"And is she puttin' out anything, because I'd like to have me some of that," another one added.

"Man, you don't want her," Antonio advised. "She's more uppity than that bitch Janine."

I walked away from the front door and headed down the hallway to Janine's bedroom, but before I made it there, she leaned out from one of the spare rooms that she'd turned into a den.

She looked at me, I walked in, shaking my head in disgust, and she closed the door behind me.

"Girl, did you know those idiots were out there getting high?" I asked, sitting down on the sofa next to her and resting my handbag on the floor.

"Yeah, I did."

"And you're okay with that?"

"No, I'm outraged. But what can I do?"

"Put that fool out! And his friends, too."

"It's just not that simple."

"I'm not saying it is, but how long are you going to allow this? Because now this joker is doing drugs and acting as though this is some party place."

"And that's why I know I have to get him out of here."

"But when, J?" We were best friends and I loved her, but I was starting to tire from all this tolerance she seemed to have built around Antonio.

"Soon. Very soon."

"Well, I hope so, because Antonio has lost his mind and he's so disrespectful."

"That's why I told you I didn't think it was a good idea for you to come by here."

"I know, but since you weren't at church, I wanted to see how you were. Plus, regardless of who Antonio thinks he is, I'm not afraid of him," I said matter-of-factly, and then Antonio opened the door like some tyrant.

"Hey, I need to borrow a hundred dollars," he practically demanded.

"I don't have it," Janine answered.

"Liar."

"I'm not a liar. I really don't have it."

"Then go to the ATM."

"Why don't *you* go to the ATM?" I interrupted.

"What? I just know you're not talkin' to me."

"Well, I must be because I don't see anybody else in here begging for money."

"You need to mind your own business before you end up gettin' hurt," he said, frowning.

"Charlotte, please just leave it alone," Janine pleaded.

"No, let this rich bitch keep runnin' her mouth so I can show her who's in charge over here," he said, walking farther into the room and acting as if he wanted to hit me.

I wished he would.

"Look," Janine hurried to say, and stood up. Next she went toward her bedroom. "All I have is a fifty."

"Then give me that," he said, glaring angrily at me and following behind her.

I was totally and completely astounded by what I'd just witnessed. Janine was already allowing him to live with her scotfree and now she was giving him money? I knew she was afraid of him, but maybe her fear was worse than I realized.

I sat there for a few minutes until Janine returned to the den. Antonio followed her again.

"And just so you know, I never liked you, anyway," he declared to me.

"Then that makes two of us, because I never liked you either. As a matter of fact, I don't like any broke man I can think of."

"You know, instead of worrying about *my* business, you need to be worrying about that preacher husband of yours and all that traveling he does. Because you can bet he's got women all across the nation and you're just too stupid to realize it. Although from what I just heard from one of my boys a few minutes ago, there was a time when you were out there gettin' your freak on, too. So maybe you and the reverend got it goin' on like that."

I wanted to call him everything imaginable but I would never let him know how much he was upsetting me.

"Yeah, Ms. Thing, it's a small world after all, because it just so happens that Killer's mother used to go to Deliverance Outreach and he knows the whole story on you and some crazy dude you hooked up with a few years back and how he burned down your house."

At this very moment, I felt like crawling under the sofa because Janine knew nothing about Aaron. At least I didn't think she did, and I had planned on keeping it that way.

"I'll bet you didn't know your girl was keeping *these* kinds of secrets from you, did you, Janine?" he continued, and then strutted away, laughing.

Janine sat there for a few seconds, just as quiet as I was, and then she said softly, "Charlotte, I *did* know. I heard about it right after I moved here, but I couldn't care less. You're still my best friend and I would never judge you based on something that happened in your past. So forget Antonio. Forget everything he said, because it doesn't mean anything."

I heard what she was saying but to me his words meant everything.

They meant that as long as I lived in this gossipy little town, I would never be able to live down the horrendous mistake I'd made and that there would always be someone like Antonio who couldn't wait to remind me of it.

It was one of the things I missed about the big city of Chicago, because unlike here in Mitchell, everyone didn't know everyone.

Not everyone knew or cared about your business and that was good.

It was a true benefit I missed.

Chapter 11

JANINE

I eased farther down into the bathtub so that my entire body was completely covered with bubbles. The water was way past warm but not too hot, and I felt more relaxed than I had in a long time. Normally I would take soothing baths like this only at night because it helped me get a good night's sleep, but this morning I'd decided that it might help to calm my nerves and prepare me for another week.

Today was Monday, and of course this past weekend hadn't been one of my happiest. It also hadn't ended on the best note, not with Antonio embarrassing Charlotte the way he had last night. I'd felt so bad and it was the reason I had never brought the subject up to her. I'd heard the story more than once from a couple of women at the church, but to me the past is exactly that and all I knew was that Charlotte had always treated me like family. I was even sure that some of the versions I'd heard were exaggerated because each time I'd heard them, the story had been slightly changed. This was also the reason I never took rumors too seriously.

I leaned my head against the back of the tub and closed my eyes. It was still very early, only five A.M., so I was glad I didn't have to get dressed for a while. Although the more I thought about it, it might have been best if I left before Antonio awakened and found some new way to harass me. Worse, he might even try to finagle more money from me. I was still saddened by the fact that I'd given him anything at all, but now he was taking things too far. I knew Charlotte had been beside herself and hadn't understood why I would give him cash, but she just didn't know what I was up against. It was always so easy for people to be on the outside looking in and deciding what they would never do, what they would never, ever tolerate. But for the most part, whenever someone was so adamant on what they wouldn't put up with, chances were they had never been in the situation in the first place.

After soaking for almost an hour, I realized I'd nodded off to sleep for a few minutes. I hadn't planned to but I guess I'd been more comfortable and content than I'd realized. However, I knew it was time I washed and got out. Which is what I did, and then turned the knob to drain the water.

I stood up, stepped out, and dried myself with an oversized bath towel. Then I saturated my skin with this wonderful vanilla and almond body butter by a new company called Drippin' Nectar by Janell. I'd also been using her scrubs and oils, too, for more than a year, and I must say that I hadn't been able to find anything better. It was the reason I made sure to never run out of it.

But so much for all the pampering I'd just given myself, because just when I walked out of the bathroom and into the bedroom, Antonio came through the doorway. Of course it had been closed and he hadn't knocked or anything. He was now sleeping in the guest bedroom and I was glad of that, but I wasn't happy about him bursting in on me anytime he wanted.

"You know," he began, "that trick Charlotte has one more time to speak to me the way she did yesterday, so I suggest you put her in check."

I pulled my towel tighter around my body and went over to the dresser and pulled out my underwear, but I refused to acknowledge what Antonio was saying.

"Oh, so now you're gonna try to ignore somebody?"

I went back into the bathroom, slipped on my panties and bra, folded the towel in half, and hung it on the chrome and gold rack. Then I came back out and went directly into my closet.

"Janine, did you hear me?" he said, moving in behind me, and now I knew I'd better respond to him.

"Yes, I did hear you, but what do you want me to say? Because it's not like I can tell Charlotte what and what not to do."

"Well, you'd better. Because if you don't, your little friend is going to find herself laid up at the hospital somewhere. She talks way too much and it's all because her money has gone to her head."

"I'm sure you won't have to worry about it, because after the way you humiliated her yesterday, I doubt she'll be coming around here anytime soon."

"Good. Because I don't want her here, anyway. And since we're on the subject of what I want and don't want, maybe this is as good a time as any to tell you how things are going to be around here from now on," he said, dropping down in the chair near the window.

"Meaning what, Antonio?" I said, stopping dead in my tracks.

"Meaning, you can go and come as you please, because it's not like I want you sexually anymore, anyway. To be honest, it was never all that great. You weren't the worst I've had, but you definitely don't qualify for any first-place medals. That's for damn sure."

I swallowed hard and continued getting dressed, trying to pretend my feelings weren't hurt.

But he continued with his list of demands.

"Next I want the refrigerator to be full at all times. I've noticed how you've been slacking up on your grocery shopping, I guess trying to punish me, but that shit ends today. I want it fully stocked with the things you know I like. Then, as far as my boys are concerned, I don't want to hear any complaints about how much they're hanging around, because we're about to start us a little business venture and that means they'll be in and out of here a lot."

"What kind of business venture?" I said, turning to look at him directly.

"The kind that will make sure I'm never in the position you put me in yesterday, having to ask you for funds and you only giving me fifty percent of it. I told you I needed a hundred dollars and that's what you should have given me."

"But I didn't have it."

"Just stop it, Janine. Stop lying before you make me hurt you."

I backed away, went into the bathroom, and zipped open my makeup bag.

"Ignore me all you want to, but I'll bet you one thing. That refrigerator had better have a ton of food in it by this evening," he said, yelling at me. He yelled a few more words and I prayed he would just leave the bedroom. I prayed that he would leave me alone altogether.

But he wouldn't and instead followed behind me again.

"And just so we're on the same page . . . if you even think about calling the police, you should know that my boys are capable of doing just about anything to anyone at anytime. Your family, including that drunk for a father you have in Ohio, and your skank friend that was here yesterday."

"Antonio, how can you do this to me, knowing that I've done everything I could for you?"

"It's like I told you before, you had no business thinking you could dismiss me like I was nothing. But since you thought you could, these are the new house rules and you either abide by them or else."

I gazed at him; however, all he did was walk away.

But then he stopped and turned back toward my direction.

"Oh and one other thing, Killer might need to stay here for a few days. His girl is actin' almost as stupid as you are, and I told him he could crash here if he needed to."

I knew this should have sent me into a violent rage, but at this point I was too numb to feel anything.

"Curtis, it's so good to see you," I said after entering the house and hugging my best friend's husband. I'd just gotten off work and decided to pay them a visit.

"I'm good. And you?"

"Well, I guess you already know the story about Antonio," I said. "So actually I could be better."

"Hey, J," Charlotte said, embracing me.

"Hey, girl. I know I called on short notice and I hate dropping in like this, but I just didn't want to go home."

"Please," Charlotte said, frowning. "Don't you ever feel bad about coming over here. Not ever."

"Well, I do because I know the two of you only have a couple more days together before Curtis has to leave back out, and I didn't want to interrupt like this."

"Don't worry about that," Curtis said as we all sat down at

the island in the kitchen. "You're welcome here at any time. I know Charlotte has already told you that, but now I'm telling you, too."

"Thank you, Curtis. Knowing that I have both of you to turn to really means a lot."

Curtis sighed deeply. "So what are you planning to do about this?"

"I don't know, but I definitely can't take much more of Antonio. He's getting worse by the day."

"And what's this Charlotte was telling me about some marijuana?"

"He and his friends have started smoking it in my home, and I can tell they're not going to stop."

"You do know you can go to jail for having that junk in your house, right?"

"Yeah, I do."

"And you're okay with that?"

"No, not at all, but . . ." I paused because this was one of those times when I wanted to defend my failure to take action. I wanted to tell both Curtis and Charlotte about my sister and why I couldn't move on ousting Antonio as quickly as they wanted me to.

"But what?" Charlotte asked.

"I have a plan," I finally said.

I really didn't, at least not exactly, but I was starting to think that maybe it would be best if I just called the police to have them come wait for Antonio to gather his things and then escort him out. Charlotte had already suggested this that day we'd gone to the spa, and while I'd been hesitant then, maybe this was the only way. Maybe instead of talking about what I was going to do, thinking about how I ought to handle this, and listening to others offering the same advice over and over, maybe it was time I ended this whole mockery. Maybe it was time I ignored my fears and faced this ridiculous situation head-on the way I'd originally planned when I'd decided to give him a thirty-day ultimatum, regardless of what might happen to me in the process. Because there was a chance that maybe Antonio had realized what a wimp I was when it came to being threatened by him and he was actually only bluffing. On the other hand, maybe he really would do great harm to me the way he'd claimed.

To tell the truth, I was making myself sick, let alone everyone around me, with all this wishy-washiness, and it was time I did something, and soon.

"Aunt Janine," Matthew said, smiling after closing the door behind him.

"I wondered where you were," I said, hugging him.

"I was at the arcade with Jonathan and Elijah and Jonathan's mom just dropped me off."

"Did you have a good time?"

"Yes, we always do every time we go. Hey, Dad," he said to his father.

"Hey, son," Curtis said, bumping his fist against Matthew's, and then Matthew hugged and kissed his mom on the cheek.

"I know you have homework," Charlotte reminded him.

"Yes, but only in math and history."

"Well, as soon as you eat, you'd better get started."

"Yes, ma'am."

"Charlotte, where's Marissa?" I asked.

"In her room, I guess. She was down here when Tracy left for the day, but then she went upstairs right after you rang the doorbell."

Somehow I wasn't surprised, because although Marissa was only five, she'd never cared that much for me. She wasn't rude, but she never had much to say, and, like today, she usually migrated to her room whenever I came around. I wasn't sure why she felt this way because I'd never done anything except treat her well, but apparently she had her reasons.

When Matthew left, I saw Curtis wink at Charlotte and wondered if she still suspected him of having an affair. She hadn't talked about it since the last time we'd had lunch, but to me, Curtis seemed happy and in love with her. I knew she'd said that they were both good at putting on a façade, but I still thought they had the ideal marriage, household, and family. I would still trade places with her anytime, because she was still so much better off than I was.

Better off because she didn't have a loser like Antonio to deal with.

Although in a matter of days, maybe I wouldn't have to deal with him either.

Chapter 12

JANINE

*A*s I pulled into the subdivision and drove around the curve, I saw Killer's raggedy SUV parked in my driveway. But when I arrived in front of my condo, preparing to open the garage, I noticed another vehicle parked on the other side of Killer's, so I had no choice but to park on the street. Even then, I had to park in front of yet another car I wasn't familiar with.

When I stepped outside and onto the pavement, I went around to my trunk and pulled out two of four large paper bags that were filled with groceries. It hadn't been my plan, but Antonio had called me while I was still at Charlotte's to remind me about the new rules. So, against my wishes, I'd stopped at the store and piled up a cart with food, snacks, sodas, juices, and paper products. I'd spent well over a hundred dollars on items I didn't really want, but I'd done it just so I could have a peaceful night at home.

As I approached the front door, I heard loud rap music playing from the stereo so I knew there was no sense in ringing the bell. I had my keys in my hand but I still struggled to hold both

bags and unlock the door at the same time. But when it opened,
I walked in and looked over in the dining room where Antonio
and everyone else were sitting.

"What's up, Antonio's Girl?" Nate said.

"Yeah, what's up?" Chad added.

"Hey, what's happenin'?" Killer said, and I wondered if they
knew any other words, because this was the same thing they'd
said to me a couple of days ago and in that same order.

But actually, right now they were the least of my worries, because
I was more concerned with the ghetto-fabulous-looking woman
I saw leaning on Antonio. They all must have seen my concern
as well because Chad and Nate got up and came toward me.

"Let us help you with those," Chad offered.

"Do you have more in the car?" Nate asked.

"Yes. Two of them," I answered, but didn't take my eyes off
of Antonio and this mystery person.

"So how was your day?" Antonio finally said, staring directly
at me and then turning his attention back to the table.

And it was only then that I thought I saw a scale, some plastic bags, and . . . something white. So I walked closer to get a
better view, and sure enough, Antonio, Killer, and this woman
were weighing, separating, and bagging cocaine. I even saw a
few rocks of crack. I was shocked, of course, but before I knew
it, I burst out laughing. I knew they thought I was crazy, but this
was one of those moments when I had to laugh to keep from
crying.

"What's so funny?" Antonio asked.

But instead I raised my hand, dismissing him, and left. I
went to my bedroom and slammed the door, but of course he
stormed in behind me.

"What's the matter with you, embarrassing me in front of
my friends like that?"

"You're in my house dealing drugs and you're asking me what's wrong?"

"I told you we were starting a business and that's exactly what I meant."

"Whatever," I said, because I wasn't about to argue with him about this.

"*Whatever* is right, and if you can't treat my boys with a decent attitude, then I suggest you stay in here until they leave."

I didn't want to believe he was serious, but I knew full well he was.

"Who's that woman, Antonio?"

"A friend."

"What kind of friend?"

"The kind that knows how to stand by her man and support him in any way he asks her to. She's also the kind that knows how to satisfy me in a way that you never could."

"So let me get this straight. You're dealing drugs in *my* house, you've brought some woman you're sleeping with in *my* house, and you think I should be okay with it?"

"Exactly. Because it's like I told you this morning, you're free to do whatever you want, and, of course, the same thing goes for me."

I shook my head and flipped on the television.

"You know, it's getting to the point where I hate even having to look at you," he continued. "So maybe you're the one who needs to be searching for somewhere else to stay."

He made that ludicrously dim-witted statement and then left to go rejoin his business partners.

I sat on my bed dumbfounded because I just knew he hadn't suggested that I pack my things and move out of my own home, the one I paid a mortgage on, so that I could let him have it free and clear. I was naïve, unwise even, and a little too easygoing for my own good, but I wasn't crazy. So he was in for a rude awakening if he thought this life we were living was going to continue.

I slipped into a Mitchell University sweat suit and decided to call my father. I usually tried to speak to him at least four to five times per week, but with everything that had been going on, I realized I'd missed a few days. Not to mention I hadn't seen him in six months. Although that wasn't all bad, considering it wasn't until after my mom passed that I'd even begun speaking to him again. I now regretted the strong animosity I'd held against him for so many years, but back then I hadn't wanted a single thing to do with him. I hadn't wanted anything to do with a man who'd never worked a legitimate job and who hadn't really been there for my sister and me when we were growing up.

I could still remember my mom having to work two jobs just to make ends meet. She did everything she could, making sure my sister and I were always clothed and fed, but my father never did anything except abuse her. More verbally than physically, but there was the time he'd hit her so hard he'd broken her jawbone and that's when I'd promised him I would never speak to him again. And I'd kept that promise for sixteen years. I'd also convinced my mom to take my sister, who was two years younger than me, and leave him just before I'd gone off to college. She hadn't wanted to, mainly because of fear, but she'd finally made up her mind to do it. She'd even filed for a divorce shortly after, but not without my father terrorizing her. Eventually, though, she'd listened to me and gotten an order of protection, and thankfully, going to jail was not something he'd desired.

Today, however, I was in a different place spiritually and I was glad I'd finally been able to forgive him. It hadn't been the easiest thing for me to do, but after visiting with him a few times and realizing he was all I had left, my heart had softened a great deal. It also had saddened me to learn that he was suffering with emphysema and was barely making it on a disability check and food stamps. Of course I sent him money each month, but I knew it wasn't nearly enough. I also knew that he had to regret not staying with any one employer for more than a couple of months here and there. He was a very sad case, and I was sure that if he had it to do all over again, he would live his life a lot differently.

I picked up the cordless phone and dialed my father's number. It rang four times but he finally picked up before his answering machine connected.

"Hello?"

"Hi, Dad, how are you?"

"Well, daughter, I'm still kickin', but not too high," he said with a smile in his voice, but I knew this meant he hadn't felt too well today. "But how are you doing?"

"I'm fine," I told him, but Lord knows I wanted to tell him everything. I wanted to tell him that I was more miserable than I'd ever been in my thirty-five years, but I just couldn't see burdening him with such awful news.

"Good, good. I'm glad to hear that."

"So what'd you have for dinner today?"

"Oh, I had one of the neighbor ladies bring me a three-piece chicken dinner from the Colonel. And I enjoyed it, too. I hadn't had anything from there in a while, but after seeing one of their commercials this morning, I thought I'd give it a try."

"I had Kentucky Fried Chicken one day last week and I hadn't been there in a while myself."

"Hey, how's that young man you brought with you the last time you were here? What's his name?"

"Antonio. And he's doing fine," I said, despising the fact that I was lying to my father about him.

"Well, I really liked him, and you be sure and tell him I said hello."

"I will," I responded, and then I heard my father coughing frantically. He did this all the time, but whenever he coughed straight from his chest, it usually meant he was smoking and more than likely drinking too much liquor.

"Dad, are you okay?"

"I think I am now," he said, trying to calm himself.

"I hate hearing you like this and I don't know why you won't quit smoking, because you know what the doctors told you a long time ago."

"Sweetheart, I know you don't understand, but what else do I have? I mean, all I do is sit here day in and day out, watching television and talking on the phone to a few of my friends. And that's not all that often. So if nicotine is going to take me out of here one day, then so be it."

"I know you're lonely, and that's why I asked you to come live with me."

"And I appreciate the offer but my place is here in Ohio. Plus I don't want to be no trouble to you. I was more trouble to you than you deserved when you were a child, and now I want you to live the best life you can. I was never there for you girls the way I should have been, and I treated your mother like a dog on the street. I treated her bad and I'll have to live with a mountain of guilt for the rest of my life."

"That's all in the past and I've forgiven you for all that."

"I know you have, and there's not a day that goes by that I don't thank God for you. You're a wonderful child and I'm so proud of you. I'm proud of the woman you've become, and you know I'm always bragging to everybody how intelligent my daughter is and how she's a big-time college professor."

"Well, I don't know about the big-time part," I said, laughing, "but I do okay."

"You are big-time. You're big-time to me, and sometimes I sit here crying with joy whenever I think about you getting that academic scholarship the way you did. Especially since you weren't raised in a decent household. I mean, I know your mother was a good woman and a good role model for you, but with all the fightin' and arguing you had to witness, I don't know how you made it through."

"God was watching over me the whole time. That I know for sure."

"You're right about that, because there's just no other way to explain it."

"Dad, I have a few things I need to take care of, but in a couple of weeks or so I'm going to take a few days off to come see you. I was thinking I would wait until Thanksgiving, but I really want to see you sooner."

"Well, you know I'll be looking for you," he said, and I could already hear his spirits lifting. I could tell he actually felt as though he had something special to look forward to.

"Do you need anything in the meantime?"

"No, sweetheart, I'm good. I still have some of that money you sent me two weeks ago."

"That's fine, but you let me know if something changes."

"You worry too much."

"Only because I love you."

"I love you, too, daughter."

"Well, I guess I should let you go, but you take care of yourself, Dad, okay?"

"I will. And you do the same."

I hung up, leaned against my pillows, and cried like a baby. I was more upset about this Antonio situation than I had realized, and then now thinking about my pitiful father hadn't helped the way I was feeling. I was also saddened by the fact that my father didn't want to come live with me because he didn't want to be any trouble, yet I had allowed Antonio to almost ruin me.

I turned up the volume on my television set and flipped through the channels. At first I didn't see anything too interesting, but I stopped when I saw a young woman doing an interview with a national news correspondent. They were inside a prison and the young woman was now in tears. I listened and wasn't quite sure what she was doing time for, but I rested the selector on my comforter when I heard her say, "I begged him not to deal drugs out of my house but he wouldn't stop and now I'm doing more time than he is. He actually lied and said the whole operation was my idea. And then . . ." she said, now wailing, "he made some deal with the prosecutor and testified against me."

I sat there watching the young woman, but mostly I pictured myself in her place.

I pictured myself in an orange jumpsuit, wasting away behind bars, serving time for a crime I hadn't committed.

I had already decided that I was going to take a stance, but the young woman in front of me had officially confirmed it.

She had sealed the deal perfectly and would never even know about it.

Chapter 13

CHARLOTTE

Curtis and I both breathed deeply until our heart rates began to settle. It was bright and early Tuesday morning, we'd just made love, and we were now holding each other the way we used to when we were newlyweds. I couldn't remember the last time we'd been intimate with each other for five consecutive days, especially since as of late, our lovemaking had become practically nonexistent. But nonetheless, I was happy that Curtis was making such a noticeable effort to satisfy me.

"I've really missed you," I said.

"We've missed each other and I'm sorry that we've lost so much precious time. I know I should have worked harder at trying to forgive you, but I just couldn't seem to do it."

"We've both done things that we're not very proud of, but baby, life is too short to keep living the way we have been. We have so much to be thankful for, and I just can't see giving up our marriage and taking a chance at ruining Matthew's and Marissa's lives."

"Neither do I. Those children mean the world to me, and it's our responsibility to give them the kind of life they deserve."

"I really hate that you have to leave tomorrow," I said, already feeling sad.

"I do, too, and the thing is, I'll be gone for seven days and only home for two before I have to leave again."

"If I had known you and I were going to reconcile our differences, I would have made plans to go out with you."

"Yeah, that would have been nice, but maybe you can go out with me the next time."

"Maybe so. I'll have to make sure Matthew and Marissa don't have anything going on that I need to be here for," I said, and the phone rang. Curtis reached over to answer it.

"Hello?" he said. "Hello?" he repeated. "Hello?" he said, elevating his voice.

Then he hung up.

"Has this been happening a lot?" he said, rising and swinging his legs over the side of the bed.

"No, this is the first time I'm aware of. Nothing showed up on the Caller ID?"

"No, it registered on the screen as unknown."

"Maybe they dialed the wrong number."

"Maybe. But if they did, then why would they sit there breathing in my ear?"

"Who knows?" I said, wondering if it had been Aaron. Especially since he hadn't hesitated to call my cell phone the way he had. I'd been contemplating getting our numbers changed the way Aaron's psychiatrist had suggested but the reason I hadn't was because I knew Curtis would want to know why I was doing it.

I wanted to tell him that Aaron had contacted me, but I couldn't take the chance of bringing up Aaron's name and having Curtis focusing on the affair Aaron and I had had. Not when Curtis had finally made up his mind to forgive me. I also didn't want to take the chance that Curtis might call the mental facility where Aaron was, trying to speak to his doctor. I didn't expect that the doctor would share any privileged information with Curtis, but again, I couldn't take any chances. For all I knew, Dr. Goldstein might tell Curtis how insistent Aaron was regarding the daughter he believed he had. I wasn't sure if Aaron had shared that information with his physician or not, but I knew it was possible. Then, of course, if Curtis got wind of that and learned that Marissa might be mentally disturbed, I knew it wouldn't be beyond him to order another blood test. He would do it without hesitation and I just couldn't allow that to happen. I couldn't allow our family to be destroyed forever.

"I guess we should get busy so we can head down to breakfast," Curtis said, walking across the room.

"Yeah, we'd better because I'm sure Tracy is already cooking."

"You know, we should think about giving her a raise, because she really does a lot around here. She does everything we ask and she never complains."

"I just gave her one a few months ago, but since you and I weren't on the best of terms, I didn't bother telling you."

"Well, I'm glad, because even when there have been times when we've needed her to come on the weekend, she's been more than willing."

"She's definitely one in a million and I always make sure she knows it."

When Curtis turned on the shower I got up so I could jump in there with him, but the phone rang again. I was almost afraid to answer it, but when I saw that the area code was right here in Mitchell, I picked up the receiver.

"Hello?"

"How are you, Charlotte?" the male voice said.

"Fine."

"And the children?"

"Fine," I said with uncertainty.

"And Curtis?"

"Wait. May I ask who's calling?"

"Are you trying to tell me that you don't even recognize your own brother-in-law?"

"Larry?" I said.

"Nobody but."

"Oh. How are you?"

"I'm okay."

"Well, is there something I can do for you?"

"Actually, I'd like to speak to Curtis if he's there."

"Well . . . I don't think that's a good idea, Larry, because Curtis has made it very clear that he doesn't want you calling or coming over here."

"Even after I poured my heart out to him the way I did at church on Sunday?"

"Yes."

"Well, I guess I shouldn't be surprised."

"I'm sorry," was all I could say.

"But Charlotte, I really have changed. I'm not that same conniving addict I once was, and all I want is a chance to get to know my niece and nephew."

"I understand, but Curtis feels very strongly about not having anything to do with you."

"But how do *you* feel?"

"What do you mean?" I said, hoping Curtis wouldn't turn off the water and hear me on the phone. If he did, I would have no choice but to hang up on Larry.

"I'm asking you if you believe me. Do you believe I'm trying to be a better person, and do you think I deserve a chance to prove it?"

"Well, it's not really up to me, so regardless of what I think about you, I would never go against Curtis's wishes."

"Well, do you think you could loan me some money until I get my paycheck? I only work part-time, so I don't make much. But I'm staying at this boardinghouse and I need to make my weekly rent payment."

"I wish I could, but I can't. Curtis would kill me if I did something like that."

"But he doesn't have to know."

I sighed because even though Curtis had already predicted that Larry was only here to take advantage of us, in my heart I wanted to help him. But unfortunately for him, my hands were tied.

"I can't go behind his back doing something he's completely against."

"Charlotte, please. I won't ask you for anything else."

Just then, I heard the water turn off and the shower door opening.

"I'm really sorry, but I have to go," I said quickly, and pressed the off button on the phone.

Then I joined Curtis in the bathroom. We smiled at each other, but at the same time I felt guilty for concealing yet another piece of information from him. This bothered me because, for whatever reason, I just couldn't stop doing it. I was well aware of how much trouble this had gotten me into in the past and how all my lies and secrets had blown up in my face, but I just couldn't see telling Curtis about Larry's phone call because all it would do was send him into a frenzy and ruin the last full day we had together until a week from now.

I knew it was wrong but I decided that this was the best way to handle the situation.

* * *

"Lord have mercy, Tracy," Curtis said as he reached for the bowl of grits. "Maybe I should have married you instead of Charlotte, because you can cook your behind off."

"Why, thank you, Reverend," she said and they both laughed.

But I didn't see anything funny. I knew Curtis had only been joking, but I hated when he made comments like that to anyone.

"Aw, baby, you know I'm just kidding, right?" he said, noticing my obvious disapproval.

"Yeah, I know," I said, and Tracy set down a bowl of scrambled eggs and left us in the dining room. Whenever Curtis was on the road, the children and I usually ate breakfast right in the kitchen at the island, but when he was home, he always preferred we sit in here as a family. He'd once said something about not having the opportunity to do this with his parents and sister while he was growing up and that he was "breaking the cycle."

"Hey. I'm serious. I was just playing with Tracy and trying to give her a compliment."

"Some things are better left unsaid."

Curtis laughed and rubbed his hand under my chin. "I can't believe you're actually jealous."

"I'm not."

"Yes you are," he said, but we both fell quiet when Tracy returned with warm homemade biscuits and a plate of sausage.

"Can I get you anything else?" she asked.

"No, everything is perfect," I said, smiling. "But if you don't mind, can you call the children down here so we can say grace? Pretty soon the food will be cold."

"Sure, Ms. Charlotte, I would be happy to."

When she left Curtis laughed again. "I don't believe you."

"Shhhh," I said, because no matter how much I didn't want to hear Curtis talking to Tracy or any other woman in that manner, I didn't want Tracy thinking I had a problem with her.

Especially since I had never been the overly jealous type and had only started to feel this way once I'd begun suspecting that Curtis was messing around on me.

"You crack me up," he said. "So what do you want to do today?"

"I was thinking we could drive over to Chicago and do some shopping. We haven't done that in such a long time."

"No, we haven't, so yeah, let's do it."

"Good morning, Daddy." Marissa beamed and hugged her father.

"Good morning, baby girl. Did you sleep well?"

"Yes," she said, and then leaned over to hug me. "Good morning, Mommy."

"Good morning," I said, and wondered why she hadn't won an Oscar yet. Because she really was that good. And the way she was acting now definitely qualified as a great performance, since she never showed me any affection of any kind and we certainly never touched each other. That is, unless you counted when I did her hair and we touched in some way by accident.

"Good morning, Mom," Matthew said. "Good morning, Dad."

"Good morning," we responded together, and Curtis said grace.

"So anything special going on at school?" Curtis asked Matthew.

"Not really, except I have to finish up that feature article I was telling you about."

"Did you work some more on the last part that you e-mailed me last week?"

"Yes. You wanna read the lines I added?"

"Of course. I'll read it before you leave if we finish breakfast in time."

"Daddy, my class wrote some new words last week, too," Marissa interrupted.

"You did? Well, good for you."

"So are you going to stick with the sports section?" Curtis asked Matthew.

"Maybe. I really like writing about the football team but I'd also like to write about some of the other stuff going on at school, too."

"Good. It's better to get experience with every section of the paper if you can. That way you'll know what you're the most interested in before you get to high school. Because you are planning to work on the paper there, too, aren't you?"

"Uh-huh. My goal is to be editor in chief."

"Exactly. You should also try to make editor in chief next year while you're still in eighth grade if you can."

"Mr. Hotlen said if I keep writing as well as I have been, I'll have a real good chance at getting the position."

"I'm really proud of you, Matthew, and I thank God every day for giving us the resources to send you and your sister to private schools. I didn't have that opportunity when I was growing up and the public schools I went to in Chicago weren't very good. But the reason I turned out okay was because I was so determined to read and learn everything I could on my own. It's the reason I'm always encouraging you to read."

"What about me, Daddy?" Marissa cut in again. "Are you proud of me, too?"

"Of course I am, baby girl. I'm proud of everything you do," he said, and it bothered me that she always tried to take Curtis's focus away from Matthew. It was so obvious but I could tell that Curtis never picked up on it.

"Hey, Dad, a group of fathers are planning a camping trip for next May before we get out of school, so can we go?" Matthew asked.

"I would love that. We haven't gone since you were in Cub Scouts."

"I'll tell them to count us in and then I'll get all the information for you."

"But what about me?" Marissa asked, and I could tell she didn't like the idea of Curtis and Matthew going away together and without her.

"Little girls can't go on camping trips with boys and their fathers. But maybe you and Mommy could go somewhere that girls like to go. Maybe you could invite some of your little friends over for a sleepover."

Marissa looked at Curtis but didn't comment, and I knew it was because she would rather die than be left here alone with me. Sadly, I didn't want to be here with her either.

We finished eating, but as soon as the children went upstairs to get their jackets and book bags, the phone rang. This was the third time this morning and this time we let Tracy answer it.

"Reverend Curtis, I'm sorry to interrupt your breakfast, but it's Mary," Tracy said, referring to Curtis's assistant. "She says it's important."

"Thank you," he said, taking the phone. "Good morning, Mary, how are you?"

I wondered why she was calling so early, but by the time Curtis ended the conversation, I already knew. I'd been able to tell just from listening to his part of the conversation.

"Bad news, baby," he said. "My publicist just booked me for a live television interview this evening, and she also scheduled a live in-studio radio interview in the morning with one of the top radio talk shows in New York. We've been trying to get both for the last couple of months, so I can't pass them up."

"So when do you leave?"

"My publisher is scheduling a flight out for this afternoon, but I promise I'll make it up to you. We'll go shopping when I get back next week."

I nodded but I knew it wasn't going to happen. Not with him coming home for only two days, but I didn't argue.

"I'm really sorry, baby," he said, scooting away from the table. "But I guess I should get upstairs and get packed."

"I'll help you."

As we left the dining room, Curtis slid his arm around my waist and I placed mine around his. I was still disappointed about his having to leave, but happy we were getting along so well.

Because right now, happiness was all that mattered to me.

Chapter 14

I tried my best to stay focused on what Rebecca was saying, but as the minutes passed, my mind wandered in a thousand different directions. Rebecca was by far one of my best students, and I was always happy to consult with her on any given assignment, but today my thoughts were distracted. I was pre-occupied because today would be the end of Antonio's reign as ruler of my house. He had no idea what was to come, but this evening he would learn that I was no longer afraid to put him out and that I was willing to live with any consequences he tossed my way.

"I was trying to decide whether I wanted my business to be one that sold a product or a service, but I'm thinking I'll choose a service because if you can sell a great service, your chances of high profitability are a lot higher," Rebecca said.

"This is very true. Because even though any good product will sell, with a service, you don't have to deal with discounting to wholesalers and retailers. You can charge a straight fee and not have to share any of it with anyone."

"Exactly. I've been reading this book I found on starting a business, and while I'd love to create a cosmetics company, I've decided to go with a marketing and public relations business. I did some research, and what I found was that so many business owners don't realize how important those two aspects really are, and that they would do so much better in sales if they had someone to help them with both."

"You're right, and actually, lack of proper marketing and publicity is one of the top reasons why most businesses fail. Another is that they don't plan well enough, and that's why I gave all of you this particular assignment. The first and foremost step for any would-be business owner should be to sit down and write a business plan."

"I know. And that's why I'm so glad you assigned this for us to do, because I'm learning so much already."

"Good," I said, and glanced at the clock on my wall. It was almost four o'clock, and as soon as Rebecca and I finished our conference I was going to head out to my car.

"Well, I think that's all for now. Pretty much I just wanted to make sure you thought my business idea was a good one to work on and to make sure I was on the right track."

"It's great, and you'll do fine as always."

"Thanks so much, Ms. Turner," she said, removing her jacket from the back of the chair and putting it on.

"No problem. Come see me anytime."

"Take care."

But just as Rebecca left, Thomas, one of my colleagues stepped into my office.

"A bunch of us are going out for drinks if you wanna come."

"No, I think I'll pass. But maybe next time."

"Yeah, right," he said teasingly. "If I had a dollar for every time you told me that, I'd be rich."

We both chuckled.

"No, really. I'm going to seriously think about going out with you guys. I don't drink all that much, but it would still be nice to sit around and have a few laughs."

"Exactly. So why don't you join us tonight?"

"I can't. But like I said, maybe next time."

"We'll see."

"Enjoy," I told him, and he smiled on his way out.

Thomas had been flirting with me for more than a year but I'd made it very clear that I was very much committed to Antonio, and Thomas never took his advances any further. He was nice-looking, clean-cut, and every bit the type of man I should have been attracted to, but for some reason I wasn't. For some reason, I had never been taken with men who fell into the "Mr. Nice Guy" sort of category, but maybe it was time I rethought my position in this area. As a matter of fact, I knew for sure it was time I made drastic changes in the choices I made regarding my past relationships because none of them was anything worth bragging about.

Next I organized a few items on my desk and slipped inside of my briefcase a couple of textbooks I'd been wanting to skim through for a while now. I wouldn't add them to the current curriculum as required material, but if they contained the information I was looking for, I would certainly consider listing them on the course syllabus as additional and recommended reading.

When I removed my leather coat from the back of my door, my office phone rang.

"Janine Turner."

"Hey, we're out of chips and orange soda, so I need you to swing by the store to pick some up," Antonio said, and I closed my eyes in disgust. "And some Oreo cookies would be nice, too, because Killer just can't seem to get enough of those."

I bit my lip and said as politely as possible, "No problem. Do you need anything else?"

"Well, actually, no, but I might as well let you know now that there's been a change in plans. Killer worked things out with his girl, but Chiquita will be moving her things in tomorrow. Her aunt told her she has to find somewhere else to stay, and I'm not about to leave her hangin' like that."

"Whatever she needs is fine with me," I agreed. My first thought was to ask who on earth was Chiquita, but I knew immediately that it was the ghetto girl I'd seen yesterday, sitting at my dining room table.

"Whatever she needs?" he repeated, obviously shocked. "Well, what brought on this happy-go-lucky attitude?"

"I just don't want to argue with you anymore, Antonio. You and I have a lot of history and it just doesn't make sense for us to end up hating each other. Plus I finally decided that you and I living in the same house and living separate lives is not all that big a deal."

"Good. Because as long as you do what I say, there won't be any problems."

"I should get out of here so I can head to the store."

"Cool. See you when you get here."

I hung up the phone, grabbed my belongings, and left the building in a hurry.

About two hours later, I walked inside my condo with two grocery bags, but this time Chad and Nate didn't offer to help me carry them. Probably because they were too engrossed with what Antonio had termed their "business venture." The table was full of product and distribution supplies and Chiquita was sitting next to Antonio, eyeing me in a manner that screamed, I live here now, too, and there ain't a single thing you can do about it.

I continued into the kitchen but I could still hear the conversation Antonio and his posse were having.

"Man, if we keep moving this out the way we did the last few days, we'll be making major bank in no time," Killer boasted.

"You got that right," Antonio seconded. "All we have to do is keep working sunup to sundown and we'll have more customers than any other dealer in this city. All we have to do is keep laying low over here on this nice side of town where the police will never suspect anything, and then making sure we only sell it on the west end."

"Word," either Nate or Chad said, because I couldn't tell which one of them had spoken. "As long as we don't have any traffic in and out of here, we'll be straight. Because that's how J-Dog and his crew got busted. I mean, that was just plain stupid to have all those addicts hanging around all times of the night."

"I'm tellin' you," Killer said, "some of these fools just don't know how to operate a successful business, but what we got here is legit. We'll be rolling for a long time and it won't be long before we'll be able to branch out over in Chicago."

"Shoot," Chiquita joined in. "Before long, we'll be making millions."

"And rolling like Nino Brown on *New Jack City*," Killer added.

I shook my head at how excited they were to be selling drugs, and how they really believed they were going to get rich from doing it. They really believed the sky was the limit and that they were living the American dream.

When I put away the last of the groceries, Killer came into the kitchen.

"Thanks for picking up these Oreos for me," he said, grabbing the bag of cookies from the counter.

"No problem."

"You know, for whatever it's worth, Antonio is a fool for messin' things up with you. And I'm not talkin' behind his back,
either, because I already told him to his face how I feel about the
whole thang."

"I appreciate that," I said, feeling awkward and not knowing
fully what to say.

Then he looked me up and down from head to toe. "Umph,
umph, umph. Beautiful and smart. Antonio, man, you must be
sick givin' up a woman like this," he yelled into the other room.

"Negro, shut up," Antonio responded. "And bring your
behind back in here so you can get to work."

"For your information, there ain't *nothin'* wrong with Antonio," Chiquita announced proudly. "My baby just realized he
didn't want that ho no more because he's in love with me. Ain't
that right, Tonio?"

"That's cold, Chiquita," either Nate or Chad said. "Callin'
Antonio's girl a ho in her own house. You know you wrong for
that."

"Well, she is a ho," Chiquita reiterated. "And she bet not say
nothin' to me unless she want a beat-down. Ain't that right,
baby?" she asked Antonio, but he still wouldn't comment.

"Just shut up, Chiquita," Killer demanded.

"You shut up!" she spat back. "Because I'll say whatever I
damn well please."

"Why don't all of y'all shut up," Antonio finally said, and
looked at me when I walked out of the kitchen. He actually
seemed embarrassed and almost sorry for Chiquita's antics.

But I ignored him, her, and the rest of them and went into
my bedroom. Once there, I looked at the clock, saw that it was
ten minutes till six, and quickly changed out of my suit and
heels and into a jogging suit, socks, and gym shoes. Then I

walked back out into the living room and over to the front door.

"Where are you off to?" Antonio asked.

"Nowhere. I left my briefcase in the car."

"Well, before you head outside, can I talk to you for a minute?"

"About what?" I asked.

"Yeah, about what?" Chiquita said in an angry tone.

"Just come here," he said to me, ignoring Ms. Thing and already walking toward the hallway.

"What?" I said, entering the bedroom.

"Hey, I'm sorry for the way Chiquita disrespected you."

"Don't worry about it."

"Are you sure? Because her whole attitude was uncalled for."

"No, really. I'm fine."

"The only reason she's here is because her uncle is one of our main suppliers, and as long as he sees Chiquita happy with me, he'll keep givin' us a break on the price."

"I told you, I'm fine."

"But regardless, I wanted you to know I don't approve of the way she acted."

"I really need to get outside to get my briefcase."

"Okay, but just let me ask you one more thing. Why couldn't you just accept me for the man I was?"

"Because you're no good, Antonio. Because you're a bum who wouldn't get a real job, and because you'll never amount to anything decent for as long as you live."

"You know what, forget my apology. You're every bit the ho Chiquita said you were, and then some."

I left the room and Antonio followed behind, calling me every kind of bitch he could think of. But I ignored him and continued on outside. I could still hear him ranting and raving, but his ranting and raving stopped as soon as an army of narcotics officers rushed inside, yelling, "Police, raise your hands, stand up, and turn around slowly."

I stood outside, looking in, and then heard multiple Miranda warnings being recited to all five criminals. Antonio, Killer, Nate, Chad, and Chiquita. Interestingly enough, they all remained silent, and soon after, the officers escorted each of them out, handcuffed, one by one. They all stared at me irately, but I guess Antonio was the angriest of all because he tried to break away and charge toward me. Thankfully, two of the officers forced him facedown on the grass, but when he got up he glared at me and said, "Remember what I told you."

Then he smiled at me and I knew exactly what he was referring to. He was referring to the statement he'd made about how his boys could do anything to anyone at anytime, and how calling the police would never stop him from harming me.

And I had to admit that his words terrified me. I was trying to be as brave as possible, but I knew Antonio wasn't going to take being arrested lightly. I knew because the last thing he'd said before being forced into the squad car was, "See you real, real soon."

And the thing was, I believed him.

Chapter 15

JANINE

Three hours later, the remaining officers had finished search-ing my home and collected bags and bags of evidence. Now I was on the phone with Charlotte, telling her everything.

"J, I am so glad that this is finally over and that Antonio is out of your life forever."

"Hopefully, because he was still threatening me even in front of the police. And the fact that they found more drugs and par-aphernalia than I even knew about, Antonio and his friends are definitely looking at prison time."

"As they should be. And if I were you, I wouldn't worry about it because what can he do to you behind bars?"

"A lot. Because I'm sure Killer, Nate, and Chad are not the only thug acquaintances he has. Plus that Chiquita chick is the niece of the guy who was supplying them, and of course this guy won't be happy either once he finds out all his drugs were con-fiscated."

"Well, we'll just deal with all of that if the time comes, but for now you should just feel relieved to have your house back."

"I do. I'm still afraid, but it's good to know that I don't have to walk around here worried about what Antonio is going to say or do next."

"I still can't believe you planned to have your house raided all along and didn't tell me."

"But that's just it. My original plan was that I would call the police to come have Antonio pack his things and leave. But then he started smoking marijuana. Then he started dealing drugs. And once I saw the program last night on television I was telling you about, my mind was made up and I called the narcotics division first thing this morning when I got to work."

"Good for you."

"It usually takes a while for a drug bust, but when I explained my situation and that I could almost guarantee they'd all be sitting around this evening with everything out in the open, they told me to come home and do everything I normally do, but then at six o'clock, if Antonio and his friends were in the midst of dealing drugs, I should pretend that I'd left something in my car and come outside. That way they would know that the bust was a go, and that's exactly what I did."

"Can you believe drugs were actually all over your house?"

"No, but they were, and I feel so stupid. I know Antonio didn't work and that he's used me all this time, but I never in my wildest imagination expected him to turn out like this. I'd never known him to get involved with anything illegal and he was usually home every day when I got off work, but now I'm betting he was doing this all the time during the day. The only thing is that he was doing it somewhere else."

"Well, if he was, you'd think he would have had a lot more money than he did."

"Yeah, you would. But maybe he wasn't as deeply involved in it until he decided to start his little operation over here."

"That's probably it. Because once you told him you wanted him to leave, I'll bet that's when he decided to go full force ahead."

"I'm just glad he was bold enough to handle the drugs in front of me, because if he'd had all of that crap in my house without me knowing it and then somehow still got busted, I would be in jail myself. I mean, the thought of that makes me crazy."

"I know it's not funny, but I could see the headline now," Charlotte said, slightly laughing. "'College Professor Arrested for Crack Cocaine Possession with Intent to Deliver.'"

"Girl, can you imagine? Me being arrested, convicted, and incarcerated for months and possibly years? So that's why I did what I had to do."

"I know you're worried about how he might retaliate, but this was your only choice."

"I'm still trying to figure out what I ever saw in him and why I couldn't see the street part of him that really came out over this last couple of weeks."

"He was good," Charlotte said. "I'll give him that, because even though he wasn't the most cultured man I've ever met, I would never have suspected he was some petty gangster. Not with him having that associate degree he always bragged about. And to be honest, he spoke pretty intelligently, too."

"But now that I think back on it, there had to be little signs. There had to be because people don't change this drastically so quickly. And I guess I was so caught up that I saw what I wanted to see. I've done it before and this is no different."

"Well, the bottom line is that Antonio is a part of the past and now it's time for you to move on to bigger and better things. It's time for you to start dating the kind of men who have something to bring to the table and who have a reputable background."

"Maybe. But right now I don't want to think about dating any man, period. Not even if he has millions of dollars, comes from the best of homes, and will love me unconditionally. Because, to be honest, I still wouldn't trust him."

"That's understandable, but once a few weeks or months pass by, you'll be fine and ready to give someone else a try."

"I doubt it."

"Of course you will, J. You'll see. Actually, I'm wishing Larry was a better catch than he is."

"Who's Larry?"

"Girl, I've been meaning to tell you about Curtis's brother for the past few days but we really haven't had a chance to talk. Anyway, he's in town, and while he's not Curtis's biological brother, they were very close when they were in college and even after they graduated."

"Really? And he's staying with you?"

"No. He says he's staying at a boardinghouse, but I'm not sure where because Curtis has pretty much told him to stay away from us."

"Why?"

"He used to be strung out on drugs, and according to Curtis, he's only out for what he can get from us and can't be trusted."

"That's too bad, but after what I just went through with Antonio, I think we both know that Curtis is probably right."

"I don't know. Normally I would be skeptical, but I really like Larry. And the kids like him, too."

"When did you see him?"

"He came over here on Friday night and then he showed up on Sunday morning and joined the church. He swears he's changed and wants to get to know God, and I really want to believe him."

"But Curtis still doesn't? Not even after his testimony?"

"No."

"Then if I were you, I wouldn't go against what Curtis wants. I mean, I know I'm the last person anyone should be taking advice from, but if Larry just showed up out of nowhere, you really need to be careful. Especially since you guys have money."

"Maybe. But I guess I don't like the idea of turning someone away when they need help. Not when the person is like family to Curtis."

"Has he asked you or Curtis for anything?"

"No . . . well, not exactly."

"Uh-oh."

"Okay, he didn't ask Curtis for anything, but he sort of called yesterday while Curtis was in the shower, wanting to know if he could borrow money for rent."

"And you didn't tell Curtis?"

"No, because things are going really well with us and he would have gone completely ballistic."

"You're playing with fire."

"Well, it's not like I've spoken to him again."

"And I hope you don't."

"I guess I just feel so sorry for him."

"Still."

"If you ever get to meet him, you'll see what I mean. He's such a likable person."

"You crack me up," I said, and then heard my phone ringing. "Hey, hold on a minute. Let me see who's calling."

My heart fluttered nervously when I saw Rachel County Jail on my ID screen, but I still decided to answer it.

"Hello?"

"This call is being made from Antonio, an inmate at Rachel County Jail," the recording announced. "To accept, press one. To decline, press two. To block all future calls from inmates at Rachel County Jail, please press three."

I paused for a minute, I wasn't sure why, but then I declined Antonio's call. After doing so, I returned to Charlotte.

"Antonio has the nerve to be calling me already."

"Girl, I'm not surprised, because I'll bet every dime I have that he wants you to come bail him out."

"Well, if he does, then he's crazier than I thought."

"Why else would he be calling? Because it's not like you have anything else to talk about."

"I just wish he'd leave me alone. That's all I want him to do."

"If he calls again, I would just ignore him, and if he continues, I would report it to the police department and the prosecutor."

"This is never going to be over with," I said, terribly frustrated.

"Yes it will be. It might take time, but eventually this will come to an end."

I sighed but didn't speak.

"Hey, this is Curtis calling on the other line. He had to leave this afternoon so he could do a couple of media interviews in New York, but I'll call you back in about an hour."

"If not, then I'll talk to you in the morning."

"No, I'll call you back when I finish."

"Talk to you then," I said, and hung up.

Then I rested my body against three pillows and tried to ease my nerves. What a day this had turned out to be. I'd known it wasn't going to be an easy process, but now I wondered how long I'd have to live in fear. The narcotics detective that I'd spoken to this morning had assured me that Antonio and his friends would definitely go down, but the specific sentence would depend on the amount of cocaine, what other drugs the police were able to find, and a host of other factors. I, of course, was hoping that Antonio would be put away forever, but I knew this wasn't logical.

I kept my eyes closed but my mind wandered from one thing to another. I thought about my father and how he wasn't in good health. I thought about my sister and how she'd died a tragic death, but when I thought about my mom, I cried uncontrollably. I missed her so much and it was at times like these that I needed her the most. I needed her to hold me the way she had when I was a child and to tell me that everything actually was going to be all right. Because at this very moment, that's what I wanted and needed to hear. I needed to know that one day I would be able to look back on all that had happened and it wouldn't affect me the way it was affecting me now.

I wallowed in my misery for at least another half hour and then the phone rang again. I had a feeling it was Antonio and it was. I didn't want to speak to him, but at the same time I knew he would never stop calling and that it was probably best if I simply went ahead and spoke to him.

So I picked up the phone and pressed the number one the way the recording instructed me to do.

"Hello?" I said, sniffling.

"Janine, baby, why did you do this?"

"Because I didn't want to go to jail for something I didn't do."

"But that never would have happened because no one would have ever found out anything."

"But you were dealing drugs in my house, Antonio, and I couldn't take that chance. Not to mention I asked you to move out and you wouldn't."

"Well, baby, right now none of that even matters, and I for-give you for what you did."

Was he kidding? He was actually forgiving me? For what?

"You hear me, Janine? Baby, I forgive you, and all you need to do is bring five thousand dollars down here to bail me out and you and I will be fine. Because I'm through messin' with drugs for good. I mean it, baby, and I'm sorry I treated you the way I did."

"I don't have it," was all I said.

"Baby, why are you lying? Why are you doing this to me after all we've been through together?"

"Antonio, I'm begging you. Please leave me alone and stop calling here. Tomorrow I'm going to pack your things and take them over to your parents', but that's where my responsibility to you ends. It's over, Antonio, and I'm pleading with you to accept that."

"I'm not accepting shit," he yelled. "You hear me? And just for the record, you were never the only woman in my life. I always had somebody else from the moment I met you."

"Antonio, please don't contact me again," I said, and he laughed loudly.

"Baby, this is just the beginning. You and me, we're just get-tin' started."

He slammed the phone down and I pulled out my phone book to call a locksmith. I knew I would have to pay after-hour fees, but it would certainly be worth it. I scanned the yellow pages and felt some sense of comfort when I saw a listing for Wilson Lock & Key Specialists. Carl Wilson was the owner and a member of our church, so at least I knew him and his wife on a personal basis. I hadn't seen them in a while, but still, I felt better than I would have calling a stranger.

It only took him thirty minutes to arrive, and in the mean-time I'd already changed the password on my security system.

Carl parked in the driveway, and since I was looking out for him, I opened the door before he was able to ring the bell or knock.

"I'm sorry to have called you so late, but I really needed my locks changed as soon as possible."

"It's no problem at all and I appreciate your business," he said, stepping inside and closing the door.

"I won't go into details, but I had someone living with me, and now that he's out, he's threatening me."

"Have you contacted the police?"

"Yes. As a matter of fact, they arrested him a few hours ago."

"Oh."

"It's a long story."

"I understand," he said, checking the doorknob. "Does your back door have the same type of lock?"

"Yes."

"Well, we should be able to get these switched out in no time."

"Good. Can I get you something to drink? Water? Juice?"

"No, I'm fine. I'll just head back out to my truck to get the locks and then get this taken care of for you."

When he left, I couldn't help thinking how attractive he was. But at the same time, he was very married and totally off limits—off limits because the one thing I was dead set against was committing adultery. I was guilty of fornication, something I clearly wasn't proud of, but I would never take up with another woman's husband. Not for any reason.

After Carl finished both jobs, he handed me the new keys and wrote up an invoice.

"Is this all?" I said, scanning the bill.

"You wanna pay more?" he asked, smiling.

"No, but it is after ten o'clock."

"I waived the after-hours charge."

"Well, thanks. That helps a lot, and again I appreciate you coming to do this for me."

"Are you going to be okay?"

"I think so."

"Well, you have my number, so please don't hesitate to call if you need to."

"I will and please tell Greta I said hello and that I'm sorry for keeping you out so late."

"To tell you the truth, I don't think she would care one way or the other. Our divorce was final six months ago."

"Oh, Carl, I'm really sorry. I didn't know."

"Not a lot of people do because we haven't been to church in almost a year. It was painful at first, but our decision to split was mutual."

"Well, again, I'm sorry."

"Don't be, and like I said, please call if you need to."

"You take care of yourself."

"You, too," he said, smiling, and I stood in the doorway until he drove down the street.

I stood there wondering why I couldn't have met someone like Carl when I'd first moved to Mitchell. More so, I wondered why Greta had made the decision to give him up. Especially when a good man was so hard to find.

Chapter 16

CHARLOTTE

Ms. Charlotte," Tracy called up the stairs to me.

"Yes?"

"Marissa's principal is on the line for you."

"Thanks," I said, picking up the phone in my bedroom. "Hello?"

"Mrs. Black?" Ms. Keller said.

"Yes. How are you?"

"Well, unfortunately, I've had better days, and I'm sorry to tell you that we have a real problem here."

"Is Marissa okay?"

"She's fine, but one of the other students caught her in the girls' bathroom striking matches and waving them around and then dropping them in the toilet."

"Dear God. When?"

"Not long ago. Marissa was in one of the stalls and the young lady who went to report it to her teacher heard her striking matches, and when she pushed open the door, Marissa just looked at her and struck another one."

"Ms. Keller, I am so sorry that this has happened."

"I'm sorry, too, and I'm going to have to ask you to come pick her up. We don't have any choice except to suspend her for the rest of the week, and I'm going to have to suggest that you and your husband take her somewhere for professional counseling."

"I agree."

"She'll be waiting here in my office until you arrive."

"Thanks so much, and I should be there in about a half hour."

I grabbed my purse and headed down to the main floor and told Tracy that I had to drive over to the school to get Marissa. I didn't go into details, but I would definitely confide the situation to her when I returned because now Marissa needed to be watched at all times. This whole obsession with fire—I couldn't erase the flashbacks that were now taking control of my mind, flashbacks of our house burning down to the ground. I could still see Aaron being dragged away from the scene and being driven off in a police car. Now, though, in the present, I had to worry about my own daughter doing the same thing, and I didn't know what to do about it. Yes, there was counseling, but what if it didn't help her? What if she truly was a bad seed and was destined to commit crimes?

I rushed out of the house, into the car, and drove out of the subdivision. I needed to talk to someone, and while I knew it should have been Curtis, I dialed my mother instead.

"Mom?" I said when she answered.

"Hi, sweetheart. How are you?"

"Not good," I said with tears rolling down my cheeks.

"Why? What's wrong?"

"It's Marissa."

"Is she okay?"

"No. I mean, nothing's happened to her, but the principal

just called to say that she was playing with matches in the bath-room at school and she's been suspended."

"Where did she get matches from?"

"I don't know."

"Has she done anything like this before?"

"Yes. I didn't tell you or Curtis or anyone, but a couple of weeks ago, I came into the kitchen and caught her playing with the burners on the stove. She was waving her hand through the fire like she was enjoying it."

"Oh no. Did you ask her why?"

"No, because once I got her attention, she turned everything off and went up to her bedroom. She never even acknowledged what she was doing."

"Sweetheart, you have got to get that child some help. Play-ing with fire is not only dangerous, it's not normal."

"Mom, I'm so afraid to tell Curtis because . . ." I tried to fin-ish my sentence but when I couldn't, I pulled over to the side of the road and cried openly.

"Honey, it'll be okay. Children have problems all the time and that's what doctors and counselors are here for."

"Mom, there's something I've never told you."

"What?"

"I think Marissa might be Aaron's daughter."

"But you and Curtis had a paternity test done before she was even born."

"I know, but remember when I worked as a paralegal at the law firm and I met that really nice rich lady, Meredith Connolly Christiansen?"

"Yes, you talked about her all the time."

"Well, when Curtis found out I was pregnant, I panicked. I knew Curtis would leave me if Aaron had ended up being the father, and I just couldn't take a chance on him doing that. So . . . I had

Meredith find and pay a doctor to administer the test and give us the results Curtis needed to see."

"Oh, Charlotte."

"I know. I've done an unforgivable thing, and the lab tech is the only person who really knows what the truth is because I made sure he didn't tell me one way or the other either. I thought it would better that way."

"Well, you've got to tell Curtis about what Marissa just did at school, and then you're going to have to tell him about that paternity test. Because if he finds out on his own, he'll never forgive you."

"But Mom, I can't. I mean, I am going to tell him about the matches and the stove incident, but I just can't tell him about that paternity test."

"I can't force you to do anything you don't want to, but sweetheart, I'm advising you to tell Curtis before it's too late. Tell him so that he won't have to learn from someone else that yet another child might not be his. He almost left you after he found out Matthew didn't belong to him, so maybe if you go ahead and tell him the truth about Marissa, he'll take it a lot better."

"No he won't. He'll file for a divorce and he'll use all of this against me in court. He'll do everything he can to make sure I don't get a dime from him, and he won't think twice about taking the children away from me. He won't even care that they're not biologically his. He'll try to take them because he'll say I don't deserve them."

"What's goin' on?" I heard my father say in the background. "And who is that on the phone?"

"Mom, please don't tell Daddy. Please. I'm begging you."

"Honey, it's just Charlotte," she told my father. "She just called to see how we were doing."

"Then why are you sitting there looking all worried about something?" he asked her.

"I'm not. I guess I'm just tired."

"Uh-huh," he said, clearly not believing a word she said.

"Is he gone?" I asked.

"Yes, but you need to handle this because I won't be able to keep this from your father forever. I've lied to him enough over the years, and that's why I'm trying to prevent you from continuing to do the same thing with Curtis."

"I'll call you later, Mom," I said, pulling back onto the road. "I'm on my way to pick up Marissa now."

"You be careful and call me if you need me."

"I will, and thanks, Mom, for listening."

As soon as I walked inside the school and down the main corridor, I entered the administration office and who did I see? My daughter sitting in a chair, swinging her legs back and forth like she was the happiest person in the world and was innocent of all charges.

"Hi, Mommy," she said when she saw me, and the bubbly expression on her face gave me the creeps.

"Marissa, what have you done?"

"Nothing, Mommy. I didn't do anything. That girl in my class just doesn't like me, and that's why she told our teacher that big fat lie."

"You stay here while I go in to speak to your principal."

"Okay, Mommy," she said, and started swinging her legs back and forth again.

The secretary whose desk was just in front of where Marissa was sitting told me I could go right in to see Ms. Keller.

"Please come in and have a seat," Ms. Keller offered, and I closed the door behind me.

"She keeps saying she didn't do anything," I began.

"I know, but when she kept insisting that the other student was lying, I asked her to let me see both her hands, and when I sniffed them, I definitely smelled sulfur."

"I just don't understand why she's done this."

"Neither do I, but you have to get her in to see a child psychiatrist, and soon. I can even recommend one if you need me to."

"Yes. I would appreciate that."

Ms. Keller flipped through her Rolodex and wrote down a name and phone number. "There's something else I think you should know, too."

"Yes?"

"When the other little girl left my office to go back to class, she walked past where Marissa is sitting right now and my secretary heard Marissa whispering that she was going to set her hair on fire for telling on her."

I wanted to respond to Ms. Keller. I wanted to say something, anything, but I was too numb to force any words from my mouth. Still, though, the truth remained. My daughter was sick. She had mental issues that needed to be addressed as soon as possible, and I had to do whatever I could to help her.

"Mrs. Black, have you witnessed any other incidents like this at home?"

"No," I lied quickly, my tone straightforward.

"Have you noticed anything different about her at all?"

"Like what?"

"Well, for example, I believe her teacher told you at the last parent-teacher conference that Marissa pretty much stays to herself and that she's not very well liked by the other children."

"Yes, she did, but not every child is outgoing or wants to play around all the time. Marissa is very mature for her age, and her maturity has always been a problem for her when she's around other children."

"This is true, and she's also extremely intelligent, but her social skills are not where they need to be."

I knew she was telling the truth about Marissa, but still, as her mother, I was offended. I was offended because even though I knew Marissa was strange, I didn't appreciate hearing anyone else point this out to me.

"I'll talk to her," I said, refusing to continue our discussion.

"I hope everything works out with the psychiatrist, and please let me know if I can be of any further assistance."

When I left Ms. Keller's office, I pulled Marissa out of the chair and we walked outside the school. I did believe all that Ms. Keller had told me, but still I lifted Marissa's hands and took a whiff of her fingers to see for myself. They did in fact smell like matches, but Marissa just stared at me like she didn't understand what I was doing. She stared at me strangely and then finally said, "Mommy, can we stop at McDonald's to get some French fries and a shake?"

"No. And I want you to tell me where you got those matches from and why you were playing with them."

"But I told you, I didn't do anything. I didn't."

"Then why do your fingers smell like matches?"

"I don't know."

"Don't you know you could have set the whole school on fire, and that if you keep doing things like this, the authorities will come and take you away from us?"

I'd told her this to try and prevent any near-future disasters, and from the terrified look on her face, I could tell I had her attention.

"But I didn't do anything,"

"And since we're on the subject, why are you always so mean

to Matthew, and why do you speak so nasty to me all the time?"

"I don't."

"You do, Marissa."

"No I don't. I'm always nice to Matthew, and Mommy, I love you so much," she said, hanging on to my arm as we headed toward the car. She was so full of deception that I could barely stand her and I couldn't wait to get her home. I couldn't wait to send her to her bedroom so I wouldn't have to deal with her. If I could, I would lock her away forever.

Chapter 17

CHARLOTTE

Baby, please call me as soon as possible," I said, leaving a voice message for Curtis.

Marissa and I had arrived home about an hour ago, and right after calling the psychiatrist and scheduling an appointment for Marissa on Friday, two days from now, I'd decided it was time to tell Curtis what was going on. Not about the potential paternity catastrophe, but I would tell him everything else.

I went into the laundry room where Tracy was. I'd confined Marissa upstairs as planned, partly as punishment and partly because I wanted to speak to Tracy in private.

"I know I don't usually bother you with our family problems, but I really need to talk to you about Marissa," I said, and she laid a stack of towels on the dryer.

"Sure, Ms. Charlotte, what is it?"

"Marissa was caught playing with matches, and not very long ago I caught her doing the same thing with the stove."

Tracy covered her mouth and shook her head.

"What's wrong?"

"Ms. Charlotte, all I can hope is that you don't fire me for not saying anything before today, but for some time now I've thought that maybe something wasn't quite right with Marissa."

"And why is that?"

"Well, there have been a few small incidents, but the one that worried me the most was this summer when the new little neighbor girl down the street came over to play with her and I just so happened to be coming out of one of the guest bedrooms and walked past Marissa's room. Her door was cracked, and what made me stop to listen was when I heard her tell the little girl that she looked like a gorilla and that her parents were going to give her away to the zoo. But the worst part was when she started poking the little girl with a sharp pencil and the little girl started crying."

I shook my head in horror.

"So I had no choice but to go in and stop her," Tracy continued. "I told Marissa that what she was doing wasn't nice, but she ran over to me and said that they were only playing a game and that the little girl had asked her to poke her. So I asked the little girl if that was true, and at first she didn't say anything but then she'd looked at Marissa and then told me that she had asked to be poked."

"Why didn't you tell me about this?"

"Because I didn't think it was my place and I guess I was hoping that this was a one-time situation."

"But you said there were other smaller incidents."

"Yes, like some of the things she says to Matthew, but I just figured it might be your everyday sibling rivalry. And Ms. Charlotte, please don't take this the wrong way, but sometimes she acts as though she hates you. And I don't know any five-year-olds who hate their mothers."

"I can't believe you kept all of this from me, Tracy. Not after being here with us all this time."

"I'm sorry, Ms. Charlotte, but I was afraid."

"Afraid of what?" I said, raising my voice.

"Afraid of being fired."

"Why would I fire you for telling me what Marissa was doing?"

"Because a few years ago I worked for another family, and when I told the mother that their teenage son was stealing money from one of the drawers where they used to stash a few thousand dollars, she told me I was lying and that I was only trying to blame him for something I'd done myself. Then she fired me on the spot."

"You still should have told me, Tracy."

"I know, and I'm so sorry I didn't. But I promise I won't keep anything else from you again."

"I know you won't. Because this is your last day working here. As a matter of fact, I want you out right now. Get out!" I demanded, and Tracy hurried past me in tears.

I ran my hands across the top of my head, but more than anything I wanted to scream. I was so angry with Tracy. So disappointed that she'd decided it was okay to keep such crucial information from me. Information about *my* daughter. She'd had no right, and I couldn't allow someone I didn't trust to continue working for us.

It was early evening before Curtis finally got around to returning my phone call.

"What took you so long?" I said, still frustrated and trying to digest all that Tracy had disclosed about Marissa.

"I had a late lunch with my agent and then I had a newspaper interview. Why? What's wrong?"

"Everything. Marissa's principal suspended her and I had to fire Tracy this afternoon."

"What? Why?"

"Marissa was playing with matches, and now the principal has recommended that we get her in to see a psychiatrist."

"Over one incident?"

"No. Marissa has some real emotional problems. And after hearing what Tracy had to say, she has more than I realized."

"Baby, I'm lost."

"A few days before you came home last week, I caught Marissa playing with the stove and running her hand through the fire."

"And you didn't tell me?"

"No."

"Why?"

"Because I didn't think it was something she did all the time," I tried to explain, and then I told him everything Tracy had had to say about her.

"Marissa was actually poking some little girl and calling her a gorilla?"

"Yes. And she's mean to Matthew all the time, too."

"When? Because whenever I'm around, she always seems fine with him."

"That's just it. She only acts like that when you're in town, but when you're gone, she acts like Matthew and I are her enemies."

"This is too much."

"Well, it's all true, and I've already made an appointment for her to see a doctor."

"Soon, I hope."

"I take her on Friday."

"Where is she now?"

"In her room, and that's where she's going to stay until then."

"Do you think that's a good idea?"

"Well . . . what else do you suggest?"

"I don't know, but if she's playing with matches and wanting to hurt people, you should probably keep a closer eye on her."

"I can't deal with her right now."

"You don't have a choice."

"Well, if you're so concerned about her, Curtis, then why don't you come home?"

"You know I can't do that. Not until early next week."

"What else is new?"

"Charlotte, look. I'm sorry I can't be there, but if something worse happens, I'll drop everything. All you have to do is call me."

"But with Tracy gone, I really need you to be here now."

"Why did you fire her, anyway?"

"Because she knew all those things about Marissa and she didn't bother telling us."

"Maybe she was afraid to."

I rolled my eyes toward the ceiling when I heard him say that, because this was the same lame excuse she had given me only hours ago. But I didn't care whether she was telling the truth about that or not because I wasn't buying it. The woman had certain responsibilities to this family and she clearly should have spoken up.

"I let her go and that's that."

"Well, maybe you should try to talk to her. Tracy has been with us a long time and Matthew and Marissa love her."

"I'm not talking to anybody about anything. She's gone and that's all there is to it."

"Fine. It's your call."

"Exactly."

"Hey, I hate to hang up, but it's almost time for me to head over to the church I'm speaking at tonight."

"What about Marissa, Curtis?"

"I told you I'd come home if I had to."

"Don't you even want to speak to her?"

"Put her on, but I really have to get going."

I went to Marissa's room and told her to pick up her phone. I stood there listening but her conversation was no different than usual. She was happy to hear Curtis's voice, and as always, she asked him when he would be here again. She already knew, but this was her normal routine every time she spoke with him.

When they'd hung up, I asked her if she was hungry and she said no. Then she went back to playing with one of the educational video games Curtis had purchased for her. I stood watching her for another minute and then I walked away, not knowing what to do and feeling totally defeated.

About an hour later, my cell phone rang and I was shocked to be hearing from the investigator, Mr. Perry, so soon. Especially since I'd just phoned him yesterday, right after Curtis had left, to let him know that Curtis's plans had changed and that he'd had to fly out a day early.

"I just wanted to give you an update," he said.

"Okay."

"Your husband didn't leave Chicago until this morning."

"No, you must be mistaken. I was here when the car came to pick him up yesterday for the airport."

"That may be, but the reason I know for sure that he didn't fly out until this morning is because I was on the same plane with him. Call it a freak accident, divine intervention, or whatever you want, but regardless of how it happened, I ended up on the same nine A.M. flight to New York that he was on."

"Then where was he from the time he left here yesterday afternoon until this morning?"

"That I don't know, but I do have some news that you won't be happy about."

My heart dropped instantly.

"Mrs. Black?"

"Yes. I'm here."

"There was a woman sitting at the gate with him and she sat right next to him in first class once they boarded the plane."

"Sometimes Mary, his assistant, travels with him. Especially when he goes to some of the larger cities."

"No, this wasn't Mary, because while we were all sitting at the gate, I sat nearby with my back to them and there were a couple of times someone named Mary called him on his cell phone regarding some sort of media interview and then it sounded like she was giving him some other itinerary."

"Then who do you think this woman was?"

"I don't know. But based on their conversation, I would have to say that she definitely wasn't one of his business associates, and I can guarantee you that they're more than friends. The woman seemed ridiculously taken with him, and there were times when your husband seemed uncomfortable with the attention she was giving him, I'm guessing because he was worried that someone might recognize him and realize she wasn't you."

Mr. Perry was very blunt, and while this was what I'd paid for, his report was tearing me apart.

"What did she look like?" I asked, feeling that I had to know.

"Just like you. She's about your height. Maybe about your complexion and she dresses immaculately."

"Are you staying at the same hotel as Curtis?"

"I've already checked in and settled into my room."

"What I need is for you to find out her name, address, and anything else you can come up with."

"I will. Although I can't promise you that I'll be able to do that until I return home. Once upon a time, I could have figured out a way to get her information from the airline, but that's become a lot harder since 9/11. So unless I just happen to run into her casually and get her to introduce herself, I'll have to wait until one of my assistants picks me up from the airport so that we can follow your husband's car back to Mitchell or wherever. Because once I find out where she lives, getting her name will be a piece of cake."

"And you'll call me as soon as you know something, right?"

"Immediately."

"Then I'll speak to you soon."

"I'm sorry I don't have more positive news."

"It's not your fault. I hired you to find out the truth, and that's what I expect, good or bad."

"I'll be in touch."

I was floored. I tried to imagine why Curtis would spend the last five days making love to me, professing his love, and promising that he was going to commit to being a good husband if in reality he had a woman out on the road with him.

This had always been my greatest fear and suspicion, but as of yesterday, I had sort of started to believe that I was all he needed. He'd had me believing that he didn't want anyone else and that our family was the most important aspect of his life. He'd even stood before the congregation on Sunday and proclaimed all the changes he was going to make regarding his family, and now I knew he had flat out lied. He'd lied to everyone in attendance, but most of all, he'd lied to me. I didn't know who this mysterious woman was, but what I did know was that Curtis would be sorry for hurting me the way he was. He would be sorrier than he'd ever been for anything else because I was going to pay him back in a way he would never forget. I would make sure he felt the same pain I was feeling and then some, and I knew exactly how I was going to do it.

Chapter 18

JANINE

I'm so sorry that I had to get the police involved," I said to Sadie. I'd gone to the nursing home to inform her that Antonio had been arraigned and charged with possession with intent to manufacture and deliver.

"Look, honey, you had to do what you had to do, and I support you a hundred percent."

"I know, but I still feel bad because Antonio is still your son and I know you care about him."

"Yes, but he had no right bringing drugs into your home, and now he has to face the consequences the same as any other criminal. His father and I have talked ourselves to death, and now we're just plain tired and ready to accept whatever is to come."

"If only he'd left when I asked him to."

"But he didn't, and I hope you're not feeling any obligation toward getting him out of jail, because it's just a matter of time before he contacts you."

"Actually, he already did, and he wasn't happy when I told him I couldn't do it."

"Good for you, and if I were you, I wouldn't take any more of his phone calls."

"I'm not going to, and I also told him that I was taking his clothes to your house. Is that okay?"

"That's fine, but he's still not moving back in with us."

"This is all such a mess."

"I just wish I could speak to him because I've got a few choice words I wanna say, but there's no way the nursing home is going to accept any collect calls from a correctional facility. My doctor was in this morning, though, saying I'll probably be able to go home after this weekend, so I'll get to talk to Antonio soon enough."

"See, I feel bad about that, too, because here you are trying to get well and I keep bringing you all this terrible news."

"Don't you think twice about any of that. I'm glad you came and told me everything, and I really hope that our relationship won't have to end just because things are over between you and Antonio."

"It won't. You know I care about you a lot, and that won't ever change."

"You're a real sweetheart, Janine," she said, smiling at me. "And that boy of mine is just plain stupid. He's lost the best thing that ever happened to him, and he'll regret it for the rest of his days."

"I really loved him. No one understood why, but that's truly the way I felt about him"

"His father and I did the best we could. We worked hard and gave him everything. But then maybe that's why he turned out like this. When he was growing up, we never made him do any chores, so maybe he got used to getting whatever he wanted without having to work for it and he never saw a reason to change. We did the same with both our boys, and maybe that's also why his older brother has been locked up down in Joliet for five years now."

I'd heard Antonio mention his brother, but not very often. I believe he shied away from the subject because thinking about him was too painful.

"When will he be out?" I asked.

"Not for at least another couple of years or so. They got him on armed robbery and something else. It was his first time being arrested, but he had no business going into that convenience store trying to steal anything. And to think he put a gun to someone's head," she said sadly. "I just thank God he at least had the sense enough not to pull the trigger."

I was at a loss for words, so instead I patted the top of her hand, quietly consoling her. I sat with her for another hour until she had fallen off to sleep and then I left. It was still pretty early, so I went down the hall to see Mrs. Johnson, who was playing bridge with three other residents.

"How's my favorite girl doing today?" she said, her face brightening more than it already was.

"I'm good, and how are you?"

"Can't complain. Especially since my partner and me are whipping the pants off these two young'uns right here."

I laughed because the two "young'uns" she was referring to couldn't have been more than five years younger than she was.

"I'll have to get you to teach me how to play sometime," I said.

"Whenever you say, I'll be ready."

"Well, I'll let you all get back to your game, but I'm sure I'll see you in a few days."

"You have a good weekend, sweetie."

"I will."

On my way out to the parking lot, I called Charlotte to see

what she and the children were up to because I really didn't want to go home right away, and she told me to come on over. I didn't mind being alone, but tonight I really wanted to spend some time with my best friend. When I arrived, though, I was shocked to see this strange man sitting comfortably in the family room having what appeared to be big fun with Matthew and Marissa because they were laughing uncontrollably.

"You didn't tell me you had company," I said.

"It's only Curtis's brother. Larry, this is my girl Janine. Janine Turner, this is Larry Reynolds."

"Nice to meet you," I said.

"The pleasure is all mine," he said, reaching over to shake my hand.

"Larry wanted to get more acquainted with the children, so I invited him over," Charlotte explained, and all I could think about was how she'd told me Curtis didn't want him there. I wasn't sure why she was defying his wishes, but knowing Charlotte, she had her reasons.

"So are you enjoying our city, Larry?" I asked.

"For the most part. It's not as exciting as Atlanta, but it seems like a good place to live."

"I'm sure," I agreed.

"So how was work?" Charlotte asked me.

"Fine, but I'm certainly glad the weekend is here so I can relax."

"I can imagine."

"If you're free, I was thinking that maybe we could go shopping or something tomorrow."

"I would, except tomorrow morning I'm driving Matthew and Marissa over so we can spend some time with my parents, and I'm not planning to come back until sometime tomorrow night."

"Oh, okay. Maybe we can go next weekend."

"Definitely."

"So, Janine, have you always lived in Mitchell?" Larry asked.

"No, actually, I just moved here about two years ago to take a position at the university."

"Really? What do you do?"

"I'm a professor in the business department."

"That's great."

"What about you?"

"Well, once upon a time I used to manage about twenty people at one of the top CPA firms in Georgia, but now I work part-time for UPS."

"UPS is a good company," I said, but I could tell he was embarrassed about his change in employment status.

"Yes, it is, and I plan on having a management position there, too, at some point. I had a few problems in the past, but my master's degree still ought to count for something."

"I'm sure it will," I said, but I couldn't deny the fact that I was shocked about his educational background. He spoke intelligently, but I guess I couldn't help focusing on his previous drug habit.

"Uncle Larry," Marissa said, "make that face you made again."

"What? Like this?" he said, making some crazy expression even Charlotte and I had to chuckle at.

"Mom, can I bring down my Xbox and hook it up to the big TV so Uncle Larry and I can play one of my games?" Matthew asked.

"Go ahead."

"I wanna play, too," Marissa whined.

"And you will," Larry assured her.

"J, are you hungry?" Charlotte said.

"You know, I hadn't thought about it before now, but actually I am."

"We ordered Chinese and there's still a lot of it in the kitchen if you want some."

"I do," I said, and we both left the room.

"Girl, are you crazy?" I whispered.

"Let's warm up your food and then we can go down to the lower level," was all she said, but she didn't look at me.

But as soon as we got down there and went into the rec room, I repeated my question.

"Charlotte, I'm going to ask you again. Have you lost your mind or what?"

"No. But before we get into that, let me tell you about Marissa's appointment with the psychiatrist."

"That's right. I wondered how that went," I said, eating some sweet-and-sour shrimp.

"Well, of course she wasn't happy about going, but once she met the doctor, she seemed fine. I was able to watch the entire session through a window they have set up, and all I could do was shake my head when I watched her in action. She did the same thing she always does with us. Answered every question with all the right answers."

"So did you speak to the doctor afterward?"

"Yes. We spoke privately and she told me that there was some indication that Marissa might be a slight bit unstable, but that she would know more once she had the opportunity to see her a few more times."

"I really hate to hear that."

"Imagine how I feel. And I'm still outraged with Tracy."

"I'm sure, but I can sort of understand why she was afraid to say anything," I said, because Charlotte had told me the whole story about Tracy's previous employer.

"I don't care. She still should have told me what happened."

I didn't say anything more because I could tell Charlotte had already made up her mind about Tracy and wasn't planning to change it anytime soon.

"Well, at least you're getting Marissa the help she needs, and that's what's most important."

"It is and I just pray this doctor can help her."

"What does Curtis think about all this?"

"Not much. Because, as you can see, he didn't rush right home once I told him everything. Although he's probably too busy lying up in his hotel with some woman."

"Excuse me?" I said. I was confused, but when she told me about the private investigator and the information he'd called to report to her last night, I understood why she felt the way she did.

"Wow."

"So from here on out, I'm going to do whatever makes me happy, including having Larry over to visit the children. They adore him, so why shouldn't they be able to see him whenever they want to?"

"I hear what you're saying but I still think you're making a huge mistake. Because what are you going to do if Curtis finds out about this? What if Marissa or Matthew tells him that Larry's been over here?"

"That's exactly what I want them to do. Curtis can't stand Larry, and it'll kill him to know that Larry was here in his house for hours with his family."

"I know you're upset, but I really wish you would rethink what you're doing. I mean maybe you should wait until this P.I. guy finds out who this woman really is."

"*Who* she is doesn't matter. All I needed to know was whether he was having an affair, and now I know my suspicions were right all along. But enough about Curtis and enough about me. How are you?"

"I'm okay."

"Have you heard from Antonio again?"

"Not since I told you about him calling the other night, but I did speak with the prosecutor's office today and of course they want me to testify."

"Are you comfortable with that?"

"Not really, but it's not like I really have a choice."

"It'll be fine. You'll testify, Antonio and his friends will be convicted and locked away, and that'll be that."

"Let's hope."

"And this is our lower level," Matthew said, coming down the stairs. Marissa was right behind and apparently they were showing Larry around the house. I could tell Charlotte didn't see one problem with this, but I cringed at the whole idea of it.

"Charlotte, you and Curtis really have a beautiful home."

"Thank you."

"I mean, the two of you have really arrived."

"You think so, huh?"

"No doubt. Curtis is a very, *very* lucky man."

I didn't like the way he was eyeing Charlotte, and I was glad the children hadn't noticed it.

"Can I get you anything?" Charlotte asked him.

"No, Matt and Rissa are taking very good care of me, so actually I'm good."

"Glad to hear it."

"You two enjoy your chat," he said to both of us, and then the three of them went back upstairs.

"He's known Matthew and Marissa how long? And he's already given them nicknames? And did you see the way he looked at you?"

"J, please. Girl, you're reading way too much into all of this. Larry was only being polite. Nothing more."

"So, as gorgeous and charming as he is, are you trying to say you're not attracted to him?"

"No. I'm not."

"Well, he's definitely attracted to you."

"I don't think so, and you are really cracking me up."

"Laugh if you want to, but I've got a bad feeling about this."

"You worry too much," she said, dismissing my theory.

But the reason I was so worried was because I knew Larry was interested in a whole lot more than just getting to know the children.

And if Charlotte thought otherwise, she was in for a rude awakening.

Chapter 19

CHARLOTTE

I wasn't sure why Janine was so concerned about Larry because, whether she believed me or not, I wasn't attracted to him. At least not in the way she was thinking. Yes, he looked good, but it wasn't like I wanted to sleep with him. I simply liked him as a person, and I had to admit that knowing how much Curtis despised him made him all that more appealing to me. He was all the revenge I needed, and I'd already begun this whole reprisal process this morning when I'd gone to the bank and withdrawn some money and then had him come by the house to get it—that is, without the children seeing him. Larry had mentioned last night that he needed transportation to get to and from his job and that he'd found a buy-here-pay-here car lot willing to accept a thousand dollars as a down payment. And since I just couldn't imagine him walking and catching the bus the way he was, not with winter fast approaching, I'd seen no choice but to help him. Then I'd decided to give him another thousand to pay his rent for the next few weeks, eat, and do whatever else was necessary.

I couldn't wait for Curtis to find out, and it was the reason I'd purposely taken the money from an account he checked regularly. He would die once he learned that I was planning to give Larry more money as time went on. I also couldn't wait for Marissa to squeal because I knew she'd be the one to tell him about Larry's visit. Curtis hadn't called yet, but chances were he would before the day was over. If not, he would definitely be calling to speak with her and Matthew tomorrow or Monday.

Now, though, we were pulling into my parents' driveway and I was really looking forward to seeing them. It had been at least a month since we'd driven over to the Chicago area and I definitely missed them.

"Mom, can you open the trunk?" Matthew said, and stepped out of the vehicle.

"Sure."

"Get my stuff, too, Matthew, okay?" Marissa added. She was already putting on the "good girl" persona for my parents, fooling them the same as usual.

As Matthew prepared to ring the bell, my father opened the door before he could do so.

"Boy, come on in here," he said, hugging Matthew. "And how's my sweet little granddaughter?" he said, grabbing hold of Marissa. "It's so good to see both of you."

"I'm fine, Grandpa. How are you?"

"For an old man, I'm doing very well."

"Hi, Daddy," I said when the children continued into the house.

"Hi, sweetheart. It's good to see you, too."

"Hey, how're my babies?" Mom said when she saw the children.

"Hi, Grandma." They were both beaming, and just knowing

166

how much love existed between my parents and my children gave my heart a warm feeling.

"Hey, sweetie," she said to me, and we hugged for longer than usual. I guess I didn't want to let go because I'd suddenly begun thinking about Marissa and her problems. I'd tried not to dwell on it, but I couldn't seem to push the whole idea of it from my mind—what was going to happen to her, and if Aaron was her father. I played both questions constantly and I was hoping for a quick and permanent solution. In a perfect world, Marissa would become the normal child she was supposed to be and Aaron would remain locked up forever, never contacting us again. I knew my thinking was total fantasy, but I still hoped for this nonetheless.

"Have the three of you eaten yet?" Mom asked.

"Yes, ma'am," Matthew answered. "We stopped at White Castle on the way here."

"For the life of me, I don't know how you children can eat at these fast-food places."

"All I had was French fries and some lemonade," Marissa said.

"Well, at least that's better than eating those little burgers they sell. Because you have to eat five of them just to get full."

We all laughed and then sat down in the great room.

"Matthew and Marissa, I've got a surprise for you in the kitchen."

"What is it, Grandma?" Marissa asked.

"Yeah, what, Grandma?" Matthew said.

"Oh . . . just a German chocolate cake I made a couple of hours ago."

"Can we have some now?" Matthew said, standing up.

"Anytime you get ready."

"I believe I'll join you," Daddy said, and they all left Mom and me sitting on the sofa.

"So how's Marissa?" Mom spoke softly.

"Pretty much the same. She's not acting any different than she always does, and of course she's always happy to be here with you and Daddy so I'm sure you won't notice any changes either."

"I feel so sorry for her because it's not like she can help the way she is."

"I know, but I'm still hoping her doctor can do something because we can't have any more of those school incidents."

"Maybe getting suspended was enough to stop her from playing with matches ever again."

"Mom, I really hope so because this whole thing is worrying me to death."

"She'll be fine. We just have to trust, believe, and stay prayerful."

"You're right."

"So how's Curtis?" she asked, and I wanted to tell her everything.

"He's good. He left New York today and flew down to Dallas, but he'll be home on Monday."

"I can't imagine doing all that traveling he does, but I'm still very proud of him. After all this time, I still tell anyone who will listen that the Reverend Curtis Black is my son-in-law, and even your daddy does the same thing."

I listened with a smile on my face, but the more Mom spoke about Curtis, the more I wanted to slander him. I wanted to tell Mom, Dad, and all of America that Curtis was the grand master of hypocrisy. I wanted to tell Mom how he was committing adultery on her daughter and that she should stop boasting about how great a man he was.

But instead I did more listening and smiling and pretended that life with my philandering husband was just peachy. I did what I was sure thousands of pastor and celebrity wives did daily just to keep up certain appearances for the public.

After chatting with my parents for another couple of hours, I kissed the children good-bye, told them to be good, and headed back to Mitchell. Traffic had been almost unbearable, something I hadn't expected on a Saturday evening, so the drive had taken me about a half hour longer than usual. Now, though, I was exiting I-90 and was only ten minutes from home.

I changed the radio dial from some talk station to Soul 106.3 and smiled when I heard Luther's one-in-a-million voice playing across the airway. He was crooning my absolute favorite, "A House Is Not a Home," and while at first I sang along with him, it wasn't long before my eyes filled with tears. I still couldn't believe he was gone, and though I'd only seen him in concert and had never met him personally, I missed him. I missed seeing him perform at award shows on television and seeing him do interviews. I missed the extraordinary music he would no longer be able to offer us, his loyal fans who supported and loved him.

When I turned onto my street, I wondered why a strange car was parked on the side opposite our house, but since I didn't recognize it, I pressed the garage door remote controller and drove inside. I'd stopped at Target right after leaving my parents, so I grabbed the bags from the backseat, walked up to the door leading to the kitchen, and went in. As soon as I did, the doorbell rang, and my first reaction was fear because now I wondered if someone had been sitting in the vehicle I'd seen, waiting for me to get home. I also wondered if the person knew no one was here with me and this caused my hesitation to escalate. But then the doorbell rang three more times and I decided to see who it was. I'd also decided I wouldn't let any strangers in for any reason.

"Who is it?"

"Larry."

I frowned because we hadn't talked about his coming over, and as a matter of fact, he knew the children were going to be away at my parents' and that he wouldn't be able to see them again until sometime next week. So this surprise visit of his made me a bit nervous.

"Hi," I said, opening the door halfway.

"So you made it back?"

"Yeah, just now."

"I know, that was me sitting in my car," he said, pointing out to the street.

"Oh, so you already picked it up?"

"Yes, and I can't thank you enough. Having my own ride makes a huge difference and I wanted to tell you in person."

"I'm glad everything worked out for you," I said, not knowing what else to say.

"You know, it's not exactly eighty degrees out here, so aren't you going to invite me in?"

"Well, actually, I need to get a few things done around here and then get to bed because I'm planning to go to church in the morning."

"I promise I won't keep you long. Really."

"Okay, but only for a few minutes."

"You are truly an angel, Charlotte," he said, entering the house and taking a seat in the living room. "And I just hope Curtis knows how blessed he is. I hope he knows any man would be happy to have you."

"That's very nice of you to say."

"I mean it. And I also hope he's not taking you for granted."

"He doesn't," I hurried to say, even though I didn't believe my own response.

"Well, that's good to know, but I gotta tell you, it's hard for me to believe Curtis has changed for the better."

"What do you mean by that?"

"Well, for one thing, the Curtis I always knew never thought twice about messing around with a ton of beautiful women. He slept around on Tanya all the time and I can even remember him telling me point-blank that he just couldn't help it. He just couldn't see himself sleeping with only one woman. He wanted to, but he used to say that his desire for sex was much too strong."

I wanted to comment, but given the fact that I was one of those women he was talking about, I chose not to say anything. I still felt guilty for sleeping with someone else's husband, and I'd finally gotten my chance to apologize to Tanya about a year ago. I hadn't known how she was going to respond, but unlike Anise, Tanya had told me that she'd forgiven me and that I shouldn't worry about it.

"Umph, umph, umph," he said, laughing and pulling out of his coat jacket what looked to be a can of beer. "Good ole Curtis."

"Larry, have you been drinking and driving at the same time?"

"Not exactly. I mean, unless you call beer a real drink."

"You really ought to be more careful."

"Oh, I'll be fine," he said, his voice slurred.

Oh my God, he was suddenly sounding tipsy, and now I knew I wanted him out of here.

"Larry, I hate to cut our visit short, but I really need to get busy."

"It's still early. You've got plenty of time."

"I know but if you don't mind—"

"As a matter of fact, I do mind," he said, moving over to the love seat where I was sitting and breathing directly in my face.

I scooted away from him. "Larry, please."

"Okay, I'm sorry. I'm way out of line, but can I help it that I've wanted you since the first day I laid eyes on you? And I gotta tell you, these feelings I have are driving me insane. You know what I mean, baby?"

Baby?

"So how about it?"

"How about what?"

"You and me. How about we waltz our little behinds right on upstairs and take care of each other? Because I can promise you Curtis is definitely getting his needs fulfilled."

"Larry, you're drunk and I'm going to have to ask you to leave," I said, getting to my feet.

"No, I think I'd rather stay. Besides, I just got here and it wouldn't be polite for you to kick me out this soon. Right?"

I stared at him dumbfounded and wondered what I'd gotten myself into.

"Okay, look. If you don't want to be with me, that's fine, but I do need a favor."

"What kind of favor?"

"I need a little more money."

"How much? And for what?"

"Another couple thousand."

"I don't have that kind of money around here."

"Well, then just give me what you do have and I'll get the rest on Monday when the bank opens."

"Larry, I can't, okay? Curtis is already going to scream bloody murder about you being over here."

He turned up his beer can again, slurping in a filthy manner.

"Oh really? Then why did you invite me over last night? Because you'd been saying over and over that Curtis didn't want me here. So tell me, Charlotte. Why'd you do it?"

"So that you could spend time with the children."

"Right."

"Larry, please. You really have to go now, so let me walk you to the door."

"See, what I think is that you decided to use me as a pawn. Maybe you wanted to make Curtis jealous or maybe just piss him off. I don't know. But either way, I'm okay with it. The only thing is, I expect to be paid for my services."

Right then and there I wanted to die. Larry had found me out and now he was trying to use his newfound discovery against me.

"So, like I said, I need more money."

I opened my mouth, planning to tell him no again, but the phone rang.

"Answer it," he said, and his tone was cold.

"It'll just go to voice mail."

"I said answer," he demanded, now standing up.

I obeyed him and went to the kitchen. Before I picked up the phone, he was already standing next to me.

I closed my eyes when I saw that it was Curtis.

"Hello?" I answered.

"Hey, what's goin' on?"

"Not much. How are you?"

"Just got back from my speaking event and I'm exhausted. I had a full day and I can't wait to get home on Monday."

"I can't wait for you to get here either," I said, not caring at all about the fling he was having because the matter at hand with Larry was dominating my priorities.

"Where're Matthew and Marissa?"

"Remember I told you I was taking them to my parents."

"Oh yeah. I forgot. Maybe I'll give them a call over there."

"I think my parents were taking them to a movie, so you might have to talk to them tomorrow," I said, and Larry kissed me on the side of my neck in multiple spots. I wanted him to stop but he wouldn't.

"Sounds good," Curtis said. "I'll just wait until then. So what else did you do today?"

"Not much, but I'm planning to go to church in the morning."

"Reverend Tolson is out of town, isn't he?"

"Yes, so one of the associate ministers will be preaching," I said, cringing because Larry was now caressing both my breasts. I jerked away from him and he smiled slyly.

"Well, I hate to run, but I'm about to crash so I won't be so tired for the service I'm speaking at in the morning."

"Okay, well, I guess I'll speak to you tomorrow sometime."

"I'll call you in the afternoon, and hey?"

"Yeah?"

"I love you, baby."

"I love you, too."

I hung up wondering how Curtis could live with himself. I wondered how he could call and tell me that he loved me, knowing that someone else was there with him.

"Wasn't that sweet? The two of you professing your love for one another."

"Larry, why are you doing this?"

"Because, I told you, I need more money."

"And I told you, I don't have it."

"Let me see your purse."

"No," I said, leaving him standing where he was.

But he grabbed my arm, stopping me in my tracks.

"Look. Enough is enough. Either you give me the money or you give me something else I want. But regardless, I'm not leaving here empty-handed."

"I don't have anything else."

"Of course you do," he said, rubbing his hand between my legs. "You've got plenty."

"Larry, stop it!" I said, shoving him away. "I'm a married woman and you're supposed to be Curtis's play brother."

"What does being married have to do with anything?"

"A lot."

"Money or sex," he said, ignoring me. "Take your choice."

"All I have is maybe three hundred dollars," I finally admitted.

"Then give me that. And I'll take those earrings you have on, too."

"You can't be serious."

"As a heart attack."

I paused but decided I wasn't removing my diamond studs.

"I would take that ridiculously huge ring on your finger but Curtis would probably try to kill me over something like that."

Hmmph. Here he was worried about what Curtis might do to him, but what he didn't know was that I would fight him to the death for my wedding ring. Curtis had gotten it for me right after he'd received his second book deal, and I wasn't planning to part with any one of these four carats.

"Larry, please go."

"I want those earrings and I want them now."

"I'm not giving you *anything*," I said matter-of-factly. "And if you don't leave, I'm calling the police."

"No, I don't think you will," he boasted, and flicked open a deadly-looking knife.

"Oh my God," I said.

"Let's go upstairs," he instructed, and I did what he told me.

When we arrived, I opened my jewelry box and he took out a string of cultured pearls, a sapphire ring, and a diamond tennis bracelet.

"Where's Curtis's stash?"

"Larry, please don't do this," I pleaded, but he slid over to Curtis's side of the dresser and went through each drawer.

"Well, well, well. What do we have here?"

"That's Curtis's favorite cross. He never takes it off, but he was in such a hurry he must have left it."

"Really? Well, it's mine now."

"Okay, Larry, I'll get you more money. I'll get you whatever you want, but please don't take that cross."

"Why not? Because maybe if I wear this, I'll get the Holy Ghost just like Curtis," he laughed.

I was horrified because if Larry took that cross, there would be no way for me to explain its whereabouts. Not to mention the reason it was so special to Curtis was because it had belonged to his favorite elder board member and he'd given it to Curtis just before he'd taken his last breath and right after Curtis had prayed for him.

Larry placed the cross in one of his pockets, seized another couple of minor pieces, and then looked at me.

"I think that should do it. For now, anyway."

"Then will you please leave?"

"I'm going. And maybe next time you'll be more careful with who you try to use. Acting like you wanted to help me when all along you were only trying to pay Curtis back for whatever he's done to you. Although I'll bet you won't tell him about tonight, now will you?"

I went down the stairway silently and opened the front door.

"Oh, and I'll call you about the rest of my money on Monday," he said, kissing me on the cheek.

I slammed the door and tried to imagine what Curtis would do if he ever found out about this. Learning that Larry had been over here was one thing, but discovering that he was now extorting cash and jewelry was something different.

Which meant I had to keep yet another secret from him.

Chapter 20

JANINE

As soon as I entered the house, I immediately removed my panty hose. Since her children were gone and Curtis was still on the road, Charlotte and I had driven to church together. Actually, I'd swung by to pick her up for service and then we'd gone to dinner right afterward.

For the first time in a long while, I was feeling pretty upbeat and we'd laughed and chatted for more than a couple of hours. We talked about everything but I still wondered why Charlotte had gotten this uneasy look on her face when I asked her about Larry. I'd wanted to know if she was planning to have him back over, and while she'd said no, she'd seemed sort of nervous. I wasn't sure why, and since she'd changed the subject so quickly, I hadn't gotten a chance to ask any more questions.

After slipping on something a lot more comfortable than the fitted suit I'd had on all day, I went to the kitchen to get a glass of Welch's sparkling white grape juice and brought it back to my den. I turned on the television, but when I glanced toward the bottom of the entertainment center, I noticed a couple of my photo albums and reached over and pulled them out.

I opened the largest one and the first photo I saw was the one of my mother holding me in her arms. She must have been so happy then because she was smiling widely. I'd always cherished this shot because there were many days, even as a grown woman, that I wished I could turn back time. I wished I could return to the days when life had been simple for me and I hadn't had to concern myself with any problems. I knew, thanks to my father, that these days had not been the best for her, but as a baby, I'd been sitting on top of the world and hadn't known one thing from another.

Next I flipped through a few more pages until I came across a picture of my sister and me when we were three and five respectively. Even then we were as thick as thieves and I missed her so much. I missed her terribly, and as of late I found myself thinking about her every waking moment. I knew it was because of what I was going through personally, but there were also times when I wished I hadn't begged her to leave her boyfriend, because if I hadn't, maybe she'd still be here.

I flipped through to the end of the book, reminiscing about my younger years, and thought about my father. I'd told him that I was going to come see him, and first thing tomorrow I was going to make my airline reservation for one week from now.

When I finished looking at the last photo album, I set it down and went to my bedroom to find something to wear to work tomorrow. I rummaged through one end of the closet to the other and finally settled on a navy blue pinstripe pantsuit that I wore way too much. It was definitely time for a new wardrobe, and now that Antonio was out of here, I was going to treat myself. I'd wanted to start yesterday and it was the reason I'd asked Charlotte about going shopping, but next week would be soon enough. My plan was to purchase at least five suits, a few separate dress pants and blouses, and it was time for a couple of pair of new boots. I also needed a new winter coat as well as a few cashmere sweaters. I didn't like spending excessively on clothing, even less now that Antonio had maxed out one of my credit cards, but I was really feeling as though it was time I did something for me.

I pulled out a matching shirt and laid it, along with my suit, on the back of the chair. Then I turned on XM Radio's smooth jazz channel and went into the bathroom to wash off my makeup. But as soon as I did the phone rang.

"Hello?"

"How are you?"

"Carl?"

"Yes, and I hope it's okay that I'm calling."

"Yes, it's fine."

"Good, because I just wanted to make sure those locks I installed were working out for you."

"They are," I said, and then neither of us said anything.

"Okay, the truth is," he finally said, "I haven't been able to stop thinking about you and I was wondering if you'd like to have dinner with me sometime."

"Maybe eventually, but I have to be honest with you. I just ended a terrible relationship and it's not like I'm feeling all that great about men right now."

"That's understandable. I went through the same thing myself when Greta and I separated. I won't bother you with the details now, but I will say that after a few months I finally realized that I couldn't blame all women for Greta's mistake."

"This is true, but my breakup is still very new and it's going to take me some time to sort things out."

"Well, just think about it, and if you don't mind, I'll still give you a call every now and then."

"I'd like that."

"Good. Also, I hope I didn't catch you at a bad time and I apologize for not asking you that right when I first called."

"No. I was pretty much just preparing for work tomorrow. Charlotte and I went to church and then to dinner and I just got home about an hour or so ago."

"I need to get back to church myself."

"It certainly won't hurt."

"You and Charlotte are pretty close, huh?"

"We are."

"That's great, because we all need friends when we're going through trials. My brother was certainly there for me when I needed him, and it really made an amazing difference."

"I know the feeling, because no matter what happens, I always know I can count on Charlotte."

"Well, I'd better not keep you on the phone, but just think about what I said and I'll be in touch."

"I look forward to it, and you have a nice evening, Carl."

"You, too, Janine."

I hung up and wondered if he could be trusted. I wondered if he was truly the decent man he was portraying himself to be or if he was an impostor like Antonio. There was no way to know for sure, but at least he owned his own business and I'd never heard anything except positive remarks about him from other church members. Still, I needed to know what happened between him and his wife. Not that it was any of my business, but if I was going to consider having dinner with him, I would have to learn a bit more about his past. I'd wanted to ask Charlotte this afternoon what she knew about him, but I'd decided against it because I didn't want her thinking I was trying to rush into another relationship with someone I didn't know much about. I hadn't even told her he was the person I'd called to change my locks, and wasn't planning to, at least not yet, anyway.

I finished removing my eye makeup, foundation, and pressed powder and then I dried my face with a large towel. But the loud knock on the front door alarmed me. It wasn't a normal knock, and all I could pray was that Antonio hadn't sent over one of his goons to terrorize me. I wanted to see who it was but I didn't think it was safe to leave my bedroom.

Still, the person banged on the door like he was crazy and I went into the living room.

I tiptoed closer to the door, and while I wasn't planning to say anything, my heart dropped when I heard Antonio's voice.

"Janine, I know you're in there, so open up the door."

I still didn't move or say anything.

"I'm asking you nicely. Open up the door so I can talk to you."

Again, I stood there, now not able to move, and it was at least sixty seconds before Antonio yelled louder than before.

"Open up this damn door, Janine!"

I stood in place and prayed that he would leave.

"If you think getting your locks changed is enough to save you, baby, you are sadly mistaken."

I winced because now I knew he'd already tried his key and was outraged that it hadn't worked. I was thankful that I'd taken care of this the same night he was arrested.

I jumped when I heard the next thud and it sounded like he'd kicked the door with his foot.

"You raggedy bitch. Those people downtown are talking about giving me ten years and I'm not going out like that."

Oh God, please, please make him leave.

And after another five minutes or so of ranting, he finally did. I peeped through the window and saw him skid off in some car I'd never seen before and I felt relieved. That is, until my phone rang again. I was hoping it was Charlotte, but it wasn't. It was a number I didn't recognize, and I decided that if it was Antonio, it might be better to answer so he could end this rampage he was on.

"Hello?"

"Why didn't you open the door like I asked you?"

"Because you and I are through with each other, and if you don't stop bothering me, I'm going to call the police."

"I don't care who you call. But I'm telling you this. You'd better find some way to help get me out of this mess."

"And how am I supposed to do that?"

"When you get on the stand to testify at the trial, you can tell them that Killer, Nate, and Chad forced me to deal drugs with them and that the only reason you told the police I was involved was so the three of them wouldn't realize that you and I planned this whole bust from the beginning."

If I hadn't been on the phone listening to Antonio personally, I would have sworn I was dreaming. Because I just didn't want to accept this lie he had concocted and how he thought I was going to perjure myself in court.

"But that's not true," I said.

"So what? And it's not like you really have a choice. Either you get me off or you suffer the consequences. As a matter of fact, I want you to go tell one of those detectives your side of the story tomorrow because that way they'll just drop the charges and I won't even have to be tried."

"I'm hanging up now. And I'm asking you to please not call or come by here again, because this is not my fault or my problem."

"It *is* your fault because you had no business snitching to those narcs. You should have kept your mouth shut, but since you didn't, you're going to fix this."

"Good-bye, Antonio."

"Janine, I'm warning you. I'm not going to prison because of you. And since I had to have one of my girls and a couple of my boys bail me out, you owe them every dime of that money."

I hung up before he could say another word, but my phone rang on and off for the next hour until the police arrived, filled out a report, and told me that it was time I filed for an order of protection. The sad part, though, was that one of the officers made it clear that some men had no regard for court orders and that I should do whatever I had to to protect myself. I hadn't liked the sound of what he was saying, but I knew he was telling the truth. I knew that if Antonio wanted to do harm to me, the law wouldn't be able to stop him. I knew dodging and hiding from him wouldn't work. I knew my greatest fear had been confirmed.

That there wasn't a single human being on this earth that could protect me.

Chapter 21

JANINE

I wasn't sure if it had been the right thing for me to do or not, but at this point I couldn't see where I had anything to lose. I didn't know much about Carl Wilson, at least not enough to invite him into my home the way I was doing now, but the bottom line was that I was afraid to spend the rest of the evening alone. I was afraid that Antonio would stop at nothing to get what he wanted, and sadly enough, Carl was the only man I could think to call. There was Thomas, at the university, but the last thing I wanted was for any of my colleagues to know about the predicament I'd gotten myself into. I'd also thought about calling Charlotte and then going over to spend the night with her and the children, but I feared that Antonio might follow me. I couldn't take a chance on him trying to hurt them, too.

So here I sat with Carl, who seemed more than happy to be here with me.

"I feel really bad about involving you in all this, but I didn't know who else to call."

"It's no problem and I'm just sorry to hear that someone is threatening you the way this Antonio person is."

"The thing is, I don't think he's ever going to let up. When I spoke to him on the phone, he sounded so angry and so vindictive."

"And there's nothing the police can do about it?"

"No, because in order to arrest him, they'd have to catch him here. Although I'm guessing with the order of protection, all I'll have to do is report to them any of the times he comes."

"I just don't understand some men."

"Neither do I, because I was good to Antonio. I treated him the way I wanted to be treated, and now this is the thanks I get."

"If you don't mind my asking," he said, repositioning his body on the sofa we were both sitting on, "why was he arrested in the first place?"

"Drugs."

"Now, that's pretty deep."

"Tell me about it."

"Was he using them or selling them?"

"Both. He was definitely using marijuana and then selling cocaine, but to be honest, I didn't even know he was doing marijuana until a couple of weeks ago because up until then he'd never brought any around me."

Carl shook his head and I could tell he was trying to figure out that thousand-dollar question: How in the world had I gotten mixed up with such an awful person?

"Before you even ask, I may as well go ahead and tell you that I don't know why except I really did love him."

Carl smiled and slightly chuckled.

"What?" I asked.

"I guess I just have a hard time trying to figure out why good people seem to end up with such losers. And don't think I'm only referring to you, because actually I was thinking more about my own situation than anything else."

"Are you saying Greta is not the fine Christian woman we all know her to be?" I asked, now smiling myself.

"Hardly."

"Okay."

"I could certainly tell you some stories, and the only reason I won't is because the last thing you need right now is to hear about my madness."

"Please go ahead."

"Are you sure? Because I know that's not why you called me over here."

"I'm positive."

"Well, to start, Greta is far from being a Christian anything, let alone a fine Christian woman. That is, unless hypocrites somehow fall into that category."

Interestingly enough, I was already raising my eyebrows and I couldn't help wondering what the skinny was on her.

"I see she had you fooled, too," he continued.

"Apparently so."

"Shoot, that woman has done everything from sleeping with her married boss, to aborting a child that probably wasn't mine anyway, to running off two years ago for two weeks with some guy she met at the health club and who she was sure she was in love with."

"Gosh, Carl, I really had no idea and I doubt that anyone else at the church did either."

"I'm sure, because I never told anyone except my brother about the horrible things she did. I never even told my parents until the divorce was final. Mainly because I was too ashamed."

"Was she always like that?"

"Not the first couple of years, but after that it just seemed like she was bored with me. She started complaining about the fact that we didn't go out enough and that she needed more excitement in her life. Which of course I tried to work on, but going to dinner, going to the movies, and going to visit friends just wasn't enough. I even tried taking her to plays in Chicago but she still wasn't happy."

"That's too bad, because the boring life she thought she had is all I've ever wanted."

"Yeah, but at the same time you ended up with this Antonio character and he definitely doesn't sound like the dinner-and-movie type either."

"Well, believe it or not, for a long while he was. He was content with just being with me, but the problem was, I never pushed him to do anything he didn't want to do and I provided everything he needed."

"Then what happened?"

I sighed at first, but then I told Carl everything. I wasn't completely sure this had been the right thing for me to do, but he seemed so sincere. His demeanor was calm and his caring attitude couldn't be ignored. He was the type of man one couldn't help feeling at peace with.

"Amazing."

"And pitiful, huh?"

"No, just amazing because I can't imagine allowing any woman to take care of me like that."

"Maybe, but as you can see, some men expect it."

"And now he has the nerve to be threatening you?"

"Yeah, but now it's not because I wanted to break up with him. It's because he's facing prison time."

"As he should be."

"Tell him that."

"I wish I could."

"No, actually I'm just kidding, because I don't want you conversing with Antonio for any reason. He's crazy and the last thing I would want is for you to end up hurt because of me."

"Well, just so you know, I'm not afraid of him, and if he tries to harm you while I'm around, he'll figure that out pretty quickly."

Now, even more than when he'd first arrived, I regretted calling Carl, because while he was a pretty relaxed individual, he was making it very clear that he'd have no problem confronting Antonio. I guess this should have made me feel somewhat protected, but it was so unfair exposing him to such chaos.

"Carl, I'm really sorry."

"About what?" he said, confused.

"Dialing your phone number."

"Hey," he said, moving closer to me and placing his hand on my knee. "There's nothing for you to be sorry about, and from this day forward I hope you'll continue calling whenever you need to."

"I appreciate that. More than you know."

"If you'll remember, I called you earlier, anyway."

"Yeah, but not so you could put your life in danger."

"Like I said, I'm not afraid, so don't you worry about that."

We sat and chatted for a while until I realized it was now after eleven o'clock. I hadn't planned on keeping him here this long but already three hours had passed, and to be honest, it really didn't feel like it. Maybe because I was thoroughly enjoying his company and I hadn't thought about my dilemma nearly as much. It was all still in the back of my mind but I wasn't as shaky as I had been earlier.

"You know, I really think I'm going to be okay now, so please don't feel obligated to stay any longer."

"Oh, so does that mean you're kicking me out?" he said, smiling.

"No, of course not. But I don't want to burden you any more than I already have, either."

"Just to be safe, maybe I should stay until morning."

"I don't think that's a good idea."

"No, let me explain. I don't mean in the same bed. I'm just saying that maybe it's a good idea I stay just in case Antonio decides to pay you another visit."

"I don't know," I said, feeling a bit uneasy, because regardless of how favorably I felt toward Carl, I didn't know if allowing him to spend the night was the right thing.

"Why? Are you worried that I'll try to take advantage of you sexually?"

"No, I'm not saying that at all, but . . . ."

"But you don't trust me."

"I'm not saying that either."

"Actually, your hesitation is understandable and I guess I don't blame you. But if you change your mind, my offer still stands. Even if it's a week from now."

"You're such a sweet man, and thanks again for everything."

He drank the last of the sparkling juice I had gotten for him about an hour ago, and then he pulled on his leather jacket. I stared at him because, for whatever reason, I hadn't noticed how tall he was. I knew he was over six feet, but now that I was paying closer attention, I was sure he had to be at least six two or three.

"I know you have my business number, but let me give you my home number and cell as well," he said, removing a business card from his wallet and writing on the back of it.

"I really owe you," I said, preparing to open the door for him.

"Not at all. Although if paying me back will make you feel better, you can do it by going to dinner with me."

"I guess that's the least I could do, huh?"

"Tomorrow around six?"

"Six is fine."

"Is there any food you like in particular?"

"Pretty much any restaurant you pick will work for me."

"Really? Then I take it you won't mind McDonald's or Burger King at all."

"Whatever," I said, and we both laughed.

"I'll figure something out by tomorrow."

We stood staring at each other until I finally looked in another direction. Whether I wanted to admit it or not, there was obvious chemistry between us. Chemistry that was stronger than I'd been willing to acknowledge, and the kind that frightened me. Why? Because the last time I'd connected with someone so quickly was when I'd met Antonio.

"I think by now you know that I'm really feeling you as a person. I like you a lot and I haven't said that to another woman since my divorce."

"I like you, too, and maybe once I have my life back in order we can spend more time together."

"I hope so, and tomorrow will certainly be a start."

We gazed at each other again but then Carl pulled me closer.

"I'm sorry, but . . ." he said, and then kissed me on the lips. "I just couldn't leave without doing that."

I pulled slightly away from his grasp, but after a few seconds I couldn't resist, kissing him again. We kissed passionately and I knew I was in trouble. I knew Carl might end up being no different than the men I'd dated in the past or possibly worse, but all I could do now was have faith.

Over the past few days, I'd been praying that I would eventually find my soul mate, the man I was supposed to spend the rest of my life with. I hadn't been thinking I'd find him this soon exactly, but I'd been praying just the same.

So maybe Carl's being here was God's way of saying, "Janine, after all these years, you finally decided to consult Me about your relationships, and that's all I've been waiting for you to do. You finally realized that trying to handle things on your own isn't the best thing for you."

As Carl strode down the walkway and got inside his car, I never took my eyes off him. Partly because I wanted to make sure Antonio wasn't lurking somewhere in the dark, making plans to attack him, and partly because I hated to see Carl go.

Needless to say I couldn't wait for our dinner date.

Chapter 22

CHARLOTTE

I don't wanna wear that ugly outfit," Marissa said, whining, and I wanted to shake her silly. It was her first day back to school since being suspended, and she was getting on my nerves.

"Well, it's not like you have a choice," I said.

"I wanna wear my Dora dress."

"Marissa, how many times do I have to tell you that your Dora dress is dirty?"

"Well, it wouldn't be if you hadn't made Tracy go away. She would have washed it already or taken it to the cleaners."

"But you still wouldn't be able to wear it to school."

"So."

I breathed deeper than normal but continued combing her hair. I was so tired of fighting with this child, and the fact that I was still troubled by Larry's Saturday night visit was only compounding my frustration.

"Marissa, hold your head up straight so I can finish what I'm doing."

"No," she said, jerking away from me.

"Marissa, get your butt back over here and sit it down in this chair before you make me spank you."

"If you do, I'm telling Daddy."

Before I knew it, I had snatched Marissa by her arm and practically slammed her into her seat.

But her only response was, "Ha, ha. Didn't hurt."

I knew she was sick but I was starting to think there was no hope for her. Not counseling, not medication, not anything.

"If you don't put on that uniform, I'm taking your television, DVD player, and CD player out of this room."

"*Noooooo!*" she said, jumping out of the chair like a maniac. "I hate you, Mommy. I hate you and I wish you were dead."

"Marissa, for the last time, I'm warning you. Get back over here."

"No! And I'm not wearing that stupid outfit either."

"One . . ." I began counting as if it would make any difference. "Two . . . three . . . four . . ."

"I hate you," she said, now throwing her stuffed animals against the wall and screaming at the top of her lungs. "I hate you and I wish Daddy had married Tracy instead of you."

Oh, how I wanted to slap her as hard as my strength would allow, and it was taking every ounce of control I had in me not to do it. I wanted to hurt her the way heavyweight champions wanted to hurt their opponents. I wanted to knock her out in the first round and then explain my actions later.

"You know what, that's it," I said, dropping the comb on her desk. "Because nothing would make me happier than to hear all your schoolmates laughing at your messy hairdo."

"I hate you," she screamed again, and then threw herself onto her bed face forward.

When the phone rang, however, she leaped across the room to answer it.

"Hi, Daddy," she said. "When are you coming home? No, I'm getting ready for school and Mommy is combing my hair. It's real pretty because Mommy combs hair better than any other mother in the whole wide world. Daddy, did you buy me something? *Yeahhhhh*, thank you, Daddy. Matthew is in his room getting dressed. I love you, too, Daddy. Matthew," she yelled to her brother. "Daddy wants to speak to you. Oh, and Daddy, Uncle Larry was over here Friday night for a really long time," she said, glaring at me. "Mommy invited him over and we had so much fun with him. And then on Saturday, before we went to Grandma and Grandpa's, he came by here again and Mommy gave him this white envelope. But she went to the bank before that and Matthew and I stayed at home until she got back."

"Hang up, Marissa," I heard Matthew telling her all the way from his bedroom.

"Bye, Daddy. I'll see you after school."

When she hung up the phone, she sashayed over to the chair and sat down the way I'd been begging her to. At the moment, she acted as though we were best friends.

"Mommy, can you finish my hair, please?"

My first thought was to send her to school looking the way she was, but I went ahead and finished her other ponytail.

"Mommy, why did you make Tracy leave?" she started up again.

"That's really not your concern, and all you need to know is that we'll be hiring someone else very soon."

"But I don't want someone else. I want Tracy."

"Well, that's just too bad, Marissa, because she's not coming back."

"I still hate you and that's why I told Daddy Uncle Larry was over here."

"I don't care what you told!" I exclaimed, because my whole plot had revolved around the fact that I wanted her to blab to her father anyway. But what I hadn't counted on was the fact that she must have been standing at the top of the stairway when Larry had showed up to get the money. I'd thought she was in her bedroom, minding her own business, but I should have known better. It was true that originally I'd wanted Curtis to find out about the money because I'd been hoping to upset him in a major way, but now that Larry had taken other valuables and was expecting even more money today, I'd decided that the most Curtis should know about was the visit.

But this little heifer right here had ruined everything and now I had to find some way to do damage control. I wasn't sure how I would manage it but I would have to come up with something good and fast.

"Mom," Matthew said, walking into the room. "Dad wants to speak to you."

"Tell him I have to finish Marissa's hair and then get you guys off to school, but I'll call him after that."

I was already panicking, and the more I dwelled on the money and the jewelry, I just didn't know how I was going to get out of this.

"Dad, Mom says she'll have to call you back once we leave for school," he said, and then told Curtis good-bye and pressed the off button. "He says he'll just see you when he gets here."

"Have you got everything packed in your book bag?" I asked.

"Yes."

"Good. If you want, you can watch television until I finish up here and then I'll fix a quick breakfast."

"Yes, ma'am."

Matthew left the room and my mind wandered back to Larry.

But not for long.

"I'm not wearing that ugly uniform," Marissa announced for the umpteenth time, even though she knew the outfit was mandatory.

But to her surprise, I was sure, I didn't even bother arguing with her. Instead, I was going to unplug her DVD player and CD player and physically carry both of them right out of here. I'd certainly done it before and I had no problem doing it again.

I was also calling her psychiatrist to see if we could secure an earlier appointment. We'd scheduled the second one for this coming Friday, but after her ridiculous episode this morning, I wanted to get her in tomorrow or Wednesday. She was completely out of control and it just seemed to me that she needed something more than a one-hour session. Something had to be done, and the sooner it happened, the better off we'd all be in the long run.

After dropping the children at their schools, I added a load of clothing to the washer, another to the dryer, swept the kitchen floor, and called an employment agency. We had to find another housekeeper, and quick, because all of Tracy's former duties were really starting to irritate me. Yes, there had been a time when I'd done all of the above. But not anymore. Not when Curtis earned more than enough to pay someone else to do it.

I'd told them exactly what I was looking for, and before I'd hung up, one of the representatives had told me they'd be pulling a list of candidates together and then faxing them over to me. I, of course, couldn't wait, and I was hoping to start interviewing before the end of the week.

Before I'd finished folding the first set of clothing, the phone rang and I rushed back to the kitchen because I'd also called Marissa's doctor and was hoping that's who was calling me back.

"Hello?"

"How are you?"

It was Larry and now I was sorry I'd even answered.

"What is it I can do for you?"

"I want my other seventeen hundred dollars."

"It's not going to happen."

"Oh, I think it will. Either that, or I'll be paying Curtis a visit when he gets home. And you know he won't like hearing that you gave me his favorite cross as a gift and that you did it just to hurt him."

"Larry, you know that's not true. You took that cross the same as you took everything else, because there is no way I would have voluntarily given it to you."

"I'm sorry, sweetheart, but that's not how I remember it. As a matter of fact, I can't wait to tell ole Curtis how once you dropped off the children in Chicago, you invited me back over on Saturday so we could get our freak on. And it won't be hard for him to believe my version of the story once I describe every detail of his bedroom and tell him how you couldn't wait to undress me."

I listened to Larry go on and on until finally I dropped down in the chair closest to me. I listened but at the same time I tried to figure my next move and I decided that no matter what Larry said, it would all come down to either Curtis believing some crackhead or he would instead believe me.

"It's your word against mine and I'm not giving you any more money."

"Look, bitch, I need that money," he yelled. "I need it *right* now."

"Why, Larry?" I took a chance on asking. "What do you need it for? Drugs?"

"You seem like a pretty smart girl, so what do you think?"

"Curtis was right about you all along."

"Bet you wish you had listened to him. But since you didn't, I need that money."

"Well, I'm not giving it to you, and if I were you, I would leave town while I'm still able."

"So you really don't think Curtis will believe my story, huh?"

"He won't."

"You're sure about that?"

"Positive."

"Not even once I tell him the exact time he called you on Saturday night? Because if my memory serves me correctly, it was 7:27 P.M. on the head, and all he'll have to do is check his outgoing call history to confirm what I'm saying. Plus I think my story will be even more convincing once I repeat your whole conversation with him, word for word. So for the last time, I need my money."

I closed my eyes and set the phone down on the table for a few seconds. I did this because I knew Larry had his whole scheme mapped out to a T and wouldn't hesitate to do all that he said he would do. But the thing was, I'd already been down this blackmail road a few years back with Aaron and I'd learned the hard way that all the lying, conspiring, and plotting I'd done had only made things worse. I'd learned this because in the end, Curtis had discovered all of my skeletons. Maybe not the paternity test, thank God, but he'd definitely found out about everything else.

"Maybe you think this is some sort of game," he said. "And you need me to show you in person that it isn't."

"Curtis will be here any minute," I said, even though I knew he wouldn't be home for another three or four hours.

"Then I suggest you head out to the bank before then."

"No," I said, staying my course.

"*No?* Okay, fine. But just know that I'll be having a nice long chat with Curtis before the day is out."

"Good-bye, Larry," I said.

But even when I'd hung up, I didn't move. I'd remained at the table and it wasn't until the phone rang again that I wondered how much time had passed by.

I pressed the button on the cordless, but when I heard a dial tone, I realized it was my cell phone. So I reached over and pulled it out of my purse.

"Hello?"

"Hi, baby."

"Aaron, why are you calling me?" I asked, my nerves already racing.

"Because I want to speak to my daughter."

"Aaron, if you call here again—"

"You'll what? Tell Curtis?"

"Why can't you just accept that you and I don't have a child together?"

"You should just be glad I haven't called your home number, and the only reason I haven't is because I'm trying to give you an opportunity to leave Curtis and bring my daughter to Michigan without him knowing. You can even bring Matthew, too, because it's not like Curtis is his real father, anyway."

"You're sick."

"No, I just want what's mine. I want my daughter and I'll do whatever I have to to see her."

"Why can't you just—" I began, but he interrupted me.

"My doctor is coming down the hallway, but I'll be in touch with you again real soon. Bye, baby."

For the life of me, I didn't want to believe this was happening. Not back-to-back, all in one hour. But the fact of the matter was, I clearly wasn't dreaming, and I was glad I'd already decided what I was going to tell Curtis regarding Larry.

For the first time in a long while, I was going to tell him the truth.

At least most of it, anyway.

Chapter 23

CHARLOTTE

Curtis had just called to say he was about twenty minutes from our house, but now I was on the phone with Dr. Mason, describing Marissa's latest episode.

"We can definitely get her in tomorrow for another appointment."

"Is there some sort of medication you can prescribe for her? Because I just don't see how we can go on with her the way she is."

"That's a tough question, because even though she does show signs of social withdrawal, flattened emotions, and irrational behavior, I'm still not sure prescribing antipsychotic medication is the answer. Not to mention my other hesitation stems from the fact that only one in forty thousand children are affected by schizophrenia, and this is what that category of meds are used for."

"Well, Doctor, something is definitely wrong with her. It's almost as if she has two personalities, and you never know which Marissa is going to show up."

"She's very good at concealing her feelings, but the reason I was able to pick up on at least a touch of instability was because no matter what we talked about, her emotions remained the same. She kept the same upbeat tone of voice and smile, even when there was nothing for her to smile about. Her whole disposition seemed more like a cover-up, and I could see how most people would never notice it unless they were paying close attention."

"I can't tell you how much it hurts knowing that your child isn't normal."

"I understand, but I promise I'll do everything I can to help her."

"Thank you."

"Also, I know you answered no on the patient questionnaire regarding any family history of mental illness, but are you sure there isn't anyone you can think of? Either on your side or your husband's?"

"No."

"Because if she does have some form of psychosis, this would at least help explain why she's showing symptoms at such a young age."

"As far as I know, neither her father nor I nor any of our family members has ever had problems like this."

I felt bad because even though I was telling the truth about Curtis's medical history and mine, I couldn't stop thinking about Aaron or his phone call to me this morning. If only I could come clean, Dr. Mason might be in a much better position to help Marissa, but I just couldn't bring myself to do it. I just couldn't fathom the idea of crazy Aaron being the father of my child.

"I just thought I'd double-check."

"Is there a certain time you'd like me to bring her in tomorrow?" I said, changing the subject.

"Normally I would just have you schedule with my secretary

but since I have my calendar right here, let's go with, say, four o'clock?"

"That'll be fine, because that way she won't have to miss any school."

"We'll see you then."

"Thanks so much."

I nestled my body against the sofa in the family room and didn't move a muscle. I was so tired of dealing with one problem after another, tired of lying at a moment's notice, tired of hiding truths that were critical to the people I loved. Lying had slowly but surely become a comfortable and normal way of life for me, but over the last few days, particularly after Larry's visit on Saturday, I'd been thinking how it was finally time to put an end to it. I knew I wouldn't be able to confess all my secrets all at once, but I was hoping to make at least a small start this afternoon. Actually, I would get my chance in a few minutes, because Curtis was now entering the house.

I got up and went over to greet him.

"Hey, baby," he said, kissing me, and I was dumbfounded. I didn't understand why he seemed happy and content, not when Marissa had told him about Larry being over here two days in a row.

I looked at him strangely, but once he'd thanked the limo driver and closed the door, he embraced me again and for some reason I burst into tears.

"This is about that Larry situation, isn't it?" he asked.

"Curtis, I am so sorry. I made a terrible, terrible mistake and I'm sorry I didn't listen to you."

We walked into the family room, Curtis with his arm around me, and we took a seat. Then I shed more tears.

"Baby, we've all made mistakes, and as long as you've now cut all ties with Larry, I'm going to forget about this."

"But there's more."

"Like what?"

At first I paused when I thought about the woman Mr. Perry had seen Curtis with at the airport, but actually, if he would forgive me for what I was about to tell him, then I would be willing to forgive him as well. Although my forgiving him would be totally contingent on Curtis's agreement never to see her again.

"I don't even know where to begin."

Now Curtis was silent, and I knew he was wondering how severe my news was going to be.

"Having Larry over wasn't the only thing that happened."

"Wait a minute. You didn't sleep with him, did you?"

"No. Absolutely not. But I did give him two thousand dollars, and then on Saturday night he came back over here threatening me. He was here when you called and he pulled a knife on me."

"What? Did you call the police?"

"No."

"Why?"

"Because I let him in voluntarily."

"I don't believe this," he said, standing and walking toward the fireplace.

"And, Curtis, that's not all."

"Well, what else could there be?"

"He took some of my jewelry and . . . your cross."

"He what?!"

"I know, baby, but there was no way I could stop him."

"See, that's the very reason I told you he wasn't welcome here."

"I know and I'm sorry."

Curtis groaned with anger.

"Okay, look," he finally said. "Maybe if we convince Larry that we're going to have him arrested, he'll tell us where he pawned everything, because I guarantee you that's exactly what he did so he could get money for drugs."

"If he did, then I think he already spent the money, because he called here today in a rage trying to get more."

I watched Curtis sit back down next to me, but his calm nature wasn't adding up. He was too relaxed and too understanding about all of this, and it was so unlike him.

"Actually, I have something to tell you, too, and as much as I hate to say it, you're not going to like it."

"Okay," I said, relieved that he had decided on his own to tell me about his mistress and that she was now completely out of his life.

"I wanted to tell you this when I came home last Friday, but no matter how hard I tried, I just couldn't do it."

I didn't know what to say so I didn't respond.

"I've been having an affair on you for five years now."

Again, I didn't say anything, but his words were killing me. I'd known he was seeing someone but I'd had no idea he'd been doing it since Marissa was born.

"Her name is Tabitha," he continued. "And for the most part, she's been traveling with me the entire time to almost every city I've gone to."

"Curtis, no," I said, my eyes tearing up again, because what he was telling me was that this Tabitha person had spent more time with him than I had.

"But the thing is, I've been trying to break it off with her. Honest. But she's not having it."

"Why can't you just tell her it's over and leave it at that?"

"Because, baby, she's pregnant, and she's threatening to go public with it."

"Pregnant?" I thought I heard myself say, but I wasn't sure because I was now having an out-of-body experience. I was devastated, to say the least, and now I knew why last week Curtis had had this sudden change of heart. I now knew why he'd treated me so kindly and why he was so adamant about saving our marriage.

"Being with her all these years was completely irresponsible, but I was so hurt over you being with Aaron. I was so hurt that every time I was with Tabitha I felt justified and like you deserved what you were getting. But now I know I was wrong."

I heard my cell phone ring and went into the kitchen to get it. "Hello?"

"Mrs. Black." It was the private investigator.

"I know your husband is probably home, but can you talk?"

"Yes. Go ahead."

"I followed his limo to the woman's residence when they dropped her off, and her name is Tabitha Charles. He was there with her for about an hour, but in the meantime I had my assistant do a title search."

"And?"

"The house is in her name and your husband's. But it's only been that way for the last three years, because before that she owned it with another man with the same last name as hers, possibly her husband. I don't know that for sure, but I'll definitely find out."

Now I knew what it felt like to have your heart ripped straight from your chest.

"I really appreciate you calling, and actually there's no need to find out anything else."

"Are you sure?"

"Yes," I said, because if there was more news, I didn't want to hear it.

"I think your retainer will cover just about everything, then, but I'll send you an invoice either way."

"Thanks so much for everything."

"Call again anytime," he said, and I closed my phone.

"Who was that?" Curtis asked when I returned to the sofa.

"The private investigator I hired to follow you."

"Then you already knew?" he said.

"Yes, but I didn't know she was pregnant, and until a few minutes ago I didn't know you'd gone behind my back and purchased a house with her."

"It wasn't like that."

"Then how exactly was it, Curtis?"

"She and her husband got a divorce, and even though the judge ordered her husband to pay alimony, he told her that within two years she would either have to sell it or pay him his half of the equity. So I helped her by signing a new loan and then she was able to pay what she owed him."

"Gosh, you're actually having a baby with another woman," I said without realizing it. "I can't believe you let this happen to us."

"I know, and baby, I'm sorry. I'm so sorry I don't know what to do, and I promise you this will never happen again," he said, taking one of my hands with both of his. "We've both had affairs and hurt each other in more ways than one, and I don't want to go on like this. I'm finally ready to commit to you forever, and I give you my word that you won't ever have to worry about me being with any more women."

"So what is this Tabitha wanting from you?"

"At first she kept pressing me about leaving you and marrying her, but when I told her I would never do that, she said she wanted money."

"How much?"

"Fifty thousand dollars' cash and then twenty percent of my income for child support."

"How did she come up with that?"

"According to her, that's what the percentage is in Illinois for one child."

"And you know for sure she's pregnant?"

"Well, yeah."

"How many months is she?"

"Three."

"So she's not showing yet?"

"No, but neither did you in your first trimester."

"I want to see proof, and if she is pregnant, you might as well tell her that you want a blood test."

"But if she is, then I already know it's mine."

"How?"

"Because I know she hasn't been with anyone else."

"All of this is making me sick," I said, pulling away from Curtis. I knew my situation with Aaron hadn't been much different, but this baby news was tearing me apart.

"We have to keep her quiet because the last thing we need is another scandal."

"This is pathetic."

"I'm already helping her pay her mortgage and utilities, but I know she's going to expect more as time goes on."

"Well, that's too bad, because she's not getting another dime until we prove that she's really pregnant."

"She'll never go for that."

"Well, it's not like she has a choice."

"Baby, can you ever forgive me?"

"This is a hard one."

"I realize that, but don't you think it's time we leave the past exactly where it is and move on?"

"It's not that easy," I said, but I had to admit that my conscience was getting the best of me. The reason: I still didn't know who Marissa's biological father was and this meant I didn't have the right to judge Curtis or be angry with him. I didn't have the right because I was just as guilty.

But I would never tell him that.

I wished I could and I actually sort of wanted to, but now that he might be having a baby with someone else, I didn't see a reason to ruin my opportunity at securing the upper hand. Curtis was now in beg mode and probably willing to do whatever it took to make me happy, and I wanted to keep things that way.

It was better to keep the focus on the terrible thing he'd done versus my own list of past transgressions.

Better and also a lot easier for me.

Chapter 24

JANINE

"Antonio showed up at your house on Sunday, today is Tuesday, and you didn't bother calling me?" Charlotte said when I called her. I'd known she wasn't going to be happy.

"I didn't want to bother you with this. It's bad enough that I'm having to deal with all this craziness, let alone involving you."

"I am so upset with you," she said. "I mean, you know how I feel about you and that I will do anything I can to help you. Anything, J."

"Well, if it makes you feel any better, I did file for an order of protection and I had Carl come over to sit with me for a few hours after that."

"Carl? Carl who?"

"Carl Wilson."

"From church?"

"That's him."

"How did that come about?"

"I didn't tell you this, but he was the locksmith I called the night Antonio was arrested."

"Okay . . . but what does that have to do with him coming to your rescue?"

"See, that's why I wasn't planning to tell you about him."

"Well, actually, I'm fine with you seeing him. I like Carl and he's certainly a much better man than that drug dealer you just got rid of."

"I was afraid to be home alone and I couldn't think of another man I could call."

"So then I guess you know he and Greta got divorced?"

"Yeah, he told me, but I hadn't heard it before then."

"From what I understand, girlfriend was a real trip."

"It sounds like it, but Carl seems really nice."

"He is. At least, he's always seemed like a decent person to me."

"That's why I gave in and agreed to have dinner with him yesterday. And we're doing it again tonight."

"Good for you."

"You never cease to amaze me."

"Why is that?"

"Because I was sure you were going to rag on me about going out with someone I don't know very well."

"Not at all. Like I said, Carl is a good person and I've never heard anything except great things about him."

"I hope that's true, because even though I hate admitting it, I haven't stopped thinking about him since Sunday."

"Maybe it's love at first sight."

"Yeah, right."

"I'm serious, because you never know."

"I won't go that far, but I will say that we made a strong connection with each other."

"Next thing you know, you'll be heading down the aisle," Charlotte said, chuckling.

"You crack me up. I doubt that, but even if that was a possibility, I can't do anything until Antonio is locked up."

"I can't believe he wants you to lie," she said.

I'd told Charlotte about what he wanted me to do so that his case could be dismissed, and even I was still astonished by his request.

"He's got issues."

"And some very serious ones at that."

"Hey, it's almost eight, so I'd better get going," I said, glancing at the time on my computer. I'd gotten to work an hour early so I could add a few items to my lesson plan, but now I only had about ten minutes to get upstairs to my classroom.

"Well, make sure you call me when you get back in from dinner. You know I want to hear all the details, and then I need to tell you about the drama going on over here."

"Is everything okay?"

"I'll talk to you tonight because it's definitely going to take a lot longer than a few minutes. Curtis and I have to take Marissa to the doctor this afternoon, but I'll be home for the rest of the evening."

"I can't believe you're going to keep me in all this suspense."

"Sorry. Just call me tonight. No matter what time."

"I will. And Charlotte?"

"Uh-huh?"

"Thank you for being my friend. I know I've said this before, but this morning I realized I don't have any other woman I can confide in. I have a few acquaintances, but you're the only person I can tell everything to. Sometimes I hesitate doing so because I don't want you to think lowly of me when I'm making a potentially bad decision, but in the end, I know I can count on you to support me."

"I've always felt the same way about you, and that's why I need to talk to you about what's going on with Curtis and me."

"I should be home by ten."

"Sounds good, and you be careful because I don't trust Antonio for as far as I can throw him."

"I will. Love you."

"I love you, too."

I sniffled and batted away tears. Charlotte really did mean a lot to me, and the more I thought about it, I realized she and my father were the only two people I truly loved and who loved me back unconditionally.

I pulled on my blazer and picked up my pad folio, but then the phone rang.

"Who was that strange-looking person I saw at your house last night?"

"Antonio, I can't talk to you, and the order of protection says that you can't dial any of my numbers. Not home, not work, not my cell."

"What order of protection?"

"The one I filed after you came to my house threatening me."

"I hope you didn't."

"I did. So, please, I'm asking you again, just leave me alone."

"I will as soon as you go talk to one of those detectives."

"I can't."

"Why?"

"Because I can't."

"You're really starting to piss me off, you know that?"

"I have to go," I said, and wondered why I kept holding conversations with him. But I knew why. I was terrified of him, and somehow I knew ignoring him completely was only going to make him angrier.

"First you try to kick me out, then you have me locked up and now you're seeing some zero you obviously were seeing while I was with you."

"I just met him a few days ago."

"No you didn't."

"Antonio, what is it going to take for you to stop harassing me?"

"For you to go down to that narcotics division and tell them what I told you to tell them."

"For the last time, I can't."

"Bitch," he said, and hung up.

And I called the police again. I was now late for my class, but this was one time I honestly didn't care one way or the other. I had a more pressing matter at hand that I had to take care of. I wasn't sure calling the police was going to help me, but maybe if I reported Antonio every single time he violated the order, they would eventually find and arrest him again. I didn't know where he was living but all I could hope was that they'd be able to locate him fairly quickly. I was hoping they would lock him up and that this time no one would bail him out before his trial.

Chapter 25

CHARLOTTE

Let me speak to Curtis," Larry said. His tone was irate, but I smiled because I knew he had no idea he was wasting his time calling.

"Curtis," I yelled, and he picked up the phone. But I didn't hang up because I wanted to hear everything he had to say.

"Larry, Charlotte already told me about the jewelry and I really need that cross of mine back," he said. "I need every single piece you took from here."

"You must be crazy. Your wife owes me seventeen hundred dollars and I'm not giving anything back until I get it."

"You're as low as they come, Larry, you know that?"

"All I want is my money."

"Okay, fine. But this is the deal. You tell me where you pawned our stuff, and then I'll bring you the money."

"Don't patronize me, Curtis. I'm not stupid and I don't like it when you make it seem like I am."

"Then you tell me how this is going to work. Because all I

want is what you stole from us, and then I want you to leave Mitchell for good."

"Leave? Then you must be planning to come off of a lot more than seventeen hundred."

"You're unbelievable," Curtis said, and clicked the phone.

But Larry called again and we both picked up our extensions. Neither of us said anything but we didn't have to.

"Look, Curtis, man. I'm sorry. I lost my head for a minute, but if you want me to go, then I'm going to need a few more dollars for transportation, a place to live, and food. I'm going to need money to survive on."

"How much?"

"Five thousand, and you'll never have to hear from me again. I'll even sign a contract or whatever you want me to."

"I can't believe you've stooped to this level, Larry. I can't believe you've allowed drugs to take over your life and that you don't care about anybody."

"When can I get the money?" he said, sounding desperate.

"Where are you?"

"I'll just meet you at your bank."

"What about our stuff?"

"When I get the money, I'll give you the pawnshop receipt," he said, and I shook my head because Curtis knew him like a book. Although I was sure pawning expensive jewelry would be a given for any drug user.

"Do you know where Bank of America is, the branch on First Street?"

"Not exactly, but I don't think I'm that far from there. Is it downtown?"

"Yeah."

"What time?"

"In about an hour."

"And Curtis, man. I'm really sorry and I promise I'll make this up to you."

"Whatever," Curtis said, and hung up.

When we arrived at the bank, I didn't see the car Larry had purchased but we still went inside the bank. We were actually about twenty minutes late, so I wondered if maybe Larry had already been here and then left, thinking we weren't coming.

There weren't very many people in the teller line so we moved through it in a matter of minutes.

"I'd like to withdraw five thousand dollars, please," Curtis requested, and passed the teller a withdrawal slip along with his driver's license.

"Would you like a cashier's check?"

"No. Cash will be fine."

"For your safety, I'll have to check your signature on file, but it won't take more than a minute."

"Thank you," Curtis said, looking at me, but neither of us said a word.

We waited for the teller to return, and when she did, she counted each bill in front of us and then placed all of them in an envelope.

"Can I help you with anything else?"

"No, I think that's it. And thanks again."

"You're quite welcome," she said, smiling, and we headed toward the entrance.

I couldn't help wondering if Larry would be in the parking lot this time, but when I saw his vehicle, my curiosity was satisfied, and I pointed him out to Curtis.

"There he is over there," I said.

"Let's get this over with," he told me, and we walked toward him.

Larry rolled down his window and reached his hand out.

"Not so fast."

"I need to go," he said, scoping his surroundings back and forth like a nervous junkie.

"Where's the receipt from that pawnshop?"

"I have it right here."

"Then give it to me."

"Curtis, man, I hope you're not up to no good."

"What are you talking about?" Curtis said, frowning.

"For all I know, you might be trying to pull a fast one on me. You might be thinking you can snatch this receipt without giving me my money, but if I were you, I wouldn't do that."

"Charlotte, let's go," Curtis said, and we turned away from him.

"Okay, okay," Larry hurried to say, and pulled out the receipt. "Here it is."

"You're pitiful," Curtis said, tossing the envelope at him.

"Charlotte," Larry said, "I'm sorry for any harm I caused you and I hope that some day you'll be able to find it in your heart to forgive me."

I just looked at him and then we started toward our car.

As soon as we did, though, three squad cars flew into the parking lot, their sirens screaming, and surrounded Larry's buy-here-pay-here Mitsubishi.

Still, we kept walking, but when I turned to look back at him being dragged from his car, I saw him staring at me. The worst part was that even though I knew I shouldn't have, I sort of felt sorry for him because he looked so shocked and helpless. And shocked he should have been, because I knew he'd had no clue that Curtis had been setting him up the entire time.

Last night, while we were getting ready for bed, Curtis had decided that he was going to stop Larry once and for all when it came to trying to steal from us. He'd decided that he would trick Larry into thinking all we wanted was the jewelry and in return we'd give him the five thousand dollars. And as Curtis had suspected, Larry had fallen for it without any questions, and this proved that he really was strung out and was willing to take any chance he had to in order to buy his next hit.

"I need to give the arresting officer this receipt for evidence so they can go bring in the pawnshop owner to identify Larry. Then we'll have to go downtown so you can give a statement about the knife he pulled on you."

"I'll just wait here," I said.

When Curtis returned, we drove away, and I wondered what was going to happen to Larry. I sat wondering but it was obvious that Curtis couldn't have cared less.

After finishing up at the police department and picking up Marissa from school, we went straight to Dr. Mason's office. Curtis and I were standing watching Marissa's session through a window the same as I'd done last week.

"Why does she keep smiling like that?" Curtis asked.

"She did the same thing at her last visit. She fakes all the time."

"But she always seems like such a good child and like she's always happy."

"That's because she pretends like she's your perfect little angel, but then when you leave, she turns into a monster."

"And the doctor doesn't know what's wrong with her?"

"Not yet."

"I hear you have a big brother," Dr. Mason said, and we both fell silent.

"Uh-huh."

"And I'll bet you love him a lot, don't you?"

"Uh-huh. But sometimes I don't. I mean yes . . . I mean no, I like him, but Miranda doesn't, and sometimes she makes me say things I don't want to say to him."

"Really? And who's Miranda?" Dr. Mason said, and Curtis sat down in the seat behind him. I knew he was stunned. As was I, because even though I'd seen Marissa in action many times, this was my first time hearing her mention someone by the name of Miranda.

"Miranda is the voice I hear sometimes, and she doesn't like Mommy either."

"Really? And why is that?"

"I don't know. I keep telling her that Mommy is a good person, but Miranda says she's not."

"But you love Mommy, right?"

"Uh-huh."

"What about your father?"

"I love my daddy and Miranda loves him, too."

"Does she love anyone else?"

"She loved Tracy but she says it's all Mommy's fault that Tracy went away."

"Who's Tracy?"

"She used to take care of our house."

"And who else does Miranda tell you she likes?"

"Grandma and Grandpa."

"And do you like your grandparents, too?"

"Uh-huh."

"What else does Miranda tell you?"

"A lot of things."

"Do you think it would be okay if you tell me some of them?"

"No," Marissa said, and that smile she'd been wearing finally left her face. "I can't talk to you anymore and I want my daddy."

"Did Miranda tell you not to talk to me?"

"I want my daddy," she said, louder. "Daddy," she screamed, and Curtis and I rushed out of the room we were sitting in.

Dr. Mason opened her door right away and Marissa ran out and jumped into Curtis's arms.

"Daddy, I don't wanna come here anymore. Dr. Mason is a bad lady," she said, looking back at her.

"It's okay, sweetheart. Dr. Mason is only trying to help you."

"No she's not. She wants to hurt us. She wants to hurt you and Mommy, too, so let's go, Daddy."

"Marissa, honey," I said, "it's okay."

"I wanna go home," she repeated. "Please, Daddy."

"First Mommy and I have to speak to Dr. Mason."

"We have a playroom right here, Marissa," Dr. Mason said.

"No."

"Marissa," Curtis said, "you're upsetting Daddy and we can't leave until you let us talk to Dr. Mason for a few minutes."

"I'm sorry, Daddy. I'll go play until you finish."

Her mood had changed again, and I was glad Dr. Mason was able to witness it.

"I regret that I'm now beginning to lean more toward the idea that Marissa might have schizophrenia," Dr. Mason told us once we were inside her office. "At first when she mentioned someone named Miranda, I thought she might have multiple personalities, but when she said that Miranda was a voice, I knew Marissa had given the voice she was referring to a name."

"Do you think this voice is causing her obsession with fire?" I asked.

"It's very likely, because maybe the voice is telling her to play with the stove or play with matches."

"So where do we go from here?" Curtis asked, and I could tell he was heartbroken. I was sad as well but not as surprised.

"Well, to start, I'd like to begin seeing her for at least an hour every single day, and chances are I'll have to begin medicating her."

"And there's no other way?" Curtis asked.

"It's my medical opinion that she needs more thorough evaluation and some sort of med to help control the voice she's hearing."

"Will you be able to schedule all of her appointments after school?" I asked.

"Well, for right now, I think it'll be best if she didn't attend. At least not until we have a better diagnosis."

"I'm sure they'll need a written excuse," I said.

"They will, and I'll have my assistant type one up today and fax it over."

"Should we tell Marissa why she's not going to be in school for a while?" Curtis asked.

"You can tell her that you want to spend more time with her and that you want her to come see me every day. Also, Reverend Black, since it seems that she enjoys trying to please you, it might be better for you to be the one to convince her that seeing me is a good thing and that you'll come with her on every visit."

"That's fine."

"Mrs. Black mentioned that you travel a lot, but if at all possible, it would be much better for Marissa if you were in town for as long as you're able to be."

"I'm scheduled to leave again on Thursday, but of course Marissa's well-being is my priority and I'll do whatever I have to."

"Good. That will mean a lot more than you know."

"Are there any harsh side effects with the medications you're considering?" I asked.

"Yes, so we'll have to monitor her very closely. Some meds can make a patient's symptoms much worse and even cause a person to become suicidal. So we may have to try several before we find the right one."

"She's only five years old . . ." Curtis said, his voice trailing off.

"I know," Dr. Mason tried consoling him. "It's tough. But as I've already assured Mrs. Black, I'm going to do the best I can to help her."

"Why do you think this is happening to her?" Curtis asked, and I prayed Dr. Mason wouldn't bring up anything about heredity.

"We just don't know for sure. Some studies show that genetics may be part of the cause, and some even show that a viral condition may be the culprit."

"Well, as far as I know, my family has no history of anything like that."

"Then chances are Marissa is simply one of those rare cases."

"We should probably go see about Marissa," I interjected.

"That would be good, and my assistant will be in touch first thing tomorrow with the next few session times," Dr. Mason promised.

"Thanks again," I said.

"Yes," Curtis added. "Thank you for everything."

We found Marissa sitting patiently and reading a book and she looked so peaceful. She looked as normal as any other child. However, unfortunately, she was anything but.

Unfortunately, she was as different as any person could be.

Chapter 26

JANINE

How are you, Dad?" I said when my father answered the phone. I'd been thinking about him a lot today and decided I would call him before leaving work.

"I think I'm coming down with a cold, but other than that, I'm pretty good."

"How's the weather there?"

"Pretty chilly as of late, but that's to be expected in October. They say we're going to have a rough winter and I believe it."

"I heard the same thing for our area and I'm not looking forward to it."

My father laughed. "I can believe that, because you never liked cold weather. Not even when you were a child."

"But strangely enough, I've lived in the Midwest all my life."

"That's because we all get used to what we get used to, and for the most part, there's no changing that."

"So have you eaten yet today?"

"I had some coffee for breakfast and then a little something for lunch, but Joe Bell called and said he was gonna bring by some barbecued ribs in about an hour."

"Joe Bell, the man that used to come to our house all those years ago?"

"That's him. I hadn't heard from him since maybe back in the eighties, but now he's living here with his daughter and son-in-law."

"Well, Dad, that's really nice."

"It is, and I was really glad to hear from ole Joe. We used to have some wild times back in the day."

"I can imagine," I said, because I still remembered how my father and Mr. Bell had been inseparable drinking buddies. I also remembered how Mr. Bell's wife had divorced him, too, shortly after my mother had left my father but I was still glad my father had been able to reconnect with Joe after all this time.

"So how are you, daughter?"

"I'm okay, but I guess it's time I told you that Antonio and I broke up."

"Oh, sweetheart, I'm so sorry to hear that."

"Don't be, because Antonio is not the person you thought he was or the person I portrayed him to be."

"He didn't hit you or anything, did he?"

"No," I said, even though he had grabbed me rather violently that day he'd come to the university, but I didn't bother burdening my father with that information.

"I hope not, because I wouldn't wanna have to come all the way to Illinois to handle that boy. I know I'm too weak to do anything, but I know a few strong young men around here who would be glad to rough him up."

"Really, Dad, I'm fine."

"Where is he now?"

"I didn't want to tell you this, but he was dealing drugs from my house and I had him arrested."

"Well, good for you, and I hope the judge throws the book at him."

"It looks like he'll definitely get some time, although I'll feel a whole lot better once he's sent away."

"He's not bothering you, is he?"

"He's called a few times," I said, but decided it wasn't worth telling my father about his recent visit to my doorstep or the way he was continually threatening me.

"I hate to see you going through this, and not being able to help you makes me feel like a failure."

"This is not your fault, so please don't feel that way."

"Well, maybe it is, because it wasn't like you ever had a good male role model while you were growing up, and maybe that's why you ended up with someone like this Antonio."

"That's just not true."

"I watch a lot of TV talk shows and there have been many times when women have been on talking about all the wrong men they keep choosing, and almost every time you find out that their father was a bad example. You find out that by choosing a no-good man, these women followed in their mothers' footsteps. It happens all the time. My own mother, God rest her soul, used to say your childhood can make you or break you, and she was right. She was more right than I ever imagined."

I knew he had a point but I'd never wanted to accept that. I'd never wanted to believe that I wasn't smart enough to find the right companion, but now I wondered otherwise.

"I'm going to be fine, Dad, so there's no reason for you to blame yourself or worry about anything."

"Do you want me to come there?"

"You know I've wanted that for a long time."

"I know, but until now I didn't want to be a burden to you. Now, though, I'm worried about you being there all alone."

"Well, actually, I'm not all alone because I do have my best friend, Charlotte, and her husband and the people at church."

"But no one's in the house with you, right?"

"No, but I have a security system and it's always set, even if I'm home during the daytime."

"I still don't like it."

"Well, if it makes you feel any better, I'll be there on Saturday. That's the real reason I called. My plane will get in around ten in the morning, and once I get my luggage and pick up a rental car, I should be at your place before twelve."

"I can't wait to see you. And this time I just might fly back with you."

"I really hope you do."

"Uh-oh, that must be ole Joe on the doorbell, so I'd better go. But you call me if you need me. You hear?"

"I will, and tell Mr. Bell I said hello."

"You take care, sweetheart."

"Bye, Dad."

I smiled when I thought about seeing my father four days from now and then I packed up my belongings and left my office. On the way out, my phone rang.

It was Carl, so now I had an even bigger smile on my face than a few seconds ago.

"So how are you?" I said.

"Well, I could be better."

"Why is that? What's wrong?"

"Nothing except I can't seem to get any work done."

"Did something happen?"

"You happened. I can't stop thinking about you and it's so embarrassing."

I laughed. "Well, if it's any consolation, I've been thinking about you all day, too."

"I feel like some twelve-year-old boy who has such a huge crush on some little girl in class that he can't concentrate on anything else."

"I know the feeling, but I have to admit it's a little scary."

"Why? Because we haven't known each other for very long?"

"Yes, and also because I don't ever again want to feel the kind of pain I've had to endure with Antonio."

"That's understandable, and you'll see soon enough that I'm definitely not in the business of hurting people. By the way, you haven't heard from him again, have you?"

"As a matter of fact, I did this morning." I sighed and told Carl what Antonio had said to me.

"I'm really worried about your safety, and as much as you might not want to hear this, we need to get you a gun."

"I'm so against those, but I will admit that it may be the only way I can protect myself."

"Where are you now?"

"In my car and headed out of the parking lot."

"Are you going straight home?"

"I have to stop at the beauty supply to get a couple of things but I should be home in about an hour."

"Why don't I just meet you then and we can go get this taken care of."

"I can't believe you're standing by me through all of this madness."

"Most things that come easy aren't really worth having and that includes relationships. Plus you can't help what's happening to you."

"Maybe not now, but I could have prevented all of this by

never allowing Antonio to move in with me. I never should have even dated him but I just couldn't see that back then."

"Well, what's done is done and we're not going to dwell on any of that."

"You're a sweetheart, Carl."

"I try," he said, and I smiled.

"So I'll see you shortly?"

"I'll be there. And since we're going to take care of this other situation, maybe instead of going to a restaurant the way we'd planned, we can just order something to carry out."

"That works for me."

"Bye, love."

I laid down my phone and asked myself again why I couldn't have met someone like Carl before now. Specifically before I'd made acquaintance with Antonio, but I knew there was no explanation for this.

After leaving the store, I stopped at the gas station and drove straight home. When I eased slowly into the beginning of the driveway, I rolled down my window and removed today's mail. Then I pressed the garage door remote and waited for it to open. When it rolled up, I drove all the way inside. Next I grabbed my purse, briefcase, and the other bags on the front seat and stepped out of the car.

But when I did, I heard footsteps and jerked my body around.

"You think you're so slick, don't you?" Antonio said, walking inside the garage and moving toward me. I dropped everything I was holding.

"Antonio, please don't," I said, backing farther into my car door.

"Please don't what? Please don't hurt you the way you've hurt me?"

"I'm sorry," I said for whatever it was he felt I should be apologizing for.

"You completely misused me from the very beginning, and now you're just outright trying to destroy me. You've destroyed everything I was working so hard to build up and now I'm going to prison."

"I'll do whatever you want."

"Liar."

"I will," I promised, pleading for my life.

"You think I'm stupid. I went by the nursing home to see my mother and my father told me that the police had been by their house looking for me because there's another warrant for my arrest. And that's all because of your silly ass."

"What do you want me to do?" I asked. "Just tell me and I'll do it."

Antonio sniggered like a madman so I shut up.

"But you know what's even worse? You had the nerve to try and replace me. It hasn't even been two whole weeks and you've already brought some fool in here that I know you were sleeping with behind my back."

"He's just a friend and he's not living here."

"I saw him Sunday and again yesterday. Yeah, that's right, I've been watching your every move."

"He doesn't mean anything to me," I lied, trying to reason with him.

"Shut up!" he said, slapping me across my left eye so hard I lost my vision for a few seconds.

"I'm so sorry," I said, crying.

"No, I think you're proud of the way you treated me, and that's why I decided this afternoon that you were going to pay," he said, pulling a knife from his coat pocket and flicking it open.

With lightning speed, he forced it into my abdomen. Then he yanked it out, drew it back, preparing to strike me again. As weak as I was, I tried blocking his attempts with my arms and hands, which now had slashes all across them.

However, the fight in me ended when he gouged my stomach a second time. And without warning I fell to the ground, face forward, and Antonio kicked me with all his might. He kicked me again and again, I guess until he was tired, or maybe Carl had stopped him, because suddenly I heard Carl yelling at him and then I heard what sounded like a major tussle between them. I lay there listening but my body must have gone into shock because I felt no pain.

Soon after, I heard a loud thud and then some metal object hitting the ground. I wasn't sure what had happened, but now Carl was calling my name.

"Janine, baby, just hold on," he said, turning me over. "Just hold on while I call for help."

His voice was fading in and out, and even though my vision was blurred, it looked as though tears were rolling down his face.

"Baby, they're on the way and you're going to be fine."

I tried acknowledging what he'd said, but the last thing I heard were the faint sounds of sirens and then a cluster of voices surrounding me and speaking very quickly.

Chapter 27

CHARLOTTE

Oh my God, Carl, what happened?" I said, rushing into the emergency room.

"That idiot Antonio attacked her with a knife."

"No. Please don't tell me that," I said, and Curtis sat me down in one of the chairs.

"He stabbed her multiple times and she lost a lot of blood."

"This is just senseless," Curtis finally said. "Just plain senseless."

"Oh God, please, not J," I said, my face now flooded with tears. "Please . . . please . . . please."

"Baby, hey. Let's just be prayerful and wait until we hear something," Curtis said with his arm around me.

"She was conscious when we got here, so maybe that's a good sign," Carl explained.

"How long have they been in there with her?" I asked.

"Almost two hours."

"And wait a minute," I said abruptly. "Antonio didn't get away, did he?"

"No. I pulled up just as he was stomping her with one foot after the other, but in the end, we scuffled and I knocked the knife out of his hand. Then I hit him with a steel bar I found in Janine's garage. He was out until the police arrived and then they arrested him."

"Thank God," Curtis said. "And maybe this time the judge will realize bail isn't an option."

"I just don't believe this," I said, trying to digest everything Carl was saying. "I can't believe J and I were just on the phone this morning and now she's in there fighting for her life."

"It doesn't seem real, I know, but when he kept harassing her, I started wondering how long it was going to be before he did something bad to her. I had a terrible feeling about it and that's why I'd just told her a few hours ago that we needed to get her a gun. That's why I was meeting her at her house in the first place, but instead . . ." Carl tried explaining but was too emotional.

"But the fact that you were there is what counts," I said, rubbing his back and trying to console him.

"That's right," Curtis agreed. "God allowed you to get there just in the nick of time."

"Life is so unfair," Carl said. "I mean, here I've been thinking that maybe I'd finally met my next wife, and now this."

"You know, until this morning, I had no idea you and Janine were seeing each other, but as soon as she told me, I felt really happy about it. I knew you were a good person and that's exactly what I told her."

"Well, thank you."

"What we have to do is keep our faith strong, and as a matter of fact, let's step outside for a word of prayer," Curtis suggested.

We left the emergency room and Curtis prayed for Janine's

survival and her soul. He asked God to save her and to give all of us the strength and understanding we needed. Then we went back inside.

"What's taking them so long?" I said as soon as we took our seats.

"I don't know, but all this waiting is driving me nuts," Carl admitted.

"If only someone would just come give us an update."

"I'm sure they will pretty soon now," Curtis said, glancing at his watch. "I guess maybe I should check on Matthew and Marissa to make sure the pizza arrived."

"That's probably a good idea," I said, but I knew Curtis's real reason for wanting to call home was to make sure Marissa wasn't taunting at her brother or, worse, trying to set something on fire. Normally this would have been my worry, too, but right now I was completely focused on Janine. I was trying to imagine what I would do without her and at the same time figure out why this had happened. I knew it wasn't right to question God, specifically in terms of why He'd allowed such a catastrophe, but I needed answers.

When Curtis stepped away, Carl and I sat silent for a minute but then he spoke.

"What in the world was Janine thinking?"

"You mean when she met Antonio?"

"Yes. She and I briefly discussed it, but I just don't get it."

"I never wanted her to be with him but she believed it could work. I know she shouldn't have, but I realize now that sometimes we can't help the mistakes we make."

"I guess, but she deserves only the best. A man who will treat her better than he treats himself."

"Well, after this, I don't think we'll have to worry about Antonio ever again, or at least not for a long while."

"Let's hope not, because I can't be responsible for what I might do to him."

"You really do care about her, don't you?" I said.

"I do. I don't want to say it was love at first sight because it sounds far too ridiculous for any grown man to even consider something like that, but I do think I'm in love with her."

"Being in love isn't ridiculous at all, and I think you should tell J just how you feel. You should tell her the first chance you get."

"Maybe, but I guess I'm just a little concerned that she might not feel the same way."

"And that's the very reason so many men end up losing perfectly good women, too. All because they have so much pride that they won't risk showing their true feelings."

"You're right. So we'll see."

When Curtis returned and sat back down, I asked him how the children were doing.

"They're fine. They already ate and they're watching some movie."

"Does Matthew have any homework?"

"Not a lot, but I told him to start on it right now."

"Both of you must be proud," Carl said.

"We are," Curtis told him.

"There's nothing like having your own family, but Greta just didn't want that. At least not with me."

"I'm sorry to hear things didn't work out," Curtis said.

"I'm sorry, too," I added.

"Actually, we never had a chance, because as soon as I met her, I immediately started thinking I could change her."

"That happens a lot," Curtis agreed. "Over the years, I've done premarital counseling for hundreds of couples, and you hear this more often than not."

"Greta loved to party all times of night and do a few things I won't even mention, but still none of it fazed me because I knew I could mold her into the woman she should be."

I didn't say anything, but at this very moment I realized that this philosophy probably applied to Janine as well. None of us had understood her connection to Antonio, but maybe she'd thought he would change for the better over time. Maybe she really had thought he would get a job and become the responsible man most women dreamed about.

The three of us were chatting when a doctor in full scrubs walked through the doorway. I panicked. I knew he was on his way to give us news about Janine.

"Are you the family of Janine Turner?" he asked.

"Yes, we're her closest friends in the area."

"I'm Dr. Weisman, and if you'll come into the conference room here, I'll give you an update on her condition."

We followed him inside and took seats around the table.

"We've had to make a lot of intestinal repairs, both the upper and the lower, and remove a small portion of her stomach. Then, because of all the blood loss, we had to start a transfusion. Her heart is also not beating the way it should be, so we need to monitor that as well. And then, finally, I regret that we're going to have to remove her left kidney. There's no laceration in that area but there are a number of severe bruises."

"The guy that did this to her had on pointed-toe cowboy boots and he was kicking her everywhere," Carl said.

"Then that explains it, because her kidney is now damaged beyond preservation. But the good news is that people have kidneys removed every day and they live full and normal lives."

"So is she going to be okay otherwise?" I asked.

"Her status is critical, but if we can get her through the next twenty-four to forty-eight hours, I think she'll be fine. She'll have a long recovery and a few problems along the way, but her chances are very strong."

"Can we see her?"

"Maybe in about an hour, but only for a few minutes because we need her to rest as much as possible. She mentioned the name Char and Carl, but I'm thinking she was a little confused and meant the same person."

"No, she's right," I said, smiling. "I'm Charlotte and this is Carl. Oh and this is my husband, Curtis. And the only immediate family member she has is her father, but he's sickly and lives in Ohio."

"Well, I'm glad you're here for her. And you say some guy did this?" he asked Carl.

"Yes. An old boyfriend, but it's a long story."

"Senseless," Dr. Weisman declared.

"My words exactly," Curtis told him.

"Well, unless you have other questions, that's pretty much all I have."

"Thanks so much, Doctor," I said.

"Yes, we really appreciate it," Carl said, shaking his hand, then Curtis did the same.

"We'll get you in to see her as soon as we get her situated."

"Oh, and how soon will you need to remove her kidney?"

"Once we're sure her heart is able to withstand it, so hopefully in a couple of days or so."

"Thanks again," I said, and Dr. Weisman left the room.

"I know it's not right, but I wish I'd taken Antonio completely out," Carl said, standing and pacing back and forth.

"Man, you're going to have to let that go because the angrier you get, the more this whole thing is going to tear you apart," Curtis responded. "And I'm here to tell you that it's not worth it. That fool is locked up where he should be, so what you have to do is let the police and the prosecutor handle their business. I mean, don't get me wrong, I know exactly how you feel, but trust me when I say you'll feel better trying to forget it."

"I just hate that he did this to her. She's all messed up because of him and now she's going to lose a kidney. All because she wanted him to leave her alone and he wasn't hearing it," Carl continued.

I sighed deeply and tears filled my eyes again. I was so tired of crying, tired of waiting to see what horrific thing was going to happen next, and tired of trying to understand why bad things happened to good people like Janine. I also wondered why my life seemed to be filled with so much grief, but I couldn't deny that in my case it was because bad things also happened to *bad* people. After all these years with Curtis, I was still keeping a major truth from him, he was still sleeping with other women, and I wondered when we would finally stop trying to hurt each other. Especially now, with what had happened to Janine, because her predicament screamed loud and clear just how precious life really was.

We went back to the waiting area and waited for not one but two hours, and then one of the nurses escorted us through the ICU doors and into Janine's room. As soon as I saw her, my knees weakened and Curtis grabbed hold of me. It was bad enough that multiple tubes flowed from her body and various monitors surrounded her bed, but when I moved closer and saw how badly she was cut, I turned away from her. Yes, they were only minor, but what hurt me so much was that I knew she'd tried to defend herself.

"J," I said, leaning toward her, "sweetie, it's me, Charlotte." She didn't speak but she did move her head slightly.

"J, can you hear me?" I asked, and she nodded affirmatively. "Carl and Curtis are here, too."

She tried whispering something but she couldn't.

"Janine, baby, we're all here for you," Carl said from the other side of the bed, and she nodded again. This time it even seemed like she was trying to smile.

"God's going to take care of you, so you just keep your faith in Him and you'll be out of here in no time," Curtis said.

"J, I love you and we're going to let you rest now," I said, kissing her forehead. "But I'm not leaving the hospital. I'll be here all night, so don't you worry about anything."

"Let's have another word of prayer," Curtis said and we locked hands.

It wasn't usual for the ICU to allow three visitors at one time, but I was glad they'd made an exception because Janine needed to know that we were all here for her together.

When he finished, Curtis patted Janine's hand and we turned to head out. But then Carl went back over to her.

"Janine, baby, I know this isn't the best time for you, but I can't leave here without telling you how I feel. You see, the reason you have to get better is because I'm in love with you. I didn't plan for this to happen, but that's just the way it is," he said, sniffling, and while Janine's eyes were still closed, tears streamed slowly down both sides of her face and I honestly wished I'd had a camcorder. I wished I'd been able to record such a priceless, genuine confession of love because most people would never witness or experience anything so beautiful. Few women would ever have a man look at them the way Carl was looking at Janine right now, and it was sad.

Curtis and I left the room so that the two of them could share a few moments alone, but I could still hear Carl's words. I heard them over and over and I knew I would never forget them. Better, I hoped Janine would never forget them either, and that chances were, she'd finally found what she'd been looking for.

Chapter 28

CHARLOTTE

I'd slept in a chair in the waiting room, waking almost every half hour, and my back was killing me. But still, if I'd had it to do over again, I wouldn't think twice about it. Curtis had left right after we'd gone in to see Janine, Carl had left around midnight, and now it was 6:45 A.M. and I was making my way past the ICU nurses' station.

When I walked in, I saw one of her nurses changing her IV bag and another drawing blood.

But to my surprise, Janine's eyes were open.

"Have you been here all night?" she asked in a weak, groggy tone.

"Now, where else would I be?" I said, and she smiled.

"Don't you have to get the kids off to school?"

"Curtis is home, so they'll be fine."

She didn't respond until the nurses left the room.

"Did they arrest him again?" she asked.

"Yes. And this time I don't think he'll get out."

Tears rolled down Janine's face as they had last night when

Carl had told her he loved her. I grabbed her hand and caressed the side of her face. I was trying my best to stay strong, but seeing her emotional state was making it extremely hard for me.

"I'm so sorry that this happened to you."

"I always knew he was going to hurt me. I knew it but I didn't see where I could do anything about it."

"Well, he's the least of your worries right now, and what we have to do is concentrate on getting you well."

"Where's Carl?"

"He was here for a long time, and I hope you remember the wonderful things he said to you."

"I remember him saying that he loved me."

"And I really think he does, J. Normally my skepticism kicks in big-time whenever any man claims he's in love this quickly, but Carl is different. He's a good man and I honestly believe he means what he says."

"I believe him, too, but I don't know what good I'm going to be to him or anyone else after this."

"Why do you say that?"

"Just before you came in here, Dr. Weisman told me that one of my kidneys has to be removed and he told me I may have stomach problems for a long time."

"But after all that has been taken care of, you'll be completely back to normal," I said, hating I'd missed her doctor. I'd been wanting to speak to him but I guess he'd decided to make rounds earlier than I'd expected.

"We'll see," she said.

"J," I said, gently turning her head back toward me. "Sometimes life throws some crazy curves, but it's not the end of the world. So what we have to do is stay positive. I know this is a very tough time for you but I'm going to be by your side every step of the way. Curtis and I already decided last night that when you leave here, you're coming to stay with us for as long as you need to."

She looked at me and seconds later her eyes watered again.

"I love you and I promise we'll get through this," I continued.

"I love you, too, but I feel so bad about having to inconvenience you in this way."

"It's no trouble at all, and I'm glad to do whatever I can."

"I'm going to need to call my father to let him know I won't be coming this weekend."

"Do you want me to call him now? I thought about that last night."

"No. This will kill him, so I have to come up with some other reason for postponing."

"When is Dr. Weisman planning to do your surgery?"

"First thing tomorrow morning, so I'll call Dad tomorrow night or on Friday."

I didn't agree that she should wait to tell him, but I didn't want to debate her decision because the last thing she needed was to be upset.

"Is there anything else I can do?" I asked.

"I need you to call the university, although I'm sure by now the whole incident is plastered all over the newspaper. How embarrassing."

Janine was right, but I didn't acknowledge her comment. It hadn't been on the front page the way she was thinking, but there had been noticeable mention of it in the local section.

"And my purse. I think I dropped it in the garage, so can you stop by my house to get it?"

"I'll do it once I go home and get cleaned up. Curtis is picking me up after he gets Matthew off to—" I said, and Janine coughed deeply. "Are you okay?" I asked, but she continued coughing. She held her stomach and I knew she was in severe pain.

I called in one of her nurses and after a while Janine settled down. Maybe I had held too long a conversation with her, but I was just so happy to see her alive and happy to hear that Dr. Weisman had scheduled the kidney surgery because this meant her heart had stabilized the way he'd wanted.

Before the nurse left again, she pressed a button to release what must have been some sort of painkiller, the kind that was administered intravenously, because Janine drifted off to sleep.

I kissed her good-bye and then went back to the waiting area to call my mother to tell her what was going on, and then I called Curtis to come and pick me up. I hated leaving Janine but I would be back as soon as I changed clothing, did the couple of tasks she'd asked me to do, and made sure everything was situated at home. If need be, I would even spend the night at the hospital again. I would do whatever I had to in order to keep her mind at ease.

When we arrived home, Marissa went straight to her room, Curtis went to his study, and I immediately shed my clothing and jumped into the shower. Right afterward, I dressed in a velour sweat suit and went downstairs to see if Curtis had spoken with Dr. Mason.

"Her secretary called just before we came to pick you up, and I have to take Marissa in at one o'clock," he said.

"What about the rest of the week?"

"Same time, but then it will probably change after that."

"She was awfully quiet in the car," I said.

"That's because she's not happy about having to see Dr. Mason again."

"Did Matthew ask why she wasn't going to school?"

"Yeah, and I told him the truth."

"What did you say?"

"That his sister isn't well and we want her to see a doctor."

"You didn't say that in front of her, did you?"

"Of course not."

I sat on the edge of Curtis's desk. "I'm so overwhelmed."

"Come here," he said, and I slid onto his lap. "Just remember that weeping may endure for a night, but joy cometh in the morning."

"I'm trying to believe that, but right now it seems like joy is taking a long time to show up. First it was the Larry disaster, then you told me about this Tabitha woman being pregnant, and now Janine is suffering in a hospital. And I'm worried sick about Marissa."

"But in the end, everything will work itself out," he said, kissing me.

"I should head over to Janine's to pick up a few things for her and then run a couple of other errands."

"Will you be here when Marissa and I get back from her appointment?"

"Yeah, because I'm planning to spend the night at the hospital again and I want to see Matthew at least for a little while when he gets home from school."

"Sounds good," he said.

Then, the phone rang.

"Hello?" I said.

"May I speak to Curtis?" a woman asked.

"Who's calling, please?"

"That's not important. You just put Curtis on the phone."

"Who is this?" I said, lifting my body away from Curtis.

"Why?"

"Because I need to know, that's why."

"Look, is Curtis there or not?"

"He's here, but unless you can tell me who you are, you won't be speaking to him."

"Well, if you must know, I'm the other Mrs. Black."

"Excuse me?"

"You heard me."

"I don't know who you are, but if you call here again—"

"You know who I am because by now I'm sure Curtis has told you."

"Tabitha?"

"Bravo for Charlotte. Now, can I please speak to Curtis?"

"No, I think we need to get something straight first. I'm the *only* Mrs. Black married to Curtis."

"Maybe you're the only one the few days out of the month when he's home, but I'm very much his wife when we're on the road."

"Those days are over, sweetie."

Tabitha laughed out loud. "I'm carrying Curtis's baby in my belly and you think things are over between us? Honey, our relationship will *never* be over. Not even once this child is eighteen."

"Well, just so you know, you won't be getting one cent until we see proof that you're pregnant, and after that we'll need proof that Curtis is the father."

"That's not a problem. I know whose baby this is because I haven't been with another man since I met Curtis. So if you want, we can ride to the testing facility together. We can take all the tests you want, but the bottom line is that you're about to be a stepmother."

Her words were slicing me into small pieces but I would never let her know it.

"Like I said, not one cent."

"Suit yourself, but in the meantime I expect Curtis to continue paying my living expenses the same as always."

"We'll see."

"Either you will or you'll be reading about the three of us—well, actually the four of us, counting the baby. Anyway, you'll be reading about us in the tabloids, and before I'm finished, you'll be watching me live on CNN telling the whole story."

"You make me sick."

"Likewise," she said, and I threw the phone at Curtis and folded my arms.

He looked at me and then picked it up.

"Tabitha, why are you doing this?" he asked. "I told you we would work this out like two civil adults, so why are you calling here harassing Charlotte? I did tell her. The phone calls have to stop. I don't care. If you need to contact me, call my cell phone, but under no circumstance are you to call our home number again. I don't wanna hear that. I'm asking you politely. Okay, fine, I'm hanging up. Good-bye," he said.

"I don't believe she had the audacity to call here for you. And then brag about being your other wife. I can't believe you've forced us into this stupid charade, Curtis."

"She's not going to stop calling until we agree to pay all her bills and set up some sort of monthly allowance."

"No. No way. I told you and I told her, we're not paying out any money until we have proof."

"And I told you that we have to keep her quiet."

"You should have thought about that when you decided to lay up with her. When you decided to choose a second wife without divorcing me."

"That's not even funny."

"Which is why I'm not laughing."

"So what do you want me to do?"

"Nothing."

"And let her go to the media? Let her ruin my career and my reputation?"

"I can't even talk about this anymore," I said, dismissing him and leaving the room.

"Charlotte?" he said.

But I kept walking. I left because I didn't have anything else to say.

Nothing I wouldn't regret later.

Chapter 29

CHARLOTTE

*H*ow dare that witch call our house making financial demands, I thought as I turned the key in the lock to Janine's condo and stepped inside. Then I disarmed the security system, which was still set because, thanks to Antonio, Janine had never gotten any farther than the garage. Actually, I'd had to run by the hospital on my way over here to find out the new code because I'd remembered her telling me she'd changed it.

I moved from room to room, making sure everything was intact, and then I headed toward the door leading to the garage and braced myself. When I opened it and looked through, I suddenly felt nauseous. Blood was all over the cement floor and I couldn't help imagining what Janine must have gone through.

As she'd figured, her purse was right near her car, so I picked it up and carried it back in with me. Then I sat down at the kitchen table, attempting to gather my composure. Being here and seeing the crime scene was a lot harder than I'd expected, and of course this whole Tabitha production was steadily eating away at me. So much so that my thought pattern was slipping

into ungodly territory. I didn't want to think what I was thinking, but I didn't see how I could simply allow this woman to
waltz into my life and take over. She'd been in Curtis's life for a
good while, but this had nothing to do with the children or me
and it was my duty to protect what was rightfully ours.

Of course, if she'd been the type of woman who would leave
town permanently, accept mutually agreed-upon child support,
and refrain from contacting us again, then maybe I'd feel much
better about the situation and possibly I'd be able to pretend this
had never happened. But I knew from speaking with her that
she wasn't. I knew she wanted the fairy tale. She was the type of
mistress that sleeps with a man year after year, knowing he has
a wife and family, yet she still hopes, prays, believes, and counts
on the fact that one day he is going to leave his wife and marry
her. It was the stupidest thing a woman could fantasize about,
but I knew Tabitha was all of the above. She wanted Curtis very
badly and I could tell she'd go to any extremes she had to in
order to make this happen—which is why she had to be
stopped.

It was the reason I would wait until she was around six or
seven months pregnant, invite her over to call a truce, and then
she would somehow tumble down our winding staircase by accident.

"I didn't want to bring this up in front of Marissa," Curtis said
once he and Marissa had come back from her appointment and
he'd followed me up to our bedroom, "but about an hour ago
one of the detectives who arrested Larry called me on my cell
phone."

"So?" I said, because I was still livid with Curtis for the problems he'd brought into our lives and for humiliating me the way
he had.

"You're lucky I'm even speaking to you right now," he said, hurling me a dirty look.

"Why? They found the jewelry, didn't they?"

"As a matter of fact, they confiscated it from the pawnshop and the owner already came in to identify Larry."

"Well then, what's the problem?"

"Well, the thing is, they're having to extradite Larry back to Atlanta to face a warrant in De Kalb County."

"Okay," I said, still confused and basically uninterested in this whole dialogue we were having.

"He sexually molested his daughter when she was a child, Charlotte, and she's now pressed charges against him. That's why he left there and came up here."

"I'm sorry to hear that, but what does that have to do with me?"

"Everything."

"How?"

My patience was growing thinner every second.

"I called Alicia and thankfully she says that Larry never approached her. She said Jalen had told her way back then that her father was touching her in the wrong way, but both she and Jalen were afraid to tell anyone."

"But I ask you again, Curtis, what does any of this have to do with me?"

"You brought that fool around Marissa and Matthew and he could have done the same thing to both of them. You allowed him to spend hours here even after I told you not to."

"But there's no way anything happened because I never left them alone with him."

"You'd better be glad you didn't, and Larry had better be thanking God he never laid a hand on Alicia, Matthew, or Marissa."

"Now you're just talking crazy, because Alicia wasn't even here."

"But she used to spend the night with Jalen all the time when she was a small girl. You heard him say that the first night he was over here, so what I'm saying is that he'd better be glad he didn't touch her back then."

I wanted to respond but I didn't know what I should say because he was right for being angry. I had irresponsibly brought a stranger into our home and subjected our children to a very sick individual and there was no excuse for it. Still, I didn't see where this compared even remotely to him getting another woman pregnant. I didn't see how he could have the nerve to confront me about anything, let alone something that had worked out fine. Larry hadn't harmed Matthew or Marissa, so Curtis needed to get over it.

"If it'll make you feel any better, I'm sorry," I said, but my tone was clearly sarcastic.

"You're always sorry. With you, it seems like there's always one thing after another, and that's why I—" he said, and then cut his sentence.

"That's why you what?" I yelled. "That's why you've been sleeping around and that's why you have a baby on the way?"

"You know what? I'm not doing this with you, because if I do, I'll end up saying some things I won't be able to take back."

"No, you started it, Curtis, so let's finish it. Let's talk about that tramp you've been screwing for what, five years now? Or maybe we could talk about how you were stupid enough to get her pregnant. Or even better, let's talk about the fact that you were too ignorant and selfish to even wear a condom. You hear me, Curtis, let's talk about all of that," I said, pressing my finger in his chest as hard as I could.

"You'd better stop while you're ahead." He grasped my arm and forced it away from him.

"No, I'm not stopping anything, because I'm tired of you playing Mr. Holier Than Thou when all along you've been committing one sin after another. You've done more dirt than anyone I can think of, but still you're running around here claiming to be a minister."

"Well, what about you? Huh? What about sleeping with your cousin's husband? What about sleeping with Aaron behind my back?"

"Oh, please," I said, tossing my hands in the air. "How many times are you going to keep throwing those same two ancient incidents in my face?"

"Well, if you're sick of hearing about old news, then let's talk about the fact that Marissa isn't my daughter."

Now, I knew. I'd been dreaming for two whole days. In reality, Antonio hadn't attacked Janine and Curtis hadn't just told me that he knew Marissa didn't belong to him.

At least this was what I'd wanted to believe, but then Curtis yelled at me again, forcing me to realize that I wasn't dreaming and that this was as real as real could be.

"You thought you were so smart, but after all this time you still don't know what I'm capable of," he said. "Remember a few years ago when I asked you how you thought you could con a con artist? Yet, you still tried to con me, anyway."

"Why are you saying all this?"

"Because she's not my daughter. Back then, I didn't trust you for a minute, so I made an appointment with the doctor who owned that paternity facility and I pretty much told him that if I ever found out his staff had falsified our test results, I would sue him for everything he had and report it to every news outlet in the country. And the next thing I knew he was telling every-thing."

My stomach turned viciously and while I tried to think of a quick alibi, I couldn't. I tried and tried but my brain wouldn't cooperate. So for the first time since I'd married Curtis, I had no choice but to admit what I'd done.

"I was afraid you would leave me," I finally managed to say.

"Just stop, because I don't wanna hear anything else you have to say. And you know why? Because even after I found out that you'd paid that facility to lie, I still decided to stay with you. Mainly for Matthew's sake, but of course I ended up loving Marissa just like she was my own."

"But she is yours. She's been with you since the day she was born and she loves you so much. She loves you more than she loves me."

"That's beside the point, Charlotte, because she's still *not* my daughter," Curtis roared, and I dropped down on the bed when I saw Marissa standing in our doorway. She'd gone into her room and slammed her door, so the last thing I'd expected was for her to come back out of it.

"Baby girl, how long have you been standing there?" Curtis asked, moving toward her.

But she was already crying hysterically.

"I hate you," she said, backing away.

"Marissa, please," I said, now walking closer and reaching out to her myself.

"I hate both of you," she shrieked, and backed farther down the hallway.

"Marissa, baby girl, Daddy can explain, now please come so I can talk to you."

"You're not my daddy!" she shouted, still backing away.

But then I rushed toward her, attempting to grab her into my arms.

And that's when she tumbled down the stairway, the entire winding flight and slammed her head against the huge cement pot on the floor at the bottom.

"Marissa, oh my God," I said, running after her.

"Oh Lord, no," Curtis said, hurrying behind me.

"Marissa, baby, wake up," I pleaded.

"Marissa," Curtis hollered. "Marissa."

"Baby, wake up," I repeated.

"I'm calling 911," he said, and I held her faint body in my arms. I held her and prayed that she was going to be okay. I prayed that God would have mercy on me. Mercy on our family. I prayed that He would spare my daughter's precious life.

Chapter 30

CHARLOTTE

Marissa had been pronounced dead on arrival, but I refused to believe it. I refused to believe that my five-year-old daughter had fallen to her death so quickly and so easily. I'd heard the emergency room doctor explaining to Curtis and me that the damage to her skull and brain had been too severe for her to survive, but I still couldn't comprehend that she was gone. I knew she'd gotten too close to the edge of the staircase and had accidentally lost her balance, but children fell down stairs all the time and rarely ever died from it. Not even when they hit their heads against planters.

So, to me, this just didn't make any sense. Although if Curtis hadn't started bellowing to the world that Marissa wasn't his daughter, she'd still be alive now. But no, he just couldn't shut up about it. He'd had to make his point the same as always, and now our little girl—well, my little girl—was gone and I'd never forgive him.

But then, as much as I wanted to, I couldn't deny the fact that I'd played a major part in this, too. I couldn't deny that the reason Curtis and I had been arguing in the first place was because I'd invited Larry over and one subject had led to another. But then the debate between us had become so heated we'd totally forgotten about Marissa and hadn't counted on her easing over to our room and listening to what we were saying.

"Mr. and Mrs. Black, can we get you anything?" one of the hospital chaplains asked, and I burst into tears.

"Not right now," Curtis told him. "But thank you."

"If you need anything at all, please let us know."

We'd been sitting in a small family room for at least a half hour, waiting to go in and see Marissa. The funeral home had already been notified, but we wanted to see her before they took her away.

When the chaplain left, Curtis placed his arm around me.

"Don't . . . you . . . touch . . . me," I said, moving from the love seat and over to one of the chairs. "Don't you ever touch me again."

"Charlotte, this isn't the time for that. Right now we have to support each other and figure out how we're going to tell Matthew about Marissa."

"It's your fault that she's dead, so you're the one who's going to tell him," I couldn't help lashing out at him.

"How can you say that?" he said, his eyes filling with tears.

"Because it *is* your fault."

"But how? Because you're the one who rushed toward her and that's when she fell back."

"Just shut up, Curtis!" I said, picking up a magazine and throwing it at him. "Just shut up or get the hell out of here."

"I can't believe you're actually trying to blame me for this," he said, and neither of us spoke another word for ten minutes.

We sat staring anywhere except directly at each other, but then I finally looked at him.

"If you knew about that paternity test all these years, Curtis, why are you just bringing it up now?"

I asked this because I was beginning to feel more sadness and regret than I did anger.

"I'm sorry. But you kept pressing me about this Tabitha situation and I couldn't help reminding you about what you've done to me. I told you the other day that we've both made a lot of mistakes, and now this is the result."

"I can't believe this has happened," I said, breaking down again, and Curtis pulled me up from the chair and held me tightly.

This time I didn't resist because I wanted and needed him to hold me. The road ahead would certainly be a rough one.

"Oh no," I said. "I really need to check on Janine."

"We'll go up there before we leave."

"I honestly feel like I'm losing my mind."

"What we have to do is pray for strength and understanding."

"But how? How can we understand something as tragic as this?"

"I don't know, but we have to try because we don't have any other choice. And we can't forget about Matthew. We can't forget that he's still going to need us the same as always, if not more."

I felt like crying again, and while I tried not to, I couldn't help it. I wept and wept until two nurses came to get us.

"If you'll come with us, we'll take you to see your daughter now," one of them said, and we followed them down the hallway.

But as we walked, something hit me. Only hours before, I'd been plotting Tabitha's miscarriage and planning for *her* to plummet down our staircase. I'd literally made myself believe I could coax her up to our second floor and then push her like it was nothing. I'd actually allowed my mind to veer off in such an insane direction, and I was sorry.

Sorry because, little had I'd known, Marissa was going to take the fall instead.

Chapter 31

CHARLOTTE

M om, she's gone," I said to my mother.

"Who's gone? And gone where?"

"Curtis and I just got back home from the hospital and—"

"Oh no, Charlotte, baby, I'm so sorry. Janine was such a good friend to you. But I thought you said she was doing better this morning. Better than the doctor had expected."

"No, Mom, I'm not talking about Janine. I'm talking about Marissa."

"What do you mean, you're talking about Marissa?"

"She's gone. She fell down the stairs."

"Dear God, how?"

"It's a long story, but the whole thing was an accident. She lost her balance, her body flipped multiple times around the curve, and she hit the pot sitting to the side at the bottom."

"Lord, Joe, honey, this is Charlotte and she's got some horrible news."

"Sweetheart, what's going on?" my father asked me.

"Marissa died earlier this afternoon."

"Died? No, no, no!"

"She did, Daddy."

"What happened?" he asked, and I told him the same thing I'd told Mom. "We'll be there as soon as we can get a bag packed."

"Thank you, Daddy, because I really need you and Mom to be here."

"How are Matthew and Curtis?"

"They're hanging in there," I said, looking at Matthew, who was sitting on the sofa, crying. Curtis was pacing back and forth in front of the fireplace.

"Sweetheart, you all try to hang in there, and we'll see you in a couple of hours or so."

When I hung up, I went over to Matthew, and he lay in my arms the way he used to when he was Marissa's age.

"Honey, I know it hurts, so you just let it all out, okay?"

"Why did she have to die? Sometimes she was mean but she couldn't help that something was wrong with her. She really couldn't help it, Mom."

"I know, baby."

"I always tried to be a good brother."

"Honey, you were the best big brother she could have had."

"I'm really sorry."

"Hey," I said, turning his face toward me. "This isn't your fault, so you don't have a thing to apologize for."

"That's right, son, you don't have to feel bad about any of this."

"But, Dad, I knew she needed help. I knew it for a long time but I didn't say anything because I didn't want my friends thinking something was wrong with me, too. I didn't want them thinking I was crazy, and that's why I didn't say anything. That's why I let her treat me any way she wanted to and I never got mad at her."

"Honey, I'm sorry you've been carrying such a huge weight on your shoulders, but you listen to me. Getting Marissa help wasn't your responsibility. It was mine and your father's and no one else's. Actually, it was my responsibility because your father didn't really know either."

"She was always such a good girl, Dad, whenever you were around, and that's why I used to pray that you would stop traveling so much. I used to pray all the time so we could all be happy. And I wanted you and Mom to stop hating each other so you could get back to loving each other the way you used to before Marissa was born."

Curtis and I looked at each other in horror and I knew he was just as hurt as I was. Matthew was telling us to our faces that we were lousy parents. I know he didn't mean to, but his message was coming across very clearly.

"I wanna go up to my room and lie down," Matthew said, wiping his face with both his hands.

"Honey, are you sure?"

"Yes."

"Okay then, we'll be up to check on you in a while," I said, and he hugged both of us.

"Charlotte, what have we done?" Curtis asked once Matthew was out of the room.

"Way too much, and, at the same time, not nearly enough."

"I've been so selfish. I've been that way most of my adult life and I still haven't learned. Even after losing two churches, two wives, and a mother, I still kept on my road to destruction. And now after Marissa's accident and the mistake I made with Tabitha, I'm sure I'm going to lose you, too," Curtis said, running his hands across the top of his head and still pacing.

"No you're not. Not after seeing how much we've hurt Matthew. We owe him a happy life and that's what we have to give him."

"I agree, so just tell me what to do and I'll do it," Curtis said, and I'd never seen him more humble. "I'll do whatever you want because I'm tired of living the way we have been. I'm tired of bragging about you in public and then sleeping with someone else behind closed doors. I'm forever through with that lifestyle, and while I know it's going to take time for you to believe me, I'm going to be faithful to you from now on. As God is my witness, you're the only woman in my life from this day forward."

"And I promise I won't lie to you anymore or keep secrets from you the way I have."

"We still have to deal with Tabitha, but we'll do it however you decide."

I left the sofa and fell deeply into Curtis's embrace.

And we stayed that way until we went up to see about Matthew.

Chapter 32

JANINE

The funeral had commenced yesterday afternoon and I was still feeling pretty bad about not being able to go. I knew I wasn't able to, but the idea that I hadn't been able to console or support Charlotte during the worst time in her life was causing me great pain. I had terribly wanted to be there for her the way she had been here for me. Especially since she'd still come here the day my kidney had been removed, which unfortunately had been the day after Marissa had passed. I knew it had taken everything in Charlotte to spend time at this particular hospital, the same one Marissa had been brought to, but she'd never complained. As a matter of fact, when I'd been wheeled back from recovery, Curtis and Matthew had come in to see me for a few minutes, too, and I appreciated that more than they knew.

Then there was Carl, who was sitting in my room right now, right next to my bed, and all I could do was smile whenever I looked at him. There were moments when I couldn't help thinking he was too good to be true, but on the other hand, I knew it was time I gave someone like him a fair chance. Someone who wanted to do anything they could for me and who wasn't expecting a thing in return. Someone who was nothing like Antonio.

Speaking of which, Antonio had been denied bail, so, thankfully, I didn't have to worry about him trying to attack me again. Not to mention he couldn't phone the hospital collect, so I didn't have to worry about him calling me either.

For the first time in a long time, I felt free. I knew I wouldn't be totally safe until the trial was over and Antonio had been sentenced, but I still felt a lot better than I had in weeks. It was true that I had scars I would always have to live with and one less kidney to depend on, but I wasn't going to complain. I wouldn't complain because I couldn't change my misfortunes. Today was a new day with new possibilities and it was high time I realized that, and time I learned that I really did have my whole life ahead of me and that I could be happy. I deserved to be happy and now I knew I didn't have to accept anything less. I'd learned the hard way, but the important thing was that I could now move forward.

"Are you warm enough?" Carl asked, pulling the covers closer to my neck.

"I am."

"Are you thirsty?"

"If you don't mind, I could have a little more ice water," I said, and he stood and poured some from the plastic pitcher into an oversized Styrofoam cup. "You should go home to get some rest. You've been here all day."

"My employees have everything covered with my business so I'm fine."

"I think it was better when I was in the ICU because at least then you went home at night."

"Only because Charlotte was here most of those times, and because in the ICU, the nurses were keeping full-time watch over you. But now that you're in a regular room, you're all alone."

"That's why I have this," I said, showing him my call button.

"You're funny."

"I know," I said, and we both laughed.

"I know you don't understand, but I really am here because I want to be. If you were home, I'd still want to spend all my time with you, so this is no different."

"It's a lot different because I'm lying in a hospital bed, trying to heal, and you're suffering with major back pain because of that recliner."

"Now, *that* I won't deny," he said, smiling.

"See, that's why I want you to go home."

"Not gonna happen. Not until I know you're comfortable for the night and you've fallen off to sleep."

"Well, at least you won't have to do this once I'm released."

"And why is that?"

"I'll be staying with Charlotte and Curtis, remember?"

"Yeah, and the only reason I'm not arguing about that is because at some point I will have to get back to work on a more full-time basis."

"Curtis has already told you that you can visit every day and as often as you want, and of course Charlotte feels the same way."

"It's really nice of them to open up their home to you the way they have."

"That's just how they are."

"I keep trying to imagine how they must feel, losing a child so tragically, but I know it's not possible."

"I don't think anyone can unless they've had the same experience."

I hadn't told Carl about Marissa's visits to a psychiatrist or about the emotional disturbances she seemed to be having, but I knew this was bothering Charlotte, too. I knew because she'd told me yesterday that she wished she'd gotten Marissa the help she needed a lot sooner. She'd even told me why she'd tried to ignore her symptoms and I'd been shocked. She'd told me everything about Aaron, where he was, and that he was Marissa's natural father.

I flipped through the TV channels and then looked back over at Carl, who was gazing at me.

"What?" I said.

"Nothing."

"You're staring at me and it's for no reason?"

"I guess I'm doing it because it's hard for me to believe you're everything I want in a woman."

"You still don't know that for sure."

"I know how empty I feel when I'm not with you, and that speaks a thousand words."

"Even though you're seeing me at my worst? Even though I only have one kidney and it will be months before I'm hopefully back to normal?"

"You're still just as beautiful to me as the day I met you."

"Now I *know* something's wrong with you."

"See, you're joking, but I'm trying to be serious."

"But the only reason I keep joking is because I don't want to be hurt again."

"I would never do that, and as time goes on, you'll realize that. But maybe the question is, how do you feel about me?"

My first instinct was to avoid the question as best I could, but Carl had done so much for me that I had to be honest.

"I'm to the point where if you tell me you're going to be here at three o'clock, then I start looking toward the doorway ten minutes before. And I keep looking until I see you walking through it. After that, I feel totally at peace, and like I'm actually in heaven."

"Are you in love with me?"

I didn't look away from him but I didn't answer either.

"Are you? Because I'm in love with you. I told you that the first night you were in here and I meant it."

Tears rolled down my face because I desperately wanted to believe him.

"What are you crying for?" he said, wiping away my tears.

"Because I *am* in love with you. But I'm also afraid. I'm not afraid to give our relationship a chance, but I'm afraid that I'll continue to fall further in love with you and then you'll change your mind about everything."

"If you don't change, I won't change. Okay?"

I nodded and Carl kissed me.

He kissed me and I could feel the love between us—even as I lay in my hospital bed, with bruises, cuts, and no makeup. Even though we'd never had sex and for the most part hadn't had a chance to discuss it.

We kissed and I wondered if he would in fact be my husband one day.

One Year Later

Epilogue

CHARLOTTE

*Y*ou look so, so beautiful," I said to Janine while hugging her.

"Well, if I do, it's because you were sweet enough to buy me the dress of a lifetime."

"And I would do it again in a heartbeat because you deserve the absolute best. You've been through so much over this past year, and this was the least Curtis and I could do for you."

"Carl and I will be indebted to both of you forever because this wedding has cost a fortune."

"Please. The only thing we want is for the two of you to be happy."

"And we will. I really do believe that," she said, pulling out a tissue. "We have to stop all this before I ruin my makeup."

"Well, we wouldn't want that, now would we?" I said, and we both laughed.

Then I straightened the lengthy train attached to her dress and made sure her veil was perfectly in place. She looked no differently than any of the women who modeled for the top wedding magazines and I was so happy for her. Happy because, healthwise, she'd now recovered completely, and because Carl had ended up being the man he'd said he was. He'd stood by her from beginning to end and then asked her to marry him six months after their initial meeting. Janine had still been some-what hesitant, but it hadn't taken long for her to realize that marrying Carl truly was the right thing to do. Even her father had felt the same way the moment he'd met him and had given them his blessings before passing on to his glory just two months ago.

Losing her father had been very difficult, but Janine had found comfort in knowing that he was no longer in pain and was finally resting in peace. And interestingly enough, Curtis and I were finally feeling the same way about Marissa, but now I knew my grandmother had been right when she'd told me that there was no loss greater than when a person lost a child or a parent.

But the best news had arrived two days ago, when Janine had learned that Antonio had been sentenced to twenty years with no chance of parole until he'd served at least eighteen of them. Of course, when Janine had come home from the hospital, he'd tried calling her, but she'd never answered and since he'd been forced to remain in the county jail until his trial, she hadn't had to worry about him making any more surprise visits. For a while, she'd been worried about his friends and what they might do, but thankfully, they'd never bothered her.

And then there was Curtis and me and our handsome little Matthew, who was now thirteen and one of the top honor stu-dents in the city. Not to mention he had amazing skills in foot-ball and he was only in eighth grade. We were so proud of him we could burst, and glad we had finally given him the happy home he'd wanted. Curtis and I had, at last, made a lifetime commitment to each other and we were finally living for better